BY BECKY BOHAN

Madwoman Press
1995

This is a work of fiction. Any resemblance between characters in this book and actual persons, living or dead, is coincidental.

Cover by Bonnie Liss of Phoenix Graphics, Winter Haven, FL

Edited by Diane Benison

Printed in the United States on acid-free paper

Library of Congress Cataloging-in-Publication Data

Bohan, Becky, 1952-
Fertile betrayal : a Nedra Wells, D.V.M., novel / by Becky Bohan
p. cm.
ISBN 1-886231-00-1 (paper)
I. Title.
PS3552.O488F47 1995
813'.54—dc20 95-857
CIP

First Edition, April 1995
10 9 8 7 6 5 4 3 2 1

Also by Becky Bohan

Sinister Paradise

Acknowledgments

Thanks to the late Dr. Lynn Weaver for her valuable information and her early review of the manuscript; to Dr. George Ruth, Pathologist, College of Veterinary Medicine, University of Minnesota, and Dr. Julie Smith for their time and expertise. Any errors of fact are my responsibility alone.

A special thanks to Kitty Johnson for her review, friendship, and support; to Ellen McEnvoy for her read-through; to Diane Benison for her excellent suggestions and red pen; and to Nancy Manahan for her special edit and support on the home front. Your help has been invaluable!

To my parents, Doc and Edith Bohan, and my sister Vicki,
for a wondrous childhood

I

A BIRTHING SURPRISE—AROUND THE KITCHEN TABLE—A QUESTION OF THEOLOGY

Nedra Wells entertained three observations about the Thompson farm: the house was as weather-beaten as the barn, the cattle were better groomed than the kids, and the cows couldn't make a live birth to save their animal souls. The first two were outside Nedra's professional concern. The last struck at its core.

The small town veterinarian covered a yawn with the back of her hand as her rusty Ford Ranger rattled along Main Street under the leafy roof of spreading elms and white oaks, and past the gleaming pillars of the Presbyterian Church. In her twelve years of practice, she had seen plenty of fetuses expelled by Mother Nature, but never two in a row on one small farm.

Now, on this cloudy day in late May, dam number three was in premature labor. Nedra felt certain about the outcome. The last time she'd checked the cow, the fetal heartbeat sounded as weak as a fluttering curtain. If this was another failed pregnancy, the Thompson cows would be aborting at a 100 percent level when the norm was only 5. Nedra felt a little flutter in her own chest at the thought.

The Thompsons—a widow and two kids—lived a quarter mile east of Lake Amelia, Minnesota, just on the other side of the four lane highway that cut northwest through the prairie, pointing toward the Twin Cities, ninety-some miles away. As Nedra turned into the Thompson driveway a little after six-thirty a.m. and slowed to a stop, a dog that was part golden retriever, part Irish setter, pranced around the truck barking. The dog's teeth fastened on her pant leg the moment she hopped from the truck.

"Hey, Samson, old buddy," Nedra said, thumping the dog's barrel chest a couple of times. "Sorry, no time to play now." Samson paused for a moment, then trotted over to the Ranger's front wheel, hoisted a leg, and let loose a yellow stream.

After stepping into her navy coveralls and rubber overshoes, Nedra sloshed through the mud to the barn, medical bag in hand. Her broad shoulders topped an easy, posture-perfect back and muscular legs. Her confident carriage told her clients that she could handle any creature they could throw her way, whether an Arabian stallion or a terrified tabby. Her wheat-blond hair, as shiny as a polished stone, dropped in a pony tail between her shoulders. Most people would say that Nedra, with her soft brown eyes and kind smile, was handsome. She would say it was irrelevant.

As Nedra approached the maternity pen, she saw two small forelegs and a pink nose covered with mucous sticking out of the cow. Teri Thompson and her two kids, Jeff and Jessie, stood around the animal.

"This one's got to be okay," Teri said, patting the sweaty rust-brown neck of the Hereford. Her eyes were almost as wide as the cow's. "We can't afford another loss." The white-faced cow shifted her weight from the left to right side, then settled into a balanced stance. She swung her head around and let out a moan that reverberated off the weathered timbers of the barn.

"Damn right," said Jeff, seventeen years old. Yellow hair, cut in a bowl style, peeked from under a red baseball cap turned backwards. His black T-shirt, clipped of its sleeves and neck, bulged out of baggy jeans that drooped around his lean waist. "At least old Betsy's near full term."

Nedra pulled on her shoulder-length latex gloves. She didn't share Jeff's optimism, nor his certainty of the stage of pregnancy.

The Thompsons couldn't afford artificial insemination like most breeders, so they relied on pasture mating for their herd. That meant they could never be certain about the impregnation date. By the size of the hooves, dainty as tea cups, Nedra knew that the calf was several weeks shy of nine months.

Reaching into the cow, Nedra felt for the carotid artery of the calf on the inner side of its jaw. No pulse. "Let's get the little guy out," she said, keeping her voice as smooth as possible. With a few bangs on the chest and half a dozen puffs of air into the nose, maybe she'd have the calf on its feet in minutes.

"Jessie," Nedra said to the girl hanging back at the rear of the stall, "bunch up some more straw behind the cow."

The girl stepped forward, eyes averted, and raked some long stems into place. Fourteen years old, she was as blue-eyed and blond as her brother, only her hair was long and stringy. Her knees poked through gaping tears in her jeans.

Nedra grasped the slimy forelegs and pulled. The calf's full head popped out, its eyes closed, then the shoulders. Nedra kept a firm hold on the calf, guiding the warm body toward the floor. Jeff held his arms outstretched behind the cow in case the calf slipped.

With a sloshing sound and a warm wave of secretion, the calf was out, and yet it wasn't. Teri made a little oh-oh sound. Nedra lowered the limp, wet animal to the straw. It had no hind legs. The rear quarters trailed off to two little pegs covered by red hide.

"Oh, shit." Nedra stared at the deformity.

Jeff backed away until he thumped into the side of the stall. His mother placed her forehead against the Hereford's neck.

"Oh, yuck!" Jessie said.

Nedra reached inside the cow again, checking for a possible twin. As the living tissue of the animal clamped around her arm like a warm suction cup, despair welled up in Nedra momentarily. Another loss. What the hell was going on? Feeling only the slippery tissue of the placenta and the uterine horn, Nedra withdrew from the cow. Arms at her side, she pondered the deformed animal lying on the floor. She didn't bother trying to bring it to life. It was dead and it would stay that way.

"What now?" Teri asked.

"I'll finish cleaning up here," Nedra said softly. The death of an animal always hurt. Nedra even felt a disquieting sadness at the thought that many of the animals she treated wound up at a packing plant. "I'd like to take some tissue samples of the cow for analysis. The calf...well, I'll pack it like the last one and send it to the Diagnostic Lab at the U."

"Do what you need to do," Teri said, her face sagging with resignation. "Kids, you help the doc here, and I'll go up and fix us all breakfast."

A couple of swallows swooped through the stall and out the open end of the building. The Thompson bull, Loco, chewed his cud at the gate door and peered in at the three humans laboring in silence. He flared his nostrils, then lifted his tail and dropped a load of manure. The earthy smell of digested pasture momentarily covered the odor of birth, blood, and disappointment.

"How could you!" Jessie cried when her mother was out of hearing range. "How could you?" she repeated as she yanked the cow's ear and then bolted from the barn.

⌘

"What do you figure?" Teri asked as she set a platter of scrambled eggs on the white Formica table where Nedra and the kids sat. The red garland design around the table's edge was worn away in places.

Nedra didn't know what to figure. After the last miscarriage, she had been sure that they were looking at contagious abortion caused by an infectious bacterial disease. But all tests performed at the University of Minnesota had turned out negative. They had even tested for EBA—Epidemic Bovine Abortion—even though that disease rarely appeared in the Midwest, and it was the wrong season for the carrier ticks to be active. She had called the County Extension Agent and asked him to check for other occurrences of spontaneous abortions in the area. He had come up empty. She had examined the cattle for nutritional deficiencies and found none.

"The Diagnostic Lab may have some answers for us this time," Nedra said.

"You know I can't afford much more than what you've done." Teri dropped into the red vinyl chair and pushed a patch of graying, sandy hair from her forehead. She was a few years older than Nedra, but right now she looked double her age. Her tan face was drawn, and the crows seemed to have stepped deeper at the outside corners of her azure eyes, which had a glassy look to them. Under five and a half feet, she was as solid as a Mack truck. She sighed and spooned a helping of eggs onto her plate. "I can't afford not to, either, can I?"

Nedra waved a hand in the air. "The lab fees are the only immediate expense. As for my time—you know your credit's always good with me." Nedra had aged her receivables eight months now.

The sun broke from the clouds for an instant. Its light flooded through the kitchen windows and hit the cracked and faded linoleum before disappearing. The pimpled varnish on the birch cupboards was worn down to the wood near the handles. The family had almost lost the farm to the bankers several years ago, and then struggled after Ed Thompson had fallen into the corn bin and suffocated. Teri labored feverishly to keep the farm solvent.

"What are you looking for now?" she asked.

"We've pretty much eliminated infectious disease as a cause for the two previous incidents. My best guess at this point is that we're looking at a toxin or poison of some sort."

"Poison? How?" A new voice joined the group. A screen door slammed behind it.

Nedra pivoted in her seat to take in the lanky frame of C. Mather Jensen topped by a well-worn straw Stetson. The thirty-two-year old, known as Matt, picked up a chair like it was a pail and sidled up to the table. He had bought the farm to the east of the Thompsons the year before Ed died. "Cows are curious creatures," Nedra said.

Matt held up a palm toward Teri. "Don't bother setting a plate for me," he said. "I just ate in town."

Teri ignored Matt and plopped a slice of toast on her plate.

"Maybe they spotted a bag of fertilizer, or a carton of pesticide and decided to sample the goods," Nedra continued. "When I helped my dad up north a few summers ago, we had a bull so weak it had to lean against a fence post to stay upright. Turned out he was nibbling lead paint off the side of the barn."

"Couldn't be chips," Matt said. "That barn hasn't felt a swipe of paint since the Lord..." Seeing Teri's frown, he shut his mouth and hooked his cowboy hat on the back of the chair. His stylish, dark hair was swept back off his face, which was shaven as smooth as an egg shell. He wore a red checkered cowboy shirt and a wide western belt with a silver buckle nearly as big as a flattened tin can. His eyes were deep set and gray.

"Hey, Matt," Jeff said. "Heard about our veal on wheels?" The boy went on to describe the deformed calf.

Matt whistled. "When I saw your truck in the driveway," he said, nodding toward Nedra, "I thought there might be a problem."

"I don't get it," Jessie said. "All the chemicals are in a separate shed. The cattle can't get into it."

"There are lots of sources for toxins," Nedra said. "We need to check the feed, the soil, and the water for contamination."

"What would you be looking for?" Matt asked.

Nedra chewed thoughtfully on a bit of eggs, then swallowed. "There are thousands of chemicals that could be the culprit. The trouble is, we almost have to know what we're looking for to test for it."

"Well, if it's chemical contamination," Jeff said, "we'd be croaking too. Look at this bod," he continued, flexing his triceps. "Absolutely perfect."

"Not a germ in you, I'm sure," Nedra teased. She turned to Teri. "Just out of curiosity, when were your last medical exams?"

Teri's face went blank.

That was a dumb question, Nedra realized immediately. She could just as well have asked her when she had last dined at a four-star restaurant.

"I can't really say. I suppose when I had Jessie here. You know we can't afford doctoring, and we don't have any insurance."

"Let's just send the suckers off to market while we can," Jeff said. "Those cattle are nothing but trouble."

"I don't want that kind of talk," his mother said sharply. "We may have troubles now, but good times are due."

Nedra resumed eating and contemplated her next step. "I'll come out Monday morning to check the grounds a little more thoroughly."

"We'll be waiting," Teri replied.

⌘

Nedra's tobacco-colored Ford was parked under a willow tree that served as the hub of the Thompson's roundabout. A dozen flies buzzed along invisible paths inside the truck, which had been customized with shelves and drawers and a refrigeration unit for drugs. Halfheartedly, she shooed a few flies with her hand. Most of them would be sucked out the open windows once she was on the road. After placing a pail on the passenger side floor, she returned to the rear and loaded her leather medical bag next to a thirty-three-gallon garbage bag that contained the fetus and placenta.

Jeff handed over her soiled, tightly-rolled coveralls and washed gloves, then contemplated the clouds. "This weather's got to break," he said. "The ground can't hold much more water."

"Have you finished planting?" Nedra asked.

"Yeah, but we've gotta have sun. Like yesterday."

Nedra straightened up and found herself staring into Jeff's eyes. "Have you grown since I was out here last?"

"Maybe a little," he said, blushing. "Four more inches and I'll be perfect."

"So you hope to hit six feet?"

"Yep," he grinned, "not that I have a lot of say about the matter. Unless you have something in that leather bag of yours to help."

"When you start walking on all fours and growing fur, come see me. Until then, eat your vegetables." Nedra finished stuffing the clothing into a corner of the truck. "What are your plans after graduation?"

"Work this place, I guess."

"I bet your mom appreciates that."

"I doubt it." Jeff glanced up at the house. Matt was coming down the back steps. "Those damn cows. I keep telling her to get rid of them. They eat up any chance for a profit."

"I suppose a small herd can be quite a drain on the bottom line."

"It's terrible. And she won't listen to reason." Jeff sighed and rested his eyes on the bull in his special pen. "Matt says it's the Hand of God. I'm starting to believe it."

"I take the scientific approach, not the theological."

"Shit, I'm half expecting Satan to come popping out of the rear end of the next cow. It's got me spooked. Couldn't you just condemn the herd?"

"Not without a proper cause. We'll find an answer. Some things just take time."

"Sometimes only the Lord has the answer," Matt said, approaching Nedra.

"When we die, I sure hope we get an answer sheet," Nedra replied. "I have a lot of questions."

"Strange, isn't it," Matt said, "how the cattle can't seem to give birth to a new generation. We don't always know the Lord's will."

"You know," Nedra said, slamming the back door and walking to the driver's side, "my mom always says that babies are the hope of the world. We have some problems here, but I'm far from giving up hope." She swung into the driver's seat and started down the oak-lined lane.

As Nedra passed the cemetery on the main road, she noticed the caretaker clipping the grass around the neatly planted rows of marble headstones. She lifted her hand in greeting. The man didn't see her, but a nasty pothole did. The Ford bounced almost a foot.

The test tubes on the front seat rattled in their wire holder. A half dozen sealed jars clinked together. Inside them, tissue samples from the dam swam in their small, unsettled seas of formalin.

II

A MEMORY

The currycomb made a scratchy sound as it bit through the coarse hair of the cow. Teri Thompson leaned into the stroke like she was polishing a car.

"Oh, Christ, you're not scrubbing Betsy down again, are you?" Jeff said coming around to the back of the stall. His mouth was set in an angry slash.

"I want to make her look pretty."

"What for?"

"For herself." Teri stroked the hide along the cow's sweaty neck. "She's upset. She knows her calf should be here and she's confused that it's not. She needs some special attention."

"You talk like she's human."

Teri stopped in mid-stroke and leveled a no-nonsense look at her son. "You don't have to be human to experience loss."

Jeff kicked at the straw and plunged his hands into his pockets. "I know you don't want me talking about it, but you've got to listen to reason..."

"Don't start..."

"We lose money on the cattle every year. You saw the figures from the program I ran in ag class. Given the feed, medicine..."

"I've cut the herd back to five cows and a bull. I don't see what more you can want." Teri moved around to the right side of the cow.

"Damn it. We're not even going to get sales of the calves now. Not that it's ever made that much difference. You won't sell the calves until they've eaten more than they're worth."

"They'd be out in the pasture," Teri said, her strokes hard and short now, "along with the other cattle."

"The pasture is half mud. Dad always said..."

"Don't you bring the dead into this conversation. You get on back to the house. I don't want to hear another word about it."

"You'd better hear it, or we're going to wind up losing the farm!" Jeff swatted at a fly as he stomped out of the barn.

As soon as Jeff departed, the cow let out a long, deep cry.

"Don't you worry," Teri said, patting the animal. "You'll forget soon enough."

Teri, on the other hand, knew that she could never forget her losses. She draped her arms over the cow's back and rested her forehead against the warm hide.

The Accident. That's how they always spoke of Ed's passing. It was softer than saying "when Dad died." At least it hadn't been gruesome, like so many farming accidents, with severed limbs and gushing blood.

The images flowed, as they often did, when Teri was alone.

The cascade of corn roared as loud as a waterfall, spilling down over Ed. Like a golden flood, the hard, dented seed poured and poured over him, bouncing off his billed cap, burying his arms, hiding him in a crush of yellow feed and churning dust. It came and came and never seemed to stop.

Sometimes even now, when Teri heard the sound of that spilling corn, she could feel the weight of it. For her, the pressure was internal, as though the corn was filling her up inside. It fell down her bones to her feet, piled higher, to her pelvis, to her chest, to her throat. Teri gasped for breath, fighting the images, and sank to the soiled straw.

The cow swung her head around, perhaps expecting to see her calf, and let out a deep, lonesome bellow.

III

A CHIP IN HAND—AN INVITATION

When Nedra turned her truck into the small parking lot next to her office, which was half a block south of Main Street, she saw a different kind of trouble angled across two stalls. Only one family in town had a white Lincoln Continental: the Osbornes.

Nedra stayed fixed in her seat for a few moments, trying to shake off the melancholy that had cupped its hands around her out at the Thompsons. She needed her wits to deal with the Osborne clan. Mister was the town banker. Missus was the President of the School Board—in a way, the dour boss of Nedra's lover, Annie, though Mrs. Osborne didn't know about the lover part.

With the pail of samples in one hand and her bag in the other, Nedra entered through the back door. The prior tenant of the squat building had been a dentist who had retired and moved to Florida the previous year. Nedra had taken over the lease with an option to buy for a paltry sum of money. The office sat between the physician's clinic of matching Kasota stone, a golden-hued sandstone, and the small backyard of the house Nedra shared with Annie.

Annie met Nedra at the rear entry of the office. A blue bandanna hid her coarse, rust-colored waves. It framed a fine-boned face that sported green dots of semigloss latex among a splash of freckles. She was painting the room that would soon be a kennel and postoperative recovery area. That was their fancy way of referring to a ten-by-twelve room with four cages.

"Mrs. God is here," she whispered.

"I saw." Nedra set her bag and pail on the bench against the hallway wall.

Annie glanced at the contents. "Didn't make it, huh?"

"Nope. A thalidomide calf."

"Deformed?"

"No hind quarters."

"Wow." Annie placed her hand on Nedra's shoulder and rubbed in a small circle.

Nedra soaked in the touch. That was one of the things that she loved about Annie. She didn't have to gush a lot of words. One touch, one look, and Nedra knew Annie understood what she was feeling. It was communication at its most basic and empathetic.

"I decided to make a run up to the Cities with the calf instead of waiting until Monday to send it in. It's in the truck now."

Annie's face brightened. "We could make it a short weekend."

"Sorry. It's strictly up and back. Pete and I are on call for Todd Nelson, remember?" she said, referring to vets in nearby towns, the latter of whom was on vacation.

"Sorry. I forgot." Annie made a tiny grimace.

"Want to come along for the ride at least?"

"Sure. I never pass up the chance to see the big city. And I'd like to see the lab building."

Nedra nodded toward the west end of the clinic. "How long have they been waiting?"

"Fifteen minutes. I've kept them amused with the VCR—the tapes on cat urinary tract infections and bovine hoof and mouth disease."

"Splendid. What do they want?"

"You'll see," she said, with a lopsided grin. "Your specialty. I opened up an account for them on the computer."

"Thanks. Am I too stinky?" Large sweat stains spotted Nedra's blue workshirt.

Annie crinkled her nose. "It'll be good for them to get a whiff of a barnyard...and a hard worker."

The front office held three lateral files, a work station, and the phone. A window with an oak counter opened to the reception area.

Oh boy, Nedra thought, as Lana Osborne and her offspring Carolyn rose from their seats. The girl dangled a covered bird cage from a well-manicured hand.

"Who do you have there?" Nedra asked.

"Chip, my budgie."

Nedra had never treated a parakeet in her whole life. "Take a seat," she said, motioning the pair back to the row of chairs along the wall, "while I step in the back for a moment to change."

Carolyn set the cage on the pine coffee table and joined her mother. Mrs. Osborne twisted her torso so that only one buttock came in contact with the chair cushion, as though she were afraid she would pick up unsightly stains on her white linen suit.

Nedra's private office, at the rear of the building, contained a shelf of her reference books above a rolltop desk. She picked a thick, dusty manual on small animal practice and cracked it open. She remembered its having a section on domesticated birds.

She seldom encountered fowl—even with poultry she had handled only one call in the past year. In some ways, chickens were easy to deal with, she thought, as she ran her finger down the index. You could always send the neurotic and sickly ones off to market, or have the badly diseased ones destroyed without nicking the farmer's bottom line. But parakeets were pets, and they needed to be fixed. Since they contained only a few thimblefuls of blood, you had to be absolutely perfect about drug dosages.

With the book open to the most promising page, Nedra unbuttoned her shirt, tossed it in the corner and slid a clean T-shirt over her head. Then she donned a light blue lab coat. Above the left chest pocket was a patch that read "Dr. Wells." Annie had taken it upon herself to embroider all of Nedra's coats. At first, she had put the stitches directly on the pocket, but after she saw how the garments would quickly wind up in the rag pile, usually with hideous brown splotches, she took to making patches that could be transferred from coat to coat. She added her own little flair by stitching a caduceus or a miniature Star Trek communication badge after Nedra's name. Their first date had been to a Trekker convention, so Nedra preferred the sci-fi communicator emblem to the medical profession's stuffy staff and snake.

Nedra set the book back on the shelf and, as prepared as possible, she ushered the Osbornes into the examination and surgery room. It was connected to another room that held a spare table and an x-ray machine.

"What seems to be the matter," Nedra asked, as Carolyn drew the cover from the cage.

"Chip's been, like, chewing himself until he bleeds." She wangled a finger at the bird, who jumped on board. She eased him through the tiny door.

"How old is he?"

"I purchased him two years ago for Carolyn's birthday," Mrs. Osborne explained. She clutched a Gucci purse with both hands.

Chip's small black eyes blinked twice.

"He does have a nasty sore spot," Nedra said, noting a bare patch in his indigo feathers and a spot of blood. Taking a magnifying glass, she examined the tracks of feathers around the chewed area and the follicle that seemed to be the source of the hemorrhaging.

Meanwhile, Mrs. Osborne eyed the examining room as though it were a root cellar. Clients often commented on the shiny, stainless steel surfaces of the examining table and connecting sink. Not the President of the School Board. When Nedra looked up, Mrs. Osborne turned from an inspection of the lab area next to the sink, where a rack of corked, blood-filled test tubes sat by a microscope. She seemed to have lost about twenty hours worth of tan in five seconds.

Carolyn self-consciously tossed back her long hair, encircled by a silk head band. The line-straight hair was the color of walnut shells and perfectly trimmed across the bottom. "Hey, you dumped those posters Dr. Crosby stuck on the ceiling. They were really dumb."

"Oh? I liked them, but I didn't think my patients would want baby bears and lion cubs staring down at them. I gave them all to my niece." Nedra returned her attention to the bird. "I saw one of your classmates this morning."

"Yeah?"

"Jeff Thompson. He is in your class, isn't he?"

"No way." Carolyn's voice went breathy. Chip flapped his wings. "I'm only a junior. He's a senior."

"Oh, yes, the Thompsons." Tiny muscles played tug-of-war with Mrs. Osborne's small, red mouth. She patted her French roll and folded an errant wedge of peroxided hair back into her coiffure.

Carolyn scraped the head of the budgie with a single finger and an inch-long fake nail. She had the same lips as her mother, tight with the tendency toward pouting.

"Chip has a broken shaft here," Nedra said, spotting the source of the trouble.

"Let me see," Carolyn demanded. Nedra handed the glass to her and fetched a tweezers from a cabinet.

"Gross." Carolyn's teal eyelids, heavy with mascara and eyeliner, flapped rapidly.

Mrs. Osborne turned away, but her glance fell on the jars containing specimens soaking in formalin that Nedra had taken from the Thompson cow. Annie had set them out when Nedra was reading about parakeets. "For heaven's sake, Carolyn, quit looking at that sore. I'm going to wait in the other room."

With Chip firmly in hand, Nedra plucked the broken quill out of the feather follicle. The bleeding stopped immediately. The bird squawked and tried to break away. Failing that, he pecked at Nedra's thumb. Nedra dabbed Chip with a bit of disinfectant and set him back on Carolyn's finger.

"How was Jeff?" Carolyn asked quietly.

"Fine."

"Isn't he the cutest? We're..."

"Are you about finished?" Mrs. Osborne asked. For a woman of moderate build, she filled the door frame nicely.

"Finished," Nedra said. "Don't touch the sore spot, Carolyn. A new feather should start growing right away. Within a couple of weeks, you should see a quill about this long." She held up her fingers, showing a quarter inch spread.

As Nedra entered the transaction on the computer at the front counter, Carolyn craned her neck in the direction of the work station. "A PC, huh? What software do you use?"

"Excel mostly. I use it to track client accounts. I'm just starting to set up an inventory system." The printer started to spit out an invoice. "I want to finish that project by the end of the quarter."

"Any games? We've got ton of them at home. We're gonna get..."

"It's *going to* not *gonna*, Carolyn. I do wish you wouldn't speak like some country hick." Mrs. Osborne frowned as she accepted the bill from Nedra. "Seems like a lot for three minutes of your time." Her gray eyes drilled into Nedra.

"But many years of education. You can put it on credit, if you'd like. I ask for a minimum of ten dollars a month. You should be able to clear the debt next month."

The lips of Mrs. Osborne jutted into an angry pout. "I'll pay the whole thing now." She scratched out the amount on a check—twenty dollars—and tore it from her checkbook.

"Thank you, Mrs. Osborne, Carolyn. Let me know if Chip has any more problems."

A subdued Carolyn fitted the floral cover over the top of the bird cage. The bird peeped, then blinked its flat, black eyes, before disappearing into a fabricated night.

⌘

"Any more calls this morning?" Nedra ran her finger down the appointment calendar.

"No." Annie peeled off her head cloth and shook out her hair.

"Good." Nedra said. "Let's take off after my shower."

The water hit Nedra with shocking force. She let the hot stream beat down her back before lathering up. Of everything in her office, this tiny white cubicle in the corner of the basement was what she treasured most. That old dentist had known how to live. Nedra washed herself vigorously. She let the disappointing delivery, the Thompson despair, and the Osborne arrogance sluice off her body and whirl down the stainless steel drain.

She snuggled into a clean cotton shirt and slicked back her wet hair into a pony tail. She heard the whir of a power drill in the distance.

"Is the parakeet going to be okay?" Annie asked as Nedra stepped into the hallway. Annie's moss-colored eyes grew a bit more piercing, if that were possible. She twirled the last screw of a door hinge into place.

"For the time being. As a pet in that family, its brain will probably explode from neurosis within three years."

Annie laughed softly. "Ready?" she asked, tilting a Dutch door toward the opening of the kennel.

"Ready." Nedra grabbed the oak door. Together, they eased the knuckles of the hinges into a tight fit. Annie stood on her toes, making her almost as tall as Nedra, then slid the pin into the top hinge and tapped it into place with a hammer.

"What's the story with the Thompsons?"

"Things seem to be getting progressively worse. Now the calves aren't just coming too soon, they're deformed."

"What does that tell you?" Annie pounded the last pin into place.

"That I need a miracle to close this case," Nedra said, pressing her back against the wall.

"You'll make one happen." Annie closed and opened the door a few times, then split the top part of the door from the bottom and tried each section separately. "Tah-dah!" she crowed, hands raised in triumph.

Nedra clapped. "Nice work."

"Thanks." Annie trailed after Nedra to the front office and took a seat on the desk. "They struggle so hard to make it. I wonder why sometimes."

"It's so damn frustrating. Every swing I take at this problem comes up with air. I can't hit anything solid."

"It seems like you know a lot more now than you did two months ago. Didn't you once tell me that the first step of diagnosis..."

"...is to know what the disease is not. True, we've eliminated a lot, but I don't feel any closer to the solution." Nedra leafed through her Rolodex. "Maybe Matt's right. The Hand of God is behind this."

"Which hand?"

"Maybe He has only one."

"Ha! That would fit perfectly with Matt's world view. The guy forbids card playing and any form of work on Sunday, or so Jessie wrote in one of her journals last winter."

"Just a sec." Nedra picked up the phone and punched a series of numbers. "I need to let the Lab know we're on our way." After a couple of rings, she heard the line pick up. "Randy!" she said.

"You again?" a voice boomed. "Now what?"

"I have another bovine fetus I need to run through the Lab."

"Same herd?" The voice grew quiet.

"Yeah."

"This is getting nasty, Nedra. Bring 'er right up. I'll open the Lab just for you."

"You're a sweetie. We'll be there around two."

"We? You're bringing the redhead?"

Nedra caught Annie's eye. "She says she can't make it through another day without seeing you."

"Then what's she doing in that backwater with you?"

Nedra paused. She had asked herself that question many times. "Listen, I have to go," she said, hearing the cow bells on the front door jingle. Helen Sinclair ambled into the office. "See you soon."

"Now don't you two look right at home?" Helen said in a motherly voice. "I hate to disturb you."

"No problem," Nedra said, turning from the phone. "What can I do for you?"

"Just need a case of K-D for my old girl."

"I'll get it," Annie offered as she headed for the supplies in the basement.

Helen was one half of what was known in town as the Sinclair sisters. In their early sixties, they owned a large acreage southwest of town, just on the other side of the Amelia River across from the nine-hole golf course. Helen was the quiet, thoughtful one. Eppy had a reputation as a foulmouthed eccentric. Nedra had dealt with her several times—including leasing the clinic building—and found her to be a few kicks short of a hellion. The sisters were the town's powerbrokers. Hardly a committee bloomed into being without one or the other sister holding an office on it.

"How's Patches doing?"

"As good as a twenty-year-old cat can do, I suppose."

The last time Helen's calico was in for shots, she displayed the slow and jerky gait of Godzilla. Nedra had diagnosed arthritis and deteriorating kidneys.

"Your car open?" Annie asked as she carried in a case of Kidney Diet cat food on her shoulder.

"Yes. It's out front."

"The navy Taurus, right?"

"Yes. The front would be fine. The doors are unlocked."

"Gotcha." Annie disappeared out the door.

Nedra entered the transaction into her computer and then began to print out an invoice. "Anything else I can do for you today?" she asked.

"Well, yes," Helen said, waiting for Annie who was just coming back through the open door.

"Eppy and I were wondering if you gals would like to have dinner with us tonight. It'll be a cool evening for barbecuing steaks, but we can still have some fun."

Nedra raised her eyebrows at Annie as she handed Helen the bill. In the ten months they'd been in town they'd had exactly two social invitations, both from the Sinclair sisters for dinner and dominoes. "What do you say?"

"We have to run up to the Cities," Annie explained. "Will you be up for it, Nedra?"

"If we make it a short evening."

"Whatever suits you. Six o'clock, then?" Helen's smile dipped into a Mona Lisa tease as she slipped out the door.

"Another evening of dominoes and Eppy's proclamations about life," Annie sighed. "What was it last time?"

"Testosterone poisoning as the cause of war and the Catholic Church as the instrument of world-wide terrorism against women. You have to admit it was more entertaining than her theories on parity, price supports, and the S&L bankruptcies."

"Barely."

"You don't care for her much, do you?" Nedra said, making her way to the lab area and the bottles of specimen tissue.

"Pomposity doesn't appeal to me."

"I get a bang out of her. Not many people have a mouth like hers."

Annie screwed up her eyes at her companion of six years. "You may get a kick out of her harangues, but just wait. She'll turn on you."

"Wanna bet?"

Annie patted Nedra's cheek. "Sometimes, honey, you're too trusting for your own good. Be careful."

IV

CITY BOUND—A BROTHER AND A SISTER—BARGAINING

By noon, Nedra and Annie had the dead calf packed in the trunk of their forest green Nissan. At the east end of town, they waited at a stop sign as a group of Hispanics crossed the street. Nedra raised her hand in greeting. One man touched the brim of a cowboy hat in turn. They were part of a crew that Allied Processing, Inc. had bused in from Texas to sweat on the food processing lines at a factory on the town's south side. Among its products, the plant put the chicken in chicken noodle soup and some of the oddities in the military's rations.

Lake Amelia, Minnesota, founded and named a century and a quarter earlier by Norwegian, Irish, and German immigrants, had grown from a farming community to a thriving little prairie town of about 2,400 souls. Over the years, its community leaders possessed the foresight to diversify, and attracted a canning factory with government contracts, a print shop whose presses spit out national and international publications, and a baked goods plant that had been bought out by a European conglomerate and now shipped frozen cookies and muffins across the nation.

Its stability was one reason that Nedra and Annie had been drawn to the town. Facing a dwindling income and a possible layoff at a clinic in the saturated vet market in the Twin Cities, Nedra had begun to toy with the idea of moving to a smaller community a few years earlier. Then that awful spring two years ago when her father had died and Annie was caught in school district cutbacks, they decided to start looking in earnest for a small town. Lake Amelia had a teaching position open in English/Social Sciences, and with Annie's fluency in Spanish, she was practically a shoo-in for a town that was grappling with diversity issues. That and the fact that she was willing to risk taking a job that could be eliminated in a few years if the school merged with one in a neighboring town. Not many applicants stuck around after they heard that. Annie believed she could always get a job nearby.

Nedra had felt that she could bear a small town once again. It wasn't like before, just after she had earned her degree, when her father had asked if she wanted to come home and practice with him. She couldn't. Not then. Now she had Annie and, in a way, she shared her father's practice. She had inherited most of his equipment. She could never have afforded to hang up her own shingle without it.

Nedra angled around the entry ramp, then hit the gas as the car gained the highway.

"Oh, boy," Annie said, taking in the flat land around her, "we're going to see a city skyline again."

"You know, the biggest shock after I moved to the Cities from my home town," Nedra said, "was that I couldn't see the horizon. There was always something in the way—skyscrapers or houses or malls. I felt like I was locked in a stall."

"Not me. Skyscrapers give me a sense of proportion." Annie considered the broad fields of corn and alfalfa punctuated by an occasional farmstead and the gravel roads that narrowed to the distant horizon. "Sometimes I don't know what to do with all this open space. Out here it's so...naked."

"Still homesick?"

"I have my days." Annie turned away and rolled down the window.

"Yeah, mover's remorse hits me once in a while, too. But we'll make it."

Annie said nothing.

After a moment, Nedra gave her a sideways glance. "Annie?"

"What?"

"Look at me." She put a warm palm on Annie's leg.

Annie kept her eyes on the fields that stretched for miles with rows of young plants. Large patches of the fields held standing water, or plants yellow from too much moisture. It had been a spring of unforgiving rains.

"Are you crying?"

"I'm sorry," Annie said. She wiped away a tear that was sliding slowly over her freckles. "It's just that I miss everything. The restaurants, the theater, the bookstores, the bars. Our friends." She pressed her lips together to keep them from quivering. "I miss Di and Patty. Sue and Mary. Jane."

"I know."

"It's just not the same talking to them on the phone. We're growing apart. I haven't talked to any of them for over two months. They're busy with their big city lives."

And you're stuck here with me, Nedra thought to herself. "What can we do?" she said.

"I don't know." Annie opened the glove compartment and took out a tissue. "I thought I would be stronger than this." She dabbed at her eyes and blew her nose.

"Stronger? You're the toughest lady I know." Nedra squeezed her leg. "What we're doing isn't easy, especially for an urban girl like you."

"See, that's what surprises me. I thought I could adapt better. I knew what small town life was like before I came here. After all, I spent some of my summers in villages," she said. As a third generation Socialist child, Annie had spent many of her childhood vacations on her parents' causes, whether chopping sugarcane in Cuba—via Canada—or picking coffee beans in struggling Latin American countries.

"But you knew that was just for a few months. Not the rest of your life."

"Or at least five years of it."

This was the first time Annie had reminded Nedra of their agreement. They'd stick it out for five years, then decide whether to stay or move back to the Cities. "Our agreement wasn't meant to be a prison sentence," Nedra said.

"I know."

"I don't want you to be unhappy all that time."

Annie took Nedra's hand in hers. "I'm not all the time. It's just that sometimes...I feel so isolated."

"Moving back isn't an option at the moment." Nedra felt her throat thicken and a discomforting pressure at the back of her eyes. "At least for me."

Annie lifted Nedra's hand and kissed a knuckle. "I know."

It was not the reassuring answer Nedra wanted. "Are you think of moving back?"

"I don't know. Right now I have a teaching job and mixed practice suits you. That's a lot."

"From cows to parakeets," Nedra said, retreating from the abyss. "It's more mixed than I expected."

"Just wait," Annie teased, "until some clever folks move in with a walleye farm or an ostrich ranch."

"I'm heading back to the cat and dog clinic then!" Nedra cried.

"Where do you draw the line? Fish or big birds?"

"Humans," Nedra said without missing a beat. "Other than myself."

⌘

Jeff Thompson steadied himself on the corral fence and caught the heels of his boots on a slat of wood. The thickening clouds hid the sun on its slide across the top of the sky. The wind stirred the fields of young corn, rippling the long leaves like the surface of a green sea. No matter how ramshackle the farm buildings were, Jeff thought, they had the rich earth under them, a land that could yield dozens of harvests in a man's life and carry him through season after season.

"Lunch is gonna be ready soon," Jessie said as she came up behind her brother. She folded her hands across a fence post and rested her chin on them.

"So?" Jeff didn't move. The breeze agitated the fringe of yellow hair that stuck out of his cap.

Jessie squinted in the direction that her brother faced. "What are you doing?"

"Thinking how lucky we are."

"Yeah?"

"Sure thing." Jeff put a large hand on the top of his head and worked his cap around a bit. "We've got a dad who bought it in a grain bin, a mother who cares more for her damn herd than us, cows that must be chewing weed killer, and enough bills to paper our entire acreage. What a load of shit."

"Don't talk like that."

"You're the one who came down here. You don't like it, leave."

Jessie pouted. "You used to be nice to me. Like Dad was."

"Well, I'm not Dad." Jeff had been thinking about him a lot recently. Mostly he remembered how he would crinkle up his leathery face when he stood in the full sunlight, how his laughter burst from him like an exploding balloon, how quiet he got when he was sad or angry. He had been quiet for so many weeks before he died.

"That's for sure." Jessie yanked a blade of grass from the ground and clamped it between her front teeth. "You're a zit head. A big ugly one."

"Shut up."

"Do you think mom will get rid of the herd?"

Jeff gave his sister a withering look. "She'd rather die first. Damn cattle. They aren't worth the hide on their tails, and this land..." Jeff surveyed the rise and dips of the earth, the life growing in the rows he had so carefully laid down, a cow by the pond pressing her lips to her reflection in the water. "This land could be a gold mine. A frigging gold mine." Jeff jumped off the fence and landed with a small thud. "I could make this place into something. Really something."

Jessie gave him a playful whack on the arm. With an ambling gait Jeff crossed a stretch of pasture, his kid sister flapping along behind him like a butterfly.

⌘

"It's my final offer, Teri. Use the brains that God gave you for once." Matt Jensen held a glass under the kitchen faucet and let the drinking water splash into it. "I'm offering you top dollar. No one else will, given the state of the buildings."

"How many times do I have to tell you, I'm not selling." Teri wiped her hands on her jeans and gazed out the window over the sink. She fixed her sight on her babies by the pasture fence. Jeff was a man now, and Jessie almost a woman, yet in her mind they'd always be bundled up in diapers. "I'm keeping the farm. It's a challenge at times, but it's the way I want to live."

Matt gulped down the water and then slid the empty glass on the counter. "You've got to give those kids of yours a chance. Jeff should go to college—he's a sharp kid."

"He's not interested in school." Teri slumped against the sink. What she had here were dilapidated buildings, shaggy kids with worn out clothes, and a stacks of bills. But God, it was a life of freedom, and it was worth every hardship and set back. "The farm is his life, too. Eppy Sinclair offered him a college loan and he turned her down." Teri began to scrape the skin off some carrots. Like the potatoes, these vegetables had been plucked out of the three-foot pit in the backyard that was covered with plywood, paper, and gunny sacks. They were as firm as when Teri had pulled them out of her garden last September. With the edge of her hand, she scooted the peelings into a colorful pile that would eventually be tossed in the compost heap.

"That heathen?" Matt's face went hard. "That would be like borrowing from the devil. The Sinclairs are godless people."

"They're just different, though that Eppy could die tomorrow and I wouldn't care." The pot with the boiling potatoes rattled and the lid shimmied around the rim as water gushed over the side and into the tray under the burner. "Damn!" Teri said as she lunged for the pan and lifted it from the heat. The water stopped rolling and stilled into a placid pool on the back burner.

"Now if you just sold the farm, you'd have a good income from my monthly payments. You'd have plenty of time to try your hand at something else. If Jeff wants to work the land, I could use a hired hand. Think about it, Teri."

"That would mean giving up the herd. I'm not going to do that."

"Lady, this farm is broke. You're sure going to lose everything, herd included."

"We're not broke. Besides, we can't sell the herd now, not if something's wrong with them. I won't put diseased cattle on the market and risk people getting sick."

"But you'll continue to feed them?"

"Come on," Teri said. "I want to show you something."

She led her neighbor out the back door, past the large spread of garden, to the nearby edge of the corn field. Samson trotted up to them from behind the tool shed. Teri knelt at the seam of the lawn and the black earth, then grasped a clump of dirt in her hands. "What does this mean to you?" She patted Samson, who had settled by her side.

"Cultivated land?" Matt pushed his Stetson off his forehead.

"That's the difference between you and me. This," she said, squeezing her hand into a fist, "means Earth to me. It's Life. You think you own this land. I think it owns me. It feeds me and my family—look at my garden. It feeds my cattle—look at this crop."

"You're too sentimental. You can't make good decisions if you get all tied up in emotion."

"You're too greedy."

"I'm ambitious...and I have vision. There's nothing wrong with that."

"There is if it turns your heart hard. You want to own the horizons, and you won't let a woman like me stand in your way."

"I helped you out before. I can't do that again."

Teri threw the dirt back into the field. "You didn't help us out. You took advantage of my husband. Ed never would have borrowed money from you—or sold you that prime acreage—if he had known you would hound me to death."

"Without my loan, you would have lost your farm years ago. You can thank me for keeping you afloat when the banks wouldn't touch you."

"That damn loan. I'm tired of hearing about it." Teri slapped the dirt off her hands. "Not that I saw a cent of it. I don't even know what debts Ed paid off with it."

"He had a lot to chose from."

"Well, I should have paid more attention to the finances. I let him handle everything. That was where I made my mistake."

"You're making another one now by not selling out. You won't get a better offer."

"We could have made it before without your help. Ed was just too much of a coward—he couldn't stand to lose money. I think positive. Sure we're in the hole, but we can work our way out. All it takes is time."

"Dream all you want," Matt said, extracting a business-size envelope from the pocket of his shirt. "But by summer's end, I'll be holding the deed to this land."

Teri's face went white. "What's that?"

"I'm calling in my note," Matt said. "I'm giving you thirty days notice to pay me."

"But I write a check to you every month for the interest."

"Twenty grand is the principal. I'm giving you thirty days to pay it."

"You...you can't do that." Teri said. Sensing his master's agitation, Samson jumped to his feet and began barking in deep, clipped tones.

Matt waved the envelope under Teri's nose. "Watch me. You're responsible for your husband's debts, and if you can't pay on demand, as is stipulated in the note, then you're going to have to sell this place to pay me. You can bet I'll be the first one to make an offer on the land." He stuffed the clean, white paper into Teri's hand.

"God damn you, get off my land! Now!" Teri started toward the barn, tossing the envelope to the ground. "Damn you to hell, I'll turn my bull loose on you!"

With a condescending smile that did not come quickly enough to hide his fear, Matt spun on the heels of his cowboy boots. "Don't try anything funny with me, lady," he called over his shoulder. "You owe me enough already without adding a personal injury suit to your headaches."

Samson hopped around the retreating farmer, his deep-throated barks rising in urgency and volume.

"Shut up, you mutt," Matt snarled.

"Get him!" Teri called to the dog. "Rip him to shreds!"

The discarded envelope lifted in the breeze and blew toward Matt. Samson leapt after it, snatched it up in his powerful jaws, and returned to his master with his prize.

V

AN AFTERNOON IN NECRO

A little after two o'clock, Nedra and Annie swung into the delivery area by the Diagnostic Lab attached to the Veterinary Teaching Hospitals at the University of Minnesota. The vet complex and animal holding facilities sprawled across the southern part of the St. Paul agricultural campus. The State Fair grounds spread to the southeast, and to the northeast lay acres of greenhouses and fields with crop and weed experiments. Beyond the fairgrounds and fields, the metropolis sprang up again, with its industrial parks, suburbs, and shopping malls.

Randy Bell's van was parked next to the Lab, a three-story, eight-million dollar expansion to the old building. The new building had the same sturdy and utilitarian look as the old, and it came with matching brick, but the windows were strictly modern—large, square, and tinted. They afforded the lab workers an expansive view of the horse pasture across the way.

Nedra beeped the horn, and the smaller of the two doors opened. This one was big enough for a double-decker bus to fit through. She pulled up to a loading dock in the enormous bay.

"There you are!" Randy called, as he started his wheelchair down a concrete ramp along the wall. "Need some help?"

"I can handle it," Nedra said as she undid the bungee cords holding the trunk lid down. She lifted the plastic bag with the fetus and placenta from a tub in the trunk that had started out with a couple of bags of ice. The water was tepid now.

Randy leaned forward in his wheelchair to accept a kiss from Annie.

"How's my guy?" she asked, ruffling his curly brown hair.

"Wondering what the hell the class star is inflicting on the herds of southern Minnesota."

"Good to see you, too," Nedra said as she slipped past Randy on the ramp. "It's not as though I'm carrying a cat here, you know."

"Now, now," Randy said, pivoting around and following her. "I've always admired your muscles. Got to keep them in shape."

Nedra stood by the stainless steel door of the large, walk-in refrigeration unit. "Want it in here?"

"Nah, take it right into Necro. I want to post it right away."

Nedra shifted the weight of the bag and entered the cavernous, blue-tiled Necropsy laboratory.

"The table in the corner with the black bottom," Randy directed.

"My god," Annie said, "you could fit my school's gymnasium into this room, bleachers and all." She stood in the doorway, itself high enough for a giraffe with Carmen Miranda headgear to amble through. Of course, no animals, other than humans, ever came through this portal alive. Annie gaped at the pristine lab ringed with stainless steel counters and sinks. Several steel tables of varying sizes, the biggest one larger than a king-size bed, were placed throughout the room on the white floor, punctuated by drains. She waved a hand in front of her nose. "Of course, a gym smells better than this place."

Nedra grunted as she laid the calf on the table.

"What's all the stuff in the ceiling?" Annie asked. She pointed at yellow tracks that ran across the length of the room.

"It's part of a hoist system," Randy explained. "See, they run all the way to the loading dock, and even into the refrigeration unit. We can lift a carcass right out of a truck and lay it on one of these babies," he said, patting a table, "without breaking a sweat."

"Where are the gloves?" Nedra asked.

"Over there," Randy said, pointing at a drawer, "but first let's go to the front office and get this case logged on the computer." He rolled to a side door and was through it in a moment.

"Want to come along or stay here?" Nedra asked Annie.

"After you."

In the front office, Randy wheeled behind the desk and signed on to the computer while Nedra filled out a data sheet.

"Hope this is right," Randy said, banging on the keyboard. "Where are the clericals when you need them on a rainy Saturday afternoon."

"Doing what you should be doing," Nedra said, handing him the form. "Enjoying yourself."

"I am," Randy replied. "Okay. This is case D93-178254. Ready to slice and dice."

Back at the Necropsy lab, Randy lowered the table to a suitable height. "You guys going to hang around? I'll be done in twenty minutes or so."

"Can't today, but I will help you get started." Nedra undid the tie around the top of the plastic bag. With their gloved hands, Nedra and Randy slid the fetus and the placenta out of the bag.

"Oh, mama," Randy said. "This one's a piece of work. The other two didn't have abnormalities. Why this one?" He shoved the plastic bag aside.

"Good question."

"Probably congenital. Funny it didn't abort sooner, but ol' Mom Nature has her ways." Randy inspected the head of the cadaver. "A vet down in Rochester sent up a newborn specimen last week just for kicks. A piglet with one head and two bodies. The sow must have squealed like a son-of-a-bitch when that one popped out.

"I pulled up the records on your last two cases," Randy continued, smoothing out the fingers of his latex gloves. "I didn't spot any peculiarities. I'll send these tissues through as usual. Anything special you want?"

"An extra close look in toxicology."

"Beyond blood lead and phenobarbital?"

"Whatever you can give me for free."

"Jeez, Nedra, always looking for handouts." Randy peered into the calf's mouth. "How's the rest of the herd looking?"

"Like they're ready for show at the State Fair."

"Hmmm. Environmental factors usually affect the entire herd. Whether it's a toxin or something like magnetic fields from an electrical transformer."

"Yeah. I don't believe in selective contamination. Magnetic fields, though," she pondered. "I suppose I should check that out."

Annie stood in the background listening and watching. She had seen Nedra perform several autopsies over the years. She preferred to limit those experiences to livestock where she could remain emotionally detached; watching an autopsy of someone's pet was too hard. She took a moment now to examine Randy sitting in his wheelchair orchestrating the start of another post mortem.

Of all the things that scared Annie most about Nedra taking up a small town practice, it was the physical danger of the job: the bull breaking away and goring her, the horse smashing her into the side of a stall, a cow kicking her knee. Or, as had happened to Randy, the late night emergency on a clear summer night when the moon was full and the temperature perfect. Returning home at two a.m. from helping a mare with a breach birth, he had fallen asleep behind the wheel, run off the road into a utility pole, and crushed two vertebrae in his lower back.

But a small town practice, handling large and small animals, was a life that Nedra had always dreamed about. Even when she worked at the clinic in Minneapolis, the stories that sprinkled their conversations often came from Nedra's girlhood when she went on calls with her father, taking care of large animals. It was a life that Nedra wanted, maybe not forever, but long enough to satisfy the yearning. Annie gazed at her partner conferring with a colleague.

Nedra was leaning toward Randy, a hand resting on the dead calf's shoulder and her eyes filled with both worry and the passion of professional engagement. "When do you think you'll have some answers?"

"Thursday at the earliest. I'll take the tissue samples right into Histotechnique and make sure Julie gets this in the first batch

Monday morning. I'll save the original specimens in formalin, just in case we want to go back to them. Got the blood samples from the dam?"

Nedra felt inside the plastic bag. "Here," she said, extracting a box that contained two stoppered test tubes. She set it at the end of the table.

"Good."

"Randy, you're a real pal. I appreciate your help."

"Don't get sentimental on me, Nedra," he warned as he picked up an electric saw.

"Always the tough guy." Nedra pecked him on the cheek. "We need to push off. I'm on duty this weekend."

"Run along. Leave Red behind, would you?"

"Don't tempt her," Nedra said, tearing off the gloves and depositing them in a disposal basket.

"You still here, dear?" Randy called out to Annie. "You're awfully quiet."

"I haven't taken a breath in ten minutes, that's why," Annie said. "This place smells like a slaughterhouse."

"I thought you'd be used to the aromas of the profession by now, Ms. Callahan. Your Nedra can't come home smelling too sweet."

"Wanna bet?" Nedra said. "I shower at the office."

Randy gave Annie his widest grin. "You've trained her well, I see."

"No," Annie said, "I've just managed to coat her with a thin veneer of civilization. Enough to get by in company anyway."

"Glad to hear it. Back in our study group days, we didn't know if our studies should be with her or on her."

"I hate to interrupt your character assassination," Nedra said, "but I need to get going."

"Run along," Randy said, waving at them with his free hand. "I'll talk with you soon." He turned back to the head of the malformed fetus as Nedra and Annie slipped from the lab and into their car. They heard the whir of the power saw as the automatic door rolled down behind them.

VI

A DINING ENCOUNTER

The Sinclair sisters lived in a modest split-level house on the outskirts of Lake Amelia. The well-groomed lawn stretched about thirty yards in each direction from the house. Peonies, which could be seen from the floor-to-ceiling dining room windows, fanned out in both directions from the front door. Rose bushes, tilted up from their winter burial, lined the south side. A row of blue spruce ran along the northern edge of the property, serving both as a windbreak and a privacy screen from the gravel county road. To the west lay the horse barn, a small coral, and twenty-six acres of pasture. Between the back of the house and the coral, a twelve-foot satellite dish drew in television signals from the southern skies.

After dinner Eppy was holding court as usual.

"Why on earth would I go have a dream about the Pope? I'm not even a Christian!" Eppy Sinclair trumpeted. Her eyes, as dark and absorbent as twin black holes, searched Nedra and Annie less for answers than for reassurance of their attention. The corners of her mouth, which hooked down naturally, gave her a perpetual frown. She sported a no-nonsense clip of black and silver hair and carried twenty extra pounds on her five foot four inch frame. "I was reaching into the refrigerator for ice cream. Suddenly, old John was standing in the doorway in his full white robe and that goofy hat he wears. I say to him, 'From cow juice to Fudge Swirl. Kind of like water into wine, huh?' He gave me that bland smile of his and a curt little nod."

Nedra and Annie broke into laughter.

"If I had the Pope's audience, you bet ice cream would be the last thing I'd be talking about," Eppy said.

"Jung says that everything in a dream represents some part of you," Annie said.

Eppy pondered this information for a moment. "Authoritarianism, probably. Plus a voracious appetite."

"Gals," Helen called out from the kitchen, "what can I get you to drink?"

"I'm ready to burst," Nedra said, aware that her jeans seemed to have shrunk half a size since she downed her steak and potatoes. Even with the top button of her 507s undone, she could feel the seams tatooing her abdomen. "But a beer might oil things up."

"I'll take a beer, too," Annie said. She slid her chair back from the dining room table, a smile of satiation stretched across her face.

"And you, Ep?"

"Make mine a lemonade with a splash of Amaretto." Eppy's eyes took in her two guests again. "Good combination," she explained. "Adds a touch of debauchery to an innocent drink."

"Every place we go in this world," the elder Sinclair continued, "there are too many people! They're slicing into the forests to make homes for people in California and Colorado. And the Northwest!" she cried as her palm slapped the oak table. "You should see Seattle and Vancouver! It's like developers think the Divine Destiny of every mountain is to be layered from bottom to top with designer toilets and Jacuzzies!"

"Now Eppy," Helen said, speaking across the tile breakfast counter that separated the kitchen from the dining room, "I don't know that the Pope can stop all that."

"Of course he can. He's got people breeding like insects, that's what! The suburbs of the Cities are spreading like cancer. They talk about a deer population problem on TV. Bull! The problem's with the humans crowding out the animals. Developers and their money-grubbing clients carve up prime farm land to build these planned communities, then start crying about deer wandering the streets. Hell, that's deer range! What do they expect!"

"It's a fright," her sister said. A few years younger than Eppy, her softly curled hair glowed a pale blond from a recent bleach job. Only a couple inches over five feet, she cut a slim figure in her navy slacks and flowered blouse.

"I agree," Nedra said. "We need a moratorium on development. If we need more housing, build up, not out."

"We need a moratorium on breeding!" Eppy exclaimed. "That's where I'd grab the Pope by his privates and say, 'Listen, you rich white boy, you've wrecked the world. We're multiplying ourselves into extinction!"

"Speaking of breeding," Helen said, making her way from the kitchen with a silver tray of refreshments, "we hear that Teri is still having problems with her herd."

Eppy reached for the dominoes, housed in a Harvester Perfecto cigar box that sat in the middle of the buffet like a miniature altar. She flipped up the top, revealing a picture of a bay horse and a gold stamp announcing the five cent price of the cigar. She dumped the set of double twelves on the table. "That's right. What's going on out there?"

As Helen settled into her seat, everyone joined Eppy in turning the dominoes face down on the varnished surface. The round table, like the rest of the heirloom furniture, had at least sixty years on it. The place was a homey showcase, filled with antiques that were treated not as treasures but as loyal old friends.

"I'm working on it," Nedra said. "Finding answers for spontaneous abortions isn't easy. In fact, we find the cause in only about thirty percent of the cases."

Eppy gave the bones a final stir, then began to draw her pieces. "Helen got a call from Teri after you drove off with that godforsaken fetus this morning. She says her calves are dying like Egyptian firstborn at Passover.' That phrase, I'm sure, comes from that nutty Matt. He's the most self-righteous, self-serving ass we've seen in some time. He gets more pious with every year, like the Old

Testament God gives him another of scoop of religion on each birthday cake. He should be off ranting with those Southern Baptists. Instead, the Lutherans are stuck with him." She examined the constellation of dots arrayed before her. "Now he's demanding payment on a loan he made to Teri's husband. It'll break her."

"Oh, no," Nedra said.

"I've known Teri since she was a baby," Helen said as she watched Eppy finger her double twelve domino, then slide it into the middle of the table. "She doesn't understand money. And those cattle! She can go off the edge when it comes to them."

"I've noticed her attachment," Nedra said. "What's behind it?"

"Well," Helen said softly, "Teri had a difficult childhood."

"Difficult! Hell, her father used the whole family as a punching bag. Once I pulled into the Winthrop place, I don't recall what for." Eppy rearranged her dominoes. "I had barely planted my feet on the ground when her mother came busting out the back door, that bully of a husband chasing her. She dashed around the end of my car—I had a huge navy Pontiac then—putting it between her and Winthrop. She had two black eyes and a trickle of blood coming out of her nose.

"I told them to behave like civilized people, and Winthrop glared at me and stormed inside the house. 'Where's Teri?' I asked the mother. She was blustering away, her face about as deformed as a potato.

"'Around,'" she says.

"'Where?'"

"She shrugged liked she didn't care, and most of the time I don't think she did. I headed for the barn, knowing how Teri took to animals. There she was curled up next to a cow that was lying down resting. She had that cow's ear between her fingers, rubbing it like is was a baby blanket. I'd probably be nutty over cows if I had had her upbringing. Winthrop treated her like a piece of pig shit. The cows treated her a helluva lot better."

"Then there was the episode with the State Fair," Helen said.

"God, yes." Eppy toyed with her end domino as she watched Helen make a play on her double twelve.

"Eppy and I helped Teri raise a calf for show," Helen said. "She went to the State Fair with it. Only a handful of girls were showing back then. You know how attached these kids get to their animals."

Nedra nodded. She'd seen more bawling kids than she cared to remember. They'd fawn over their animal all year long like it was a pet—whether it was a cow or pig or sheep—then when it came time to sell the animal, they'd be busted up for weeks.

"We went to the auction and bought the cow for Teri—it was a feeder. A Hereford like what she has now."

"We hauled it back down here and gave it to her," Eppy said. "She kept it at our place—Old Man Winthrop wouldn't have it on his farm. That cow sure turned out to be an expensive gift with all the grain that went down its worthless throat. But she got ten or twelve calves from it, sold them, and put the money in the bank. When she married, she took that damn cow with her and started her own herd out of her savings. Most every animal she had for a while was a descendant of that State Fair show."

"But none of those animals are around today, are they?" Nedra asked.

"Hell, her husband saw to that," Eppy said. "Ed sold them to satisfy the banker when they got into the cash squeeze a few years back."

"Who bought the original herd?" Nedra asked.

"Ultimately the grocery stores...as hamburger," Eppy said. "Sending those animals to the packing plant caused Teri more trauma than nearly losing the farm. I swear she tottered on the brink after that one. Damn bankers—and husband. They had as much sensitivity as a slab of granite." Eppy tasted her Amaretto and lemonade mix. "First thing Teri does after Ed dies is she scrapes together a few dollars and buys a cow and a bull. Those kids didn't even have decent clothes to wear but what we gave them, and Teri buys cattle. Stupid move."

"I don't know about that," Helen said. "It may have been the only way she could keep her sanity."

"If her sanity depends on a bunch of brain-dead animals, the woman needs a tailor-made straitjacket. God, I've had my fill of her and those cows."

"Now, Eppy, be charitable," Helen said.

"Charitable! I've been too damn charitable! That's part of the problem! The bankers won't touch her, and she's into me for close to forty grand. It's like giving a gambler stake money to repay a loan. I'm through with it! She's not getting one more dime out of me to keep that damn farm afloat!"

"You know she doesn't believe you."

"Well, I've told her in every way possible a dozen times over. She hears what she wants to hear, and believes what she wants to believe."

Helen stroked off imaginary dust from the smooth surface of the table. "Well, girls," she said to Nedra and Annie, "as you can see, Eppy and Teri are a bit sore at each other."

"Money troubles tend to be a great source for problems," Nedra said. "That and love."

"We can narrow it down to money for Eppy," Helen gently teased. "She's tighter than shrink-wrap."

"Not tight enough," Eppy grumped, "or I wouldn't be out a small fortune. I kick myself everyday for being such a gumpious fool."

"The calving problem is causing Teri no end of concern," Helen said. "She feels that she has no hope without them."

"It's a tough case," Nedra said, glancing at Annie and feeling her support. "I'm doing all that I can."

"Humph!" Eppy snorted. "Some folks in town are wondering if you're up to the job."

"Why?" Nedra tried not to show the sting of Eppy's words. She clicked a black tile into place, playing off of Helen's piece. "Because I'm a female?"

"Maybe that," Eppy said. "Maybe it's your being a dyke."

"Believe me," Nedra said slowly, "neither my gender nor my sexuality affects my practice of medicine in any way." She glanced over to Annie, whose fingers had frozen on the dragon design she was moving toward the center of the table.

"Everyone in this town who has more than two brain cells knows about you two," Eppy said. "Believe me, tongues were flapping like birch leaves in a tornado when you first moved to town. The vet and the teacher. Moved to town together. Put their name on the lease together. Opened savings and checking accounts together. You probably even had a peeping Tom or two just to make sure you slipped between the same sheets."

"If we'd had known people were so interested, we could have left the curtains open," Nedra said. She felt the skin under her French braid grow warm.

"Ha!" Eppy cried. "You'd probably have had the busy bodies set up lawn chairs to watch."

"If everyone was so concerned," Annie said slowly, "why is this the first we've heard about it?"

"Listen," Eppy said, "no one had the guts to talk to you face-to-face. Plus, we were so desperate for a vet we'd have hired a three-toed Martian."

"Or the Pope," Helen said.

"We may be small town, but we're not stupid. We've been advertising for a vet for two years. You're the first nibble we got. All the vets coming out of school nowadays specialize. They want to work in the Cities, have regular hours, and charge a small fortune to clip a dog's toenails."

"I think you're confusing us with physicians," Nedra said dryly. She had yet to hit thirty grand a year.

"There's hardly enough large animal work to keep a small town vet busy these days," Eppy continued. "Used to be that every farm had some livestock. Everyone's gotten rid of them except the big operators. People are too damn lazy to take care of animals. Except that damn fool Teri Thompson."

"Listen," Nedra said, "we just want to live our lives. We don't bother people about how they live their lives. We expect the same in kind."

"The school board's renewed my contract for next year," Annie said. The freckles seemed to stand out on her face. She turned to Nedra. "If there had been an issue with our relationship, I'd have heard about it."

Eppy's mouth curled up with evil delight. "Child," she said, "it was an issue. Believe me." She slid a four-six combination into place and marked her score.

Annie swung her head around to the older Sinclair. She clenched her jaw together, which tightened the smooth skin over her delicate cheekbones. It was the expression she used when deliberating on the fate of an errant student.

Eppy held up a veined and calloused hand. "They won't touch you." Her grin broadened. "I've seen to that."

"What did you do?" Annie asked. Nedra sat back and marvelled at her lover, who was now fully in her teacher mode: totally controlled, composed, and firm.

"Oh, don't worry. I told some of those damn toads on the school board who were thinking of giving you the heave-ho," Eppy cocked her eyes at her two guests, "that if they so much as blinked wrong they'd be facing a lawsuit and so much bad publicity that they'd want to erase the town right off the state map." Eppy broke into a broad, singular laugh. "I asked them how'd they like to have a few bus loads of gays in their tutus and flannel shirts caravan down from Minneapolis and march up and down Main Street. The big city media is already trying to paint us small towners as ignorant bigots over the Chicanos. Do we need to prove it to them by running a couple of quiet, hard-working lesbians out of town?"

A bubbly laugh suddenly escaped from Helen. "I think the phone lines in this town were tied up for three days after Eppy's tirade."

As Nedra looked from one older woman to the other, she considered her conversation with Annie earlier in the day. Maybe they wouldn't have to wait five years to move back to the Cities. Five minutes might do it.

"When did this happen?" Annie asked.

"Six or seven weeks after you came. Late in September, maybe."

Annie's eyes went thoughtful, then she showed that brilliant smile that had caught Nedra's attention the first time they'd met. "I remember the principal going for about two weeks without saying a word to me. Now I understand. I wonder which made him more uncomfortable, my being a lesbian or facing a scandal."

"Heh-heh," Eppy crowed. "We had his pecker in a vice. And Her Majesty Lana Osborne. She can't look me in the face to this day. As if I enjoy looking into that painted mug of hers."

"Eppy!" Helen chided.

The dark pools of Eppy's pupils deepened, and the lines around her eyes softened.

"Don't worry. People like you both just fine."

"Good," Nedra said. "We have no intention of pretending we're something we're not."

Eppy grunted in an approving sort of way. "Well, just don't make a big deal out of it. Everyone prefers to let sleeping dogs lie."

"You seem to like to kick them awake," Nedra said. "Why?"

Eppy fingered a tile. "I want you to know how things stand in this town concerning the two of you. And where Helen and I stand. You've had our support from day one."

"Why?" Nedra asked.

"Because you do," Eppy snapped. "Now, Helen, play your turn. You're holding up the game!"

VII

PILLOWTALK—PILLOWTHOUGHT

"Eppy Sinclair is a manipulative old bag," Nedra grumped.

"What?" Annie said. "I thought you got a bang out of her." She lay with her hands folded under her head. A strip of moonlight leaked between a crack in the bedroom drapes and illuminated a ribbon of her stomach flesh. Nedra's thumb traced the pale bar, then ran up her belly, between her breasts, and over the knobs of her collar bones.

"Yeah, right through my head," Nedra said. "We handled it well, though, don't you think?"

"Like pros."

"Why on earth would she go on like she did?"

"To shock us." Annie turned her head slightly. The shadows of her face deepened. "That's how she always stays the center of attention. She's always the loudest and the lewdest." Annie let out a big sigh. She rubbed her fingers lightly across Nedra's forehead. "You have a couple of lines that you could plant corn in."

"Made by Eppy's hatchet."

Annie gave Nedra a few wet smooches above her eyebrows, then a couple of soft ones. "Feel better?"

"Practically worry free."

Annie fit a knuckle between two of Nedra's ribs.

"Yowww!" Nedra howled. "I'll talk, I'll talk."

"Scared that we're going to be run out of town?" Annie snuggled in close. "That's not the worst thing that could happen to us."

"What's the worst?"

Annie smoothed her hands across Nedra's cheeks and drew her lover's face close. Annie's eyes, soft and strong, held Nedra's. "Not being with you."

Nedra smiled briefly. "Thanks. I needed to hear that."

"Listen, even if they do run us out, we'll get along. We always do. We always will."

"You'd have what you want, then. Being back in the Cities."

"I'm not sure what I want."

"I could maybe get a vet job some place, but you might have trouble. Teaching jobs are hard to find up there."

"I have career alternatives, you know."

"Yeah? Like what?"

"Hollywood starlet. Crime boss."

"Neat! Big buck careers. Short-lived, though."

"Or maybe administrative assistant to the Sinclairs. They have their fingers in so many pots, I'm sure they could use help."

"Just what we need. Our livelihood depending on them."

"In a way, it already does," Annie said.

"Or so Eppy would have us believe."

The moonlight disappeared behind a cloud. After a few moments, small pings of rain splattered against the bedroom window.

"What do you think of their stories about Teri?" Annie asked.

"It explains a lot. She's weird, but God, she works hard. I don't think I've seen anyone take better care of their cattle. I give her credit for that," Nedra said.

"Do you think you can figure out what's going on with her cows?"

"There's an answer. Science will prevail, I know it." Nedra settled her head deeper into Annie's shoulder, and Annie's arms tightened around her back. "I won't let this be my first major diagnostic failure."

"You bet. The game's not over yet." Annie bent her knee between Nedra's legs, letting her thigh press into her. Nedra felt Annie's moisture and forgot about deformed calves.

"I think a new game's just starting," Nedra said. Annie was in the third week of her cycle. Nedra could always tell by her scent, a delicate smell like saffron oil with a touch of goldenrod. Nedra began to move on her.

"Diagnosis correct," Annie cooed as she pressed her mouth to Nedra's and tightened her grip.

⌘

Annie eased her arm from under Nedra, who adjusted her head on her pillow and sank back into a heavy sleep. Their cat, Copper, wound up like a fur turban at the foot of the bed, raised her head to check out the movement, but her face plopped back into her tail before she could open her eyes. Kettle, the black tabby, stretched her legs and turned over.

The small sounds of a sleeping house became distinct now that Annie set her mind to listening. There were the delicate poofs Nedra made as she breathed, and the tiny, but determined heaves of the two cats. The venetian blinds made a dull clang as the slats bumped against the open bathroom window. Here in the bedroom, the night breeze lifted the drapes quietly, but outside the leaves rustled in the soft whoosh of the rain-laden wind.

As Annie looped a strand of Nedra's hair over the curve of her ear, she marvelled at her present contentment and wondered how strong the laces were that held it in place. While her relationship with Nedra felt as rich and permanent as the prairie land under them, the forces that worked on it were as capricious as the weather. Nedra seemed oblivious to bigotry—an animal doesn't care about the personal life of its healer. Annie, on the other hand, felt its threat rake across her at times. She was a teacher. A molder of young lives. Seemingly rational parents could buy into the craziest stereotypes and squalid fantasies when it came to sexuality. Despite Eppy Sinclair's assumption of safety and her powers of persuasion, Annie felt no reassurance. She could be fired. Then what?

Return to the big city? She would love it. But she knew Nedra would resent it, and always wonder what might have been. Then they'd both have to find jobs again in a tight market.

Could they stay on in Lake Amelia? Could they make it financially on one income for awhile? Nedra was in the process of building up her practice. By fall she thought maybe she could afford to take on an assistant. Worst case, she could be Nedra's assistant for a time. A short time. Being in a lover's employ could lead to all sorts of problems.

Best case, she could find a job in nearby Mankato. With more than 40,000 people, surely the city would have something for her. It would be a commute of under twenty minutes.

No, Annie thought. The best case would be returning to Minneapolis, but it would be a trip she'd make alone. Nedra would stay. Lake Amelia was her dream.

And Annie's dream? She didn't know any more. Once it had been a good relationship and a good job. She had both, but it wasn't enough, not in a small town. Discontent suddenly washed through her. At what point would sharing a life with Nedra mean giving up her own?

Annie turned her face toward the drapes swaying in the night breeze. After a few minutes of watching the slow movements of the muslin, Annie's eyes dropped down for a final time. As her breath deepened into the steady rhythm of a sleeper, images of angry people, crying children, and deformed animals pooled behind her twitching eyelids.

VIII

A STITCH IN TIME—NEDRA'S COLLECTION

Late Monday morning, after Nedra patched up a quarter horse that had tangled with a stretch of barbed wire, she headed for the Thompson farm. She bounced along the gravel roads that ran through the flat fields of corn and beans. The sun warmed the earth where plants lined the fields like strings of malachite.

Nedra readjusted her bones in the worn fabric seat and rested an elbow on the window frame. She was aware that her posture reflected that of her father's many years ago when the two of them had gone on calls together. They'd bump along the country roads chatting or just smelling the wild honeysuckle and contemplating the shapes of cumulus clouds. Nedra remembered sitting in the dusty Chevy truck, her eyes barely clearing the passenger's window. Invariably, her father would reach over and pat her bare leg. "This is the life, isn't it, honey?" he'd say and then grab the wheel again to navigate the dips of the road.

She could picture his huge hand on her skinny leg that was covered with the fine blond hair of childhood. His hands were magic, she used to think. They'd be inside cows, or fingering the intestines of a sow in a post mortem, or steadying a cat in a grand mal seizure. They were rough hands, cracked in winter, the hands of a hard worker and a healer. Nedra lifted her own hand off the steering wheel and sought in her fingers and palm the characteristics of her father.

As she neared the Thompson farm, Nedra saw a green and black utility truck parked across from the driveway. A man was behind the wheel, leaning his back against the door, and stretching his legs lengthwise across the seat. His forest green utility cap was pulled low over his eyes. As Nedra steered her truck to the side of the road, the line technician woke up.

"Hi. You must be Stitch," she said, approaching his truck. The thick-featured man rubbed his eyes and yawned. "Sorry I'm late," Nedra continued. "I got tied up on a case. Hope you weren't waiting long."

"Don't make a piss-pot of difference to me," Stitch Feldon replied. He took off his cap and rubbed the back of his neck. "Boss still signs my paycheck."

"Lucky you."

"He says you think there's an EMF problem out here."

"EMF?"

"Electromagnetic fields."

"Right. We're having some calving problems on this farm, and I want to see if electricity's a factor."

"That's your first mistake, lady. Magnetic fields, *not* electrical fields, cause problems." Stitch tugged on a frayed belt that looped under his pot belly like a sling. His thinning black hair was combed straight back from his ruddy face. He pointed to the line running along the driveway toward the Thompson house. "See, that there's the secondary wire running up to the house and over to the barn. It's stepped down to 120 volts. Nothing up there can cause stray voltage. Take it from an *ex-pert*." He slapped his service cap back on. "Now if we had one of those high voltage power lines—those babies carry close to a quarter of a million volts from the plant, or even one of the large transformers—that's 13,000 volts—then we'd be talking major sizzle power. Stray voltage, maybe. But those secondary wires?" He shook his head. "You're pissing on the wrong tree."

Nedra frowned. "Have you been up to the barn yet?"

"You kidding? I ain't tangling with Teri without a witness. No-siree."

"Why would you want a witness?"

"She likes to imagine things sometimes. That lady's marble bag ain't full, if you ask me."

"Hmmm. Well, hop in," Nedra said as she went to her truck. "I'll drive you up there."

"If there's EMF here," Stitch said as they bumped up the driveway to the house and farm buildings, "I'll take a knife and fork to my cap. No mustard, either."

Considering the grease on his cap, Nedra wondered if he'd tried deep frying it already.

A couple of squirrels scampered across the dirt road and up the trunk of an old red oak at the edge of the small grove. Most of the trees were hard woods of one variety or another, with a dozen walnut trees scattered among them.

"I've read that electricity—um, EMF—has been a problem with some herds," Nedra said. "There's even a higher incidence of leukemia among kids who live within three hundred feet of those small transformers."

"All hype. You've got the tree huggers trying to push us back into caves and eat grass, you've got the shysters thinking they can sue the utilities like we was the lottery or something, and you've got the faggy newsmen who make us into bad guys so they get better ratings than the schmo the next channel over. Every snook's gotta have an angle these days."

By the time Nedra and Stitch stepped out of the Ford, the screen door at the back of the house snapped open. Teri, dressed in jeans, work boots, and a white T-shirt with the 4-H logo emblazoned on the front, marched down the walk. Samson, the dog, paused long enough in his barking to water a hub cap.

"Hi, Teri," Nedra said. She noticed immediately the sunken eyes of Teri and a tightness around her mouth. "Do you know Stitch from the utility company?"

"I should," she said with a smile that fell short of her eyes. "We dated when I was in high school."

"Teri," Stitch nodded. "Looking smart, as usual."

"Sure." Teri shifted her gaze back to Nedra. "So what's the plan?"

"Stitch is going to check for magnetic fields around here," Nedra explained as she stepped toward the utility pole. "Then I'm going to take some samples of the site."

"We're at the tail end of the circuit here with a single-phase line. We won't see nothing much." Stitch positioned himself under the transformer by the machine shed. He held out a black device a little bigger than a package of cigarettes. Dirt and grease outlined the cuticles and sides of his jagged fingernails. The needle jumped slightly.

"What is that thing?" Teri asked.

"A Gaussmeter. Measures magnetic field strength."

"Let's see," Nedra said. She stepped closer to the technician and caught a whiff of his acrid body odor.

"Not even a hundred milligause. It drops off at the square of the distance, you know." Stitch eyeballed the barn. "By the time I get over there, I won't have even a full milligausse. Care to bet the farm on it, Ter?"

"Is that reading normal?" Nedra asked.

"Yessirree." Stitch made a sucking noise with his teeth. "If anything's killing those calves, it's got nothing to do with electricity." Stitch stepped closer to the barn, then stopped.

"See," he said, tilting the meter toward Nedra, "the needle ain't even moving." He walked a little ways further. "Normal here, too. The only way these cattle could be getting exposed to magnetic fields is if Teri here is hauling her babies over to the high voltage lines in the next county and parking the truck under a tower." He eyed his old girlfriend. "You doing that, Ter?"

"If you're finished," Teri said, pushing a hand through her bedraggled hair. "I'd appreciate your moving along."

"Don't get pushy, now," he said, fiddling with his meter. He checked his watch. "How about that? It's five minutes past my lunch time. I've got a tuna sandwich calling my name."

"Stitch," Nedra called after the technician, "could you write up your findings in a report for my files?"

"Sure," he called, as he headed down the driveway. "I'll put it in a report, Miss Vet. Just for you."

⌘

"Stitch Feldon," Teri said, "is a thick headed mule...and about as smelly as one. To this day he thinks he should have been my husband."

"So you jilted him?" Nedra creaked open the back door of the truck and then slid a box of jars and white envelopes close to the edge.

"In my junior year. He was several years older than me—I thought I was pretty neat, going out with a twenty-year-old. But then Ed and I started going out—he was better all around. Better looks, manners, and he knew how to talk. Ed was Stitch's younger halfbrother, you know. By different fathers."

"Really?"

"Yeah, Ed's father married a widow and took in Stitch. He never did adopt him, though. Not his flesh and blood, he said. Ed and Stitch were raised together, but mixed about as well as Cain and Abel. There was a terrible fight after my first date with Ed. I thought those two were going to kill each other. You never saw so much blood. Stitch had over seventy stitches in him by the time it was over."

"Is that where he got his name?" Nedra asked as she sorted through a junk box looking for a pen.

"Yeah. Ed didn't come out much better. It was the only time I ever saw him hurt anything, you know. Not like Stitch. He's mean. He went after me once about ten years back."

"What do you mean?" Nedra asked, facing Teri.

"Oh, I suppose you could call it attempted rape or something."

"Teri, that's awful. Did you press charges?"

"Nah. That's something you don't want to do in a small town. I clobbered him so good his head was probably ringing for days." Teri made a little laughing sound.

Nedra eyebrows shot up at the odd-pitched chuckle.

"He likes to talk smart, but I've got him scared. He knows that if he tries anything, I'm coming back at him hard." Teri took in the handful of envelopes in Nedra's fist. "So, what did they say up at the University?"

"They're running the tests now. I'll hear in a few days. The pathologist thinks we're on the right track—we're probably looking at an environmental factor since they've ruled out disease on the first two cases. This third one will be proof enough for me."

"What are you doing now?" Teri asked.

"I'm sampling the soil, water, and storage facilities to see if we're running into a toxin."

"Well, how much is this going to cost me?" Teri said in an exhausted voice.

"Nothing for my taking the samples. I'll find out about charges for additional tests. I won't do anything without your approval."

Teri nodded. "I'll come on down to the barn with you for a while," she said, "then you can be on your own. I have some baking and the wash I have to tend to. Have you had lunch?"

"Just finished." Nedra had a candy bar stashed in the small refrigerator in the truck. She preferred eating it to taking food from Teri. She felt guilty enough about the breakfasts she'd received. "How are you doing, Teri? I know these must be difficult times."

"You don't know the half of it," Teri said as she led Nedra toward the barn. "But," she continued, pasting a crooked smile on her mouth, "I can't let these setbacks get me down. Times are hard, but I'm due for good times. If only people would give me a chance."

"I'll try my best to help you," Nedra said.

The barn, empty of livestock, stood open to the abnormally cool spring winds. A breeze swept up from the pasture and stirred the straw on the floor. The interior looked like many old barns, with weathered planks of bare, gray wood. Two worn harnesses hung from hooks above the main door. Aluminum pails, ropes, chains, halters, and an assortment of dirty leather straps dangled on nails throughout the forty-by-sixty-foot structure.

"What did the cattle feed on over the winter?"

"The hay over there," Teri said, pointing at a row of bundled feed in the southwest corner. "We have a bit more up in the loft. It's from our fields, and some came from mowing the ditches. We have permission to do that."

"What about oats or corn?"

"Over there." Ten sacks of grain huddled in the corner next to the hay.

"Let's start there," Nedra said.

For almost an hour, Nedra tramped around the farm buildings, gathering up samples of feed, dirt, paint chips, water, straw. She'd scoop a sample into a jar or envelope, seal it, then write on the outside the name and location of the contents.

The machine shed was Nedra's last stop before going into the pasture and fields. Nedra felt the shed wouldn't provide answers, but she also knew that if its doors had ever been left open, the cows would have accepted the invitation if they were out of their pens.

Nedra entered the building. The tractor parked in the middle of the dirt floor was a vintage model from the Eisenhower era. The original paint, a leaf green, appeared only in spots. The rest of the exterior, sanded and painted over the years with varying shades of green, looked like jungle camouflage. The name JOHN DEERE was almost obliterated by the rounds of patch work.

The sight of the well-tended tractor came as no surprise. Given the thrift and determination of the Thompson family, Nedra expected no less. What did surprise her, however, was the display of tools arranged on pegboard across one whole side of the shop. Power drills, hammers of every head shape possible, wrenches that floated like a school of open-mouthed fish. Nedra let out a low whistle.

"Mighty impressive, isn't it?" Teri asked as she joined Nedra.

"Amazing. You must have thousands of dollars worth of equipment here."

"We do. They belonged to my husband. He spent the winter tinkering with the machines, or making some outlandish creation—like sparrows out of loops of 10-gauge wire." Nedra noticed then the coils of wire of various thickness on the south wall. "The bank took every tool and sold them at the November auction four years ago. Eppy Sinclair bought them for a thousand dollars and gave them to Jeff for Christmas. I never would have accepted them—I won't stand for charity—except they were for my son, and it was the holidays." The lines on Teri's face deepened and hung heavy. "You can only hurt a boy so much, you know. He was only thirteen then, and without a father."

"Does he use them now?"

"Some. For class projects—shop and science—and for keeping appliances fixed. He's gotten pretty handy with the machinery. He keeps old Johnnie here," she said, patting a head light of the tractor, "purring like a milk-filled kitten."

"Nice machine," Nedra said.

"You should have seen our other one. It had a few years on it, but it was nice. The bank took that one and eighty acres. They would have gotten more, except that Ed had some life insurance on him, bought through the bank. Those bankers look out for their interests, that's for sure. They wanted this tractor, too, but no one would buy it."

Nedra circled the machine shed, examining the walls and corners for possible chemicals. Cans of engine oil and fuel additives seemed to be the only obvious substances that could cause harm if ingested.

"Any chance the cows could wander in here?" Nedra asked.

"Doubt it. There's only the side door there and the big door here," Teri said, flicking her hand at the metal sliding door, set into the wall of corrugated steel.

"I don't see any chemicals or powders lying around, except those oil-based products. I'll just take a sample of them." Nedra poured a tiny amount of gasoline additive into a small jar.

With Teri back in the house, Nedra stopped at the truck to leave her current samples and to snatch a Nestles Crunch bar.

Making her way to the field next to the barn, Nedra stepped to the fence, propped her boot on the lowest wooden slat, and surveyed the Thompson property. The family farmed a hundred and eighty acres now, most of it lying to the south and east of the homestead.

Half the land was in oats and hay, the other in corn. The stalks should have been shin-high by now, but with the weather, they were only ankle-high. A few areas looked washed out, and pockets of standing water covered dips in the fields.

Nedra considered the land before her. In the flat expanses and the gentle folds of the earth, the vegetation had soaked up the sun and rain since the great glaciers had receded to the north ten thousand years earlier. This was the prairie that the bison had grazed and where the Sioux had hunted. The land was a deep, rich black—as black as asphalt or a moonless sky. And across it rolled a weather as variable and uncertain as life itself.

Now, on the western border, a low pond filled in a depression of earth. Reeds rose from the water, and a pair of mallards dived for food, their feathery butts pointing at the sky. Small boulders and rocks dotted the lowland. Since the area could not be cultivated, the Thompsons used it as pasture for their cattle.

On the far side of the strip, Highway 60 cut through the prairie, separating the Thompson land from the eastern edge of town. Closer at hand, wedged next to the highway and an intersecting main road, was another crop of sorts: neatly planted rows of marble headstones at Our Lady of Mercy Cemetery. The caretaker was nowhere to be seen today.

Nedra trudged through the pasture, looking for God knew what. The grass appeared a healthy green. The cattle, bunched under a shade tree by the barbed wire fence on the western-most side of the lot, blinked their big eyes at their physician. A few nibbled at the ground cover, but most seemed content to stand and swish the flies off their backs with their long tails.

Betsy, the cow that had most recently lost a calf, swung her head around. Nedra ran her hand along its spine, then patted her head. The whites of her eyes were clear, her hide thick and shiny, and her nose slimy. Perfectly normal, Nedra thought.

She took samples of a couple of salt licks, water from the pond, grass, bits of dirt from here and there.

"Neeee-draaaaahhh!"

Nedra, scribbling on the label of the last jar, glanced toward the barn when she heard her name called. Teri's daughter skipped down the cow path toward her, deftly placing her feet between mounds of manure.

"Hey, Nedra, whatcha doing?" Jessie said, breathing deeply. Her face was flushed a deep pink.

"Taking samples."

"Cool."

Nedra explained her methodology to the ninth-grader as simply as she could. "Why are you home so early?" she asked.

"Last week of school. We only have finals. I finished mine early." Jessie ran to the herd and tapped each cow on the head as though playing tag with them.

"Oh, that's right." Nedra remembered Annie mentioning the exams. She didn't recall anything about the kids getting out early, though.

"This is my mom's favorite, favorite cow," Jessie said, looping her arms around the animal's neck. "Her name is Lucky."

"Lucky, huh?"

"See this spot here, on her leg." The girl pointed at a curlicue of white that flared into a patch of rust-colored hair. "This looks like a horseshoe."

Nedra tilted her head as though appraising a work of art. "So it does."

"Betsy's my favorite, though."

"Uh-huh." Nedra flipped through the envelopes and jars in the pail to make sure that she had all the samples she wanted.

"Know why?" Jessie kissed the cow's ear. A metal ear tag caught the sun and reflected light like a mirror.

"Why?" God, Nedra thought, how does Annie put up with kids day after day? No wonder teachers need three months a year to recuperate.

"Suppose I was pregnant," Jessie continued, swinging under the cow's neck, "and a dead baby with no legs came out of me."

Nedra's fingers stopped between two envelopes.

"Do you think the doctors would try to save it?"

"I don't know, Jessie." Nedra felt the cool breeze blow across her cheeks and the sweet aroma of new plants fill her lungs. "Maybe."

"Wouldn't that be something?" The girl's eyes fixed on the horizon. "I'd be the mother of a freak. That's as good as being a freak itself, isn't it?"

"Why on earth would you want to be a freak, Jessie?"

"'Cuz it would be neat."

Nedra turned an envelope sideways to mark her spot. "In what way?"

"I don't know," the girl said. "It just would." Then she skipped her way across the pasture, leaving Nedra alone with the cattle and her questions.

IX

A SPICY EMERGENCY—A CLEVER BOY— NEDRA LISTENS—BLASTOFF

Late the next afternoon Nedra was operating on a Dachshund when the front door opened.

"Just me!" Annie called out. "Who do you have back here?" she asked, walking into the surgery area.

"The Miller dog. Spay job." Nedra mouthed Annie a kiss over the wiener dog, its tongue lolling at one end of the stainless steel table and its ovaries sitting in a small, pink clump at the other.

"I thought the appointment was scheduled for this morning."

"Yeah, so did I. They dropped her off after lunch and said they'd be back tomorrow around lunch. A family emergency in Austin or something."

"Oh, good! We'll have the first patient in our refurbished quarters."

"Looks like it." Nedra glanced up at Annie. "You're out late today, aren't you?"

"I had to check in textbooks and pack them away for the school year." Annie stroked the dog's long ears.

"Did you ever think," Nedra said, "but for a twist and turn in evolution, I could be stretched out on this table and the dog operating on me?"

Annie lifted her eyebrows. "I'd buy a ticket to that."

Nedra flashed Annie a smile and continued suturing. "Did you see Jessie in school today?"

"No."

"She's been at the back of my mind all day. Why would she say she wanted to be a freak?"

"It's hard to know when kids are calling for help or just talking junk."

"What's she like in class?"

"Quiet. She's a little distracted sometimes, but not any more than other kids. Really, Nedra, it's probably nothing more than adolescent babbling. She's trying to find her individuality and she hasn't figured out how to do it yet. At least she's not screwing half the boys in her grade like some of her classmates. These kids...they're in such a hurry to grow up. I just want to tell them that they have the rest of their lives to be an adult."

The street door opened again, this time to the yelps of a dog in pain.

"Oh, jeez," Nedra said, "could you check that out while I finish stitching up this girl?"

"Sure." Annie disappeared into the waiting room. A few moments later she called out. "A dog's been hit by a car."

"Bring him in here," Nedra said, tying the final knot. She ripped off her latex gloves as she made her way to the examination area. "What happened?" she asked as she scrubbed her hands.

A Hispanic boy, maybe ten or eleven years old, clasped a mutt to his chest. The strawberry blond dog looked like a mishmash of breeds: terrier, lab, cocker, and dust mop. His hind leg hung at a peculiar angle.

"What happened?" Nedra repeated.

"A car." The boy tried to talk but he broke into tears instead. His black hair fell into huge, brown eyes. His oval face was chalky with fright.

Nedra put her arm around the boy's shoulder and guided him to the exam table. "Lay him down here very gently," she said.

The boy set his pet down like an egg on a pillow.

"What's his name?" Nedra asked as she lifted the dog's upper lip and noted that the gums were a bit pale. She pressed a finger to the gums, then began counting the number of seconds for the color to return.

"Salsa."

"A spicy little guy, huh?" Nedra said. Two seconds. That meant minor shock. She quickly checked the dog's breathing pattern and slid a stethoscope on his chest to check the heart rate. "What's your name?" Nedra asked, making quick eye contact with the boy. He looked at her directly. She liked that.

"Tony Diaz." He stroked Salsa's head. "Is he going to be okay?"

"I can't make any promises, but I think he'll make it. He's awake and his trauma is minor." Nedra took out a liter bag of saline solution from under a counter and hooked it on an IV holder "How old is he?"

"Four. I got him when he was a little puppy."

Nedra inserted a twenty-two gauge catheter into the front leg vein and adjusted the drip of the solution. "So, you've been pals for a long time, huh?"

"Yeah. What about his leg?"

"I need to set it, but first I've got to stabilize him. Then I'll make him sleep while I work on him."

"Is your sister Carla?" Annie said, stepping up to the table.

"Yeah."

"I thought she might be. I've seen her at school." Annie nodded toward Nedra. "This is Dr. Wells."

"I know." Tony kept his eyes on his whining dog, who struggled to sit up.

"I'd like you to wait outside now, Tony," Nedra said as she prepared a two-percent solution of Biotal, an anesthetic drug.

"No. I want to stay here."

"Sorry," Annie said, "the doctor needs space to work." She put an arm on the boy's shoulder and steered him toward the door.

"I'll stand back here," Tony said, trying to pull away.

Nedra decided to let Annie handle the boy while she injected the dog.

"Sorry. Doctor's rules," Annie said. "Come on."

"I need to go to the bathroom first," Tony said.

"Okay," Annie said. "I'll take you downstairs. Then we'll sit in the waiting room."

"I'll let you know when you can come in," Nedra said as the door to the waiting room closed. As soon as she was alone, she checked on the Dachshund, still placidly snoring on the operating table. "I guess you won't be going anywhere for a while," she said as she went back to Salsa, now in doggie dreamland. She took him in the next room for an x-ray on the Korean War vintage machine she had inherited from her father.

Forty-five minutes later, she opened the door to the waiting room. Tony rushed past Nedra to the exam table. Salsa lay quietly with a cast running from his paw to the leg joint. Nedra left the two alone as she moved the Dachshund to the kennel.

Tony tapped the smooth plaster. "Wow," he said when Nedra stepped back into the room. "How did you do it?"

"We need to be careful with his cast for a while," Nedra said. "It's still a little wet."

Tony snatched his hand away.

"Under the plaster, here," Nedra said, pointing at the side of the leg, "I put tongue depressors, one on each side. Then I wrapped wet plaster gauze around it."

"How much is this gonna cost?" Tony asked. "My mom's gonna yell at me."

"Maybe the person who ran over your dog will help pay."

"No way. It was old lady Osborne in her white Lincoln. She's mean."

Nedra patted the dog's head. "How about if you work off what you owe?"

"Yeah?"

"Sure. How about cleaning up the kennel, feeding the animals, and washing the floors for the next couple of weeks?"

"Deal!" Tony eyed his dog again. "When will he wake up?"

"In a few hours. I think it would be a good idea to keep him overnight. He's had some trauma, and I'd like to keep him close by."

"Keep him here?"

"In the back. You can come by tomorrow morning and take him home."

"I don't want to leave him," Tony said. "I'll stay here with him. I used to camp out sometimes with my dad."

"Sorry, Tony," Nedra said. "That's not possible."

The boy started to cry again.

"Tony," Annie said, resting a hand on the boy's shoulder, "your dog will be just fine here."

Nedra remembered the childhood nights that she had sneaked into her father's office to stay with a particularly alluring dog. While they were sleeping off the anesthesia, she would rub that spot on the top of their snout that felt like warm velvet.

Annie made a little "what do you think?" face.

Nedra thought of the liability and the mischief that a boy could get into. "I'm sorry, Tony, but you'll have to leave now. I'm closing the office."

"You're going to leave Salsa alone?"

"I'll stop in during the night. And I have a monitor in the kennel so I can hear what's happening when I'm at the house.

"I don't..."

"Tony, I'm not going to argue."

"Come on," Annie said, "I'll take you home. How's that?"

"No, I don't want a ride. I'll walk." He petted the sleeping dog, then trudged out the front door.

⌘

Tony quickly stole around the side of the clinic, opened the back door without making a sound, then stepped down the basement stairs, placing his feet as carefully as a tightrope walker.

After he heard Nedra and Annie leave the clinic, he counted to one hundred, then ascended the basement stairs. He went into Nedra's office and lifted a worn afghan off the couch crammed against the outer wall. He spread the cloth next to the row of cages in the kennel. The middle enclosure on the south wall held a snoring Salsa, his eyes jerking around like jumping beans. Tony stuck his hand through the wire mesh. His short fingers slid between the dog's ears.

After a few minutes, Tony tiptoed to the front office and called his mother, telling her he was staying with a friend. He returned to Salsa's cage, opened it, and slid his dog out by pulling on the towel that he was sleeping on.

"Hey, boy," Tony whispered, "I thought you were a goner." He arranged the dog next to his stomach, lifting him gently as a bubble. A few sleepy groans escaped the mutt. Salsa adjusted his bones and let out a big sigh. His leg stuck out like a bandaged boomerang.

"This is better, huh?" Tony asked. He curled an arm around the dog. A nightlight gave everything in the room a strange appearance, as did the angle on the floor. Tony felt dwarfed in the room. All the cages glared at him like empty little prisons. Something creaked down the hall. A whirring sound started. Tony sat up. It was the refrigerator in the next room. "I'm not scared," he said, hugging his dog. With the tiny snores and warm heaving chest of his injured dog, Tony drifted into an uneasy sleep.

⌘

Nedra couldn't get to sleep. "Maybe I should have let him stay...or let him take the dog home," she said, shoving back the covers of the bed. "He's probably crying his eyes out."

"It's part of his growing up. Now relax." Annie drew the sheet and blanket back up and then stuck the edges under Nedra's chin.

"You said that his dad died. What happened?"

"Tony told me that he was killed in a car accident a couple of years ago, only six months after they moved here from Brownsville. Someone at school mentioned the situation to me a while back, but I didn't make the connection."

"Why did they stay on?"

"They're waiting for a lawsuit to be settled and the mother thought they'd have a better chance if they stayed in the area. I think there's a tidy little sum involved, over a hundred thousand. Meanwhile, she's working on the chicken deboning line at Allied Processing."

"Who else was involved in the accident?"

"No one local, if I remember right. It happened on the other side of Mankato, I believe."

Nedra glanced at the luminous numbers of the alarm clock. "It's one o'clock. Maybe I should check on Salsa. It's awfully quiet over there."

"Nedra, it's supposed to be quiet. He's sleeping."

"I know, but..."

"Jeez, I don't know why I agreed to let you get that bloody monitor. If it's not going to keep me awake with yowls from demented dogs, it's going to drive you nuts because you don't hear anything."

⌘

Tony's eyes snapped open. Where am I? he thought, halfway sitting up. His pupils adjusted to the dark and the deep shadows draping the room from the nightlight. The animal doctor's place.

He heard a click, then a soft step in the back hallway. He wanted to say *Who is it?* but the words stuck in his throat. He remembered in Texas the night he had seen the ghost of his grandfather, just as his grandma had promised he would. It was in his grandma's trailer. The ghost was like a cloud, but it had a mustache and hair as silver as a coin. Even though it was his grandfather's spirit, Tony had been scared.

Now a small light crawled along the hallway like a drunken beetle. Then a figure appeared, dark and silent, wearing a ski mask and eyes that bulged out like cooked eggs.

Tony let out a high-pitched scream. It pierced Salsa's drugged sleep. Thirty yards away, it ripped out of the speaker by Nedra and Annie's bed, shooting the women toward the ceiling as effectively as Saturn rockets.

X

A COP INVESTIGATES

Nedra and Annie bolted across their backyard to the vet clinic.

"There he is!" Tony cried as he hopped from foot to foot on the back stair of the clinic, jabbing a finger toward the northeast. "There! Over there!"

Annie drew up to take care of the boy, her slippers skidding on the small stones by the handicap ramp. Nedra continued running for another half a block until she hit Main Street. She scoped out both directions of the road, looking east and west along the newly paved thoroughfare. A few lamps punctuated the darkness with dim cones of light. No cars were parked between the freshly painted lines; nothing moved along the deserted avenue. To the east a dog went crazy, its deep-throated cries tearing sleep from the neighborhood. Within a few seconds, a whole canine chorus erupted. Nedra jogged east to the next intersection, peering into dark yards, trying to penetrate the long shadows. Clusters of leaves lifted and settled in the light breeze. Lights popped on in a few houses along the way.

Seeing nothing, Nedra turned back. When she caught sight of her clinic, she saw a black and white unit in front, its motor running. Annie stood next to it, resting an arm on the roof of the car as she talked earnestly to a cop named Donnelly.

"That was quick," Nedra said, trying to minimize her panting. She detected a faint fragrance of lilacs from around the south side of the clinic, where a solitary bush was in its last bloom.

"I called 911," Annie said. "See anything?"

"No, but I think whoever broke in ran east down Main Street."

Officer Donnelly clicked the button on the radio mike, moved her lips against the hard plastic, and droned incomprehensibly. "Steve's up on the north end," she said after she relayed information. The northern edge of town was eight blocks away, as was about every other edge of the prairie settlement. "He'll make a sweep through that side of town." The cop shut off the engine. "I'll take a look around, then meet you inside to take your statements."

The officer slipped her metal flashlight out of her service belt. She snapped on the beam and followed the dancing circle of light around the side of the office.

Five minutes later, she entered the clinic through the front entrance. "I checked the bushes and garages in the immediate area east of here," she said. "Nothing doing. The perpetrator came in through the back, right?"

"Right," Tony nodded. He stood in the waiting room with Nedra and Annie, digging his bare toes into the linoleum while the officer scribbled in a small, worn notebook.

"Why don't we all have a seat," the officer suggested, claiming the chair backed against the wall that separated the room from the entryway.

"Would you like some coffee, Joanne?" Annie asked. "Or a soft drink?"

"No thanks."

"I'll have a Pepsi," Tony said. Annie frowned and fetched one from a refrigerator in the examination room.

With a broad, pale hand, the cop flipped her notebook open to a fresh page. Her gun rode high on her hips, almost poking her in the ribs. She fastened her eyes on Tony. They were deep-set, icicle gray, almost wolf-like. "Who's the kid?"

"Tony Diaz," Nedra said.

The cop gave Nedra a hard look. "You want to tell me why you have a juvenile staying here?"

"I can't." Nedra smiled apologetically. "Perhaps Tony can clue us in."

Tony's face went hot and bright. "I wanted to stay with my dog."

Nedra lifted a hand toward the kennel. "His dog was hit by a car and needed to stay overnight. I guess Tony couldn't bear to leave him alone."

"So you have a kennel and hotel operation running simultaneously?" the cop asked, showing a row of white, slightly overlapping teeth. Her short, brown hair had gone about ten percent gray.

"How did you get in?" Nedra asked.

"Simple," Tony said, then explained his trick of sneaking in the back way. "Are you mad at me?"

"Disappointed," Nedra said. "I understand your wanting to be with Salsa, but I also need to you follow the rules of the clinic."

"God, they get so attached, don't they?" Joanne said. "Our terrier bought it two years ago. The kids moped for weeks." She turned to the boy. "You Theresa's kid?"

"Yeah."

"She know you're here?"

"No. She thinks I'm at Johnnie Rodriguez's."

"You've got a good mother, Tony," the officer said. "You treat her right." Joanne flipped a page in her notebook. "Okay, son, tell me what happened."

Tony recounted the tale, using his arms, voice, and every facial muscle to aid him.

"This light you saw," Joanne said, "was it a flashlight?"

"Yeah. A flashlight. When I yelled, the guy ran out the back door."

Although what Nedra and Annie heard over the speaker was definitely a scream, they didn't correct the boy. Annie explained how she and Nedra had found Tony on the back steps.

"Anything appear to be missing?" the cop asked. "Drugs would probably be the primary target."

"I haven't had time to look," Nedra said. "Give me a few minutes." She did a once-over of the medicine cabinets and the refrigerators while Joanne continued to question Annie and Tony.

"From what I can tell, nothing's been disturbed," Nedra reported a few minutes later.

"The perp probably didn't have time," Joanne said.

"Should I do a thorough inventory?"

"I don't think it's necessary. He apparently didn't make it past the kid."

The youngster grinned.

"Tony," Annie said, "are you sure that the person who came in here was a man?"

"Sure. Well, pretty sure. I suppose, maybe it could have been a girl."

"Well, terrific," Joanne lamented. "That leaves everyone in this town open as a suspect, except those in the nursing home and the hospital. How tall was this person?"

"I don't know. Pretty tall."

"Were you lying on the floor when you saw him."

"Yeah."

Joanne scowled. "Who all uses this door," she asked, moving toward the rear of the building. The door stood halfway open now.

"Nedra and I do mostly," Annie said. "And people in wheelchairs."

"Delivery folks, too," Nedra added. "They bring their dollies up the incline."

The cop stooped over to examine the lock on the door and the door frame. "Wasn't jammed open," she said. "Looks like a clean entry. Anyone besides you two have a key to the place?"

"Not that I know."

"Well," Joanne said, "they knew how to get in the easy way, that's for sure. I suggest you get your locks changed first thing tomorrow. I told Eppy a year ago—when the dentist was here—to get better locks. She's got better things to do than manage her property, I suppose." She shut the door and pressed the button lock on the knob. "Do you two have anything to add?"

"Not really," Nedra said. "By the time we got here, the person had taken off."

Joanne flipped the notebook closed and headed for her car, followed by Nedra and Annie. "That's about all I can do now," she said. "I suggest you either take the kid home tonight or stay with him."

"I agree," Annie said. "I'll stretch out on the couch in the waiting room. I don't want to leave him alone."

"Thanks, Annie," Nedra said, "but I'll do it. It's my responsibility."

"But I'm used to being with kids. You're not."

Before Nedra could protest further, another squad car rolled up. Joanne, who was about to step into her unit, closed the steel door and angled back toward the sister vehicle.

"Found someone?" Joanne asked.

Steve Jones crunched his black boots on the pavement as he stepped from the car. "Yep. A couple blocks away," the young, muscular officer reported, his lean checks flushed with exertion. "Running through the alleys like a tomcat."

The passenger door creaked open. Jeff Thompson rose from the car, his hair messed in swirls. Sweat dripped down his face. His eyes skimmed the assembly before him. "I didn't do anything," he said.

"What are you doing out this time of night?" Joanne said, her voice rough with authority.

"Nothing." He face became as blank as a whiteboard. "Let me go."

"What would your mother say if I had to haul you in?"

"Who cares?" Jeff blinked a couple of times. "Hey, could you turn that frigging light off?"

Steve reached in the car and flicked off the switch. The pulsating light died.

"Like I said, nothing. I was just on my way to see my girlfriend," Jeff said. "Carolyn Osborne. She lives just a few blocks away."

"Where's your pickup?" the officer asked.

"Back at the farm."

Joanne hooked her thumbs over her broad, black belt. "What did you do, fly into town?"

"I walked. I have legs, you know."

"You think we're stupid?" Steve asked, taking a step in toward the boy.

Jeff recoiled instinctively. An expression of pure loathing passed across his face, then vanished.

"It's less than a mile. I can do it ten, fifteen minutes easy. Ask my girlfriend."

"So what happened?" Joanne asked.

"I heard someone running," Jeff said, his voice filled with condescension. "I thought someone was coming after me, so I started running. Then the cop car cuts me off."

"Find him just like this?" Joanne asked the other cop. "Nothing on him?"

"Like what?"

"Ski mask? Flashlight?"

"Nothing like that."

"Hey, I haven't done anything," Jeff said. "Let me go. I have my rights."

"Tell you what," Joanne said. "I'm going to drive you home. We've had a serious incident here. Somebody tried to break into the vet clinic."

"Big deal. What does that have to do with me?"

Joanne sighed. "That's what I need to know." She stuffed her notebook in her front pocket. "Put him in my car," she told Officer Jones.

Joanne turned to Nedra and Annie. "I'll have Steve stop by his girlfriend's house before Jeff has a chance to talk to her. I'll also have him check the bushes between here and where the boy was picked up. That's about all I can do."

After the cops left, Nedra and Annie went back into the office to tuck Tony in for the night. Annie, as promised, curled up on the couch in the waiting room.

Nedra retrieved a can of soda from the refrigerator and then settled into a chair next to Annie. She popped the tab and offered her a drink. Annie declined.

"Jeff Thompson," Nedra said, shaking her head. "What do you think?"

"Innocent until proven guilty." Annie adjusted her sweat pants. "But I'd say he's up to no good, whether it's breaking in here or going after his girlfriend in the middle of the night."

"Interesting that he didn't seem to care too much about what had happened with the clinic," Nedra said.

"Interesting that he wasn't intimidated by two cops," Annie said. "The kid's got an attitude problem."

Nedra took another mouthful of the grape flavored drink. "I should start locking up some of the heavy-duty drugs I have."

"You're assuming that the person was after drugs."

"Why else break into a vet's office?"

"I don't know. Maybe someone wanted to admire the terrific paint job in the kennel." Annie yawned. "If they wanted drugs, why not break in next door? The physician's clinic probably has a better stock than you do."

"Good point."

"Like I keep telling the kids at school, drugs aren't the answer. Maybe they're not the answer here."

XI

SCHOOL CHUMS—TERI'S REFLECTIONS

Joanne Donnelly tapped on the weathered door of the Thompson home. Everything about the place seemed tired. The side porch drooped, the roof dipped. Stains like dried wounds had bled down the edges of the windows from rain mixing with the powder of crumbling sills. The frail moonlight that seeped through the haze of clouds deepened the shadows of the nearby trees and washed out the faded blue trim to a grimy gray.

"Why don't you just let me go inside?" Jeff complained.

Joanne rapped louder. "I want to talk to your mother."

A light snapped on, and Joanne heard a "Who's there?"

"Teri, it's Joanne Donnelly. I have your boy here."

The knob turned and Teri swung the door open. She appeared on the other side of the screen, hands pressing into her hips. She wore a cotton chenille robe that was worn smooth in places. She glared at her son. "What are you doing out this time of night?"

"Nothing."

Teri turned to the cop. "What's he done?"

"Nothing, I hope. May I come in?"

Teri pushed on the screen door, and Joanne caught the edge. "Get inside, buster," Teri snapped as Jeff passed in front of her.

Teri slid back a chair from the kitchen table. Sitting down, she folded her arms in front of her chest and leveled her dead-cold eyes on her son, then on the cop.

"There was a break-in at the vet clinic tonight. Jeff was apprehended nearby, running down an alley."

"Does that mean he did it?"

"Not necessarily."

Teri turned to Jeff. "Did you do it?"

Jeff gave his mother a who-me? look. "No way. If I did, I sure wouldn't have gotten picked up by the town clowns."

"Careful," Joanne warned.

"What were you doing sneaking out?" Teri asked.

"Come on. I'll be eighteen in a few weeks. I can do what I want."

"The truck belongs to me. You didn't have my permission to use it."

"Ever hear of walking, ma? You know, one foot in front of the other?"

Teri shook her head. "Didn't dare start it up, huh? You're no dummy. Were you seeing Carolyn?"

Jeff stared defiantly at his mother.

Teri's lips hardened into a scowl. "Joanne," she said, "are you charging him with anything?"

"Not unless we have solid evidence that he's the perpetrator."

"Do you need him for anything?"

"Not now."

"Get upstairs, Jeff," Teri ordered. "We'll discuss this in the morning."

The two women watched the sulky boy trudge up the steps.

Joanne set her elbows on the table. "How are you, Ter?"

"About ready to snap." The farmer rose from the table and filled a glass with water. "Want some?"

"No, thanks." She kept her eyes on Teri.

"Why not? It's the only thing I can afford to give to company. A good well and good land are about the only things this place has."

She returned to her seat. "Of course, that's what makes a good farm, isn't it? That and a decent cash flow."

"What's eating you?" Joanne asked.

"Sometimes it just seems like too much. Jeff is a handful these days—I'm thinking it might be better if he did go off to school. Jessie wants her dad back from the dead." Teri sipped the water. "The herd is having trouble and the vet can't figure it out. And that damn Matt is calling in a note when he knows I can't get the cash in thirty days."

"Christ," Joanne said softly.

"I don't know why I hang on like I do. Pride, I suppose."

"Or sheer stubbornness." Joanne slid back in the rickety chair. "Remember when we were decorating the gym for the junior prom? Ed tried to help you stick those damn plastic fronds around the basketball backboard, only you didn't want him near you. The tape wouldn't hold and the leaves kept falling down, but you wouldn't accept any help. It took you nearly an hour to cover that one stupid backboard."

"Yeah, I remember that." Teri tried on a smile.

"You had such a bad crick in your neck that night, you could hardly dance with Ed."

"He was furious, that I remember. Our first big date and I'm walking like a hunchback."

"You're a stubborn woman, Ter. Admit it."

"Nothing wrong with that."

"Maybe not for you. You've kept this place by sheer will."

"I know that. I've had a hard run of luck, but the farm won't fail me. Not now, not after everything I've been through."

The women listened to the crickets outside and the breeze stream around the house. A moth flitted by the bare bulb overhead.

"I'm worried about Jeff," Teri said at last. "He's never had a serious girlfriend before. I don't know that he knows how to behave."

"Does he know the facts of life?"

"For heaven's sake, Jo, he lives on a farm. He'd have to be as dumb as a potato in the dirt not to know about it."

"Knowing the mechanics of it is one thing. Knowing the spirit of it all is something different."

"I'm not very good with feelings." Teri traced an imaginary line on the table. "You know that. Even that day when Ed died out back..."

A second moth joined the first in a dance around the light. The refrigerator broke into a loud hum.

"What's going to happen to Jeff?" Teri asked.

"Nothing, if he didn't do anything." Joanne rearranged herself in the chair and adjusted the belt around her waist. "He's getting too damn cocky for his own good."

"I know. He's so impatient. He wants everything now, and his way. He needs to settle down a bit."

"I could toss him in jail for a night. That sometimes throws the fear of God into a kid that's not too far gone."

Teri made a sour face. "That's pretty drastic."

"Well, if there's anything I can do..."

"Thanks, but let's wait a while."

"Teenagers are as much fun as a tub of piranhas," Joanne said. "My oldest wolfs down every scrap in the refrigerator, then whines, 'Mom, I'm hungry. When are you going to get groceries?' They're as self-centered as newborns. If I had my way, I'd send all ankle-biters to the moon and bring them back when they reached thirty. No messing with toilet training or college tuition."

"I could go for that," Teri smiled.

"Well, I need to push off," Joanne said. She scraped the chair back across the linoleum and stood.

Teri followed her old friend out the back door. "I think I'll just sit outside for a while."

⌘

Teri listened as the purr of the squad car faded into the night. How had things gotten so out of control? she asked herself as she stretched her legs down the last two steps. To the south, shadows passed over the land as the moisture-laden clouds crossed the moonlight. Teri turned her head to the right and took in the sparsely lit town. A few streetlights dotted the night, like far off Christmas lights.

Of course, it would be all over town tomorrow, how the cops had picked up Jeff and brought him home. How the cops thought he had broken into the vet clinic. That was ridiculous.

And his catting after a girl in town? Teri shook her head at the thought and took another sip of cold tap water. The hormones of young boys could get hotter than frying oil. It had been that way with Ed. She never got hopped up about it and just put up with the sex stuff to please him.

She only married him because she had been stupid and gotten pregnant. No wonder things had ended so badly. God could be harsh when He'd had enough of someone. Death was something you couldn't argue with. It was a door slammed and bolted shut. It was final, final, final.

Maybe Matt was right. She should sell out while she could—it was still her decision to make, Matt's note be damned. But what would she do without her cows? What would she do, period? She had no job skills other than running a farm, and she wasn't so hot at that, either. She could waitress or be a cleaning lady or work on the line at one of the factories in town.

"Ugh," Teri said out loud. She thought of being cooped up in a building all day, of having some boss tell her what to do. No thanks. Farming was in her blood. She might be poor, but a person who rises with the sun and steps outside to work her land and to tend to her own cattle has all the riches of the world. It's a free life with the days spent in generation and harvest. Sell the farm? Never. Sell the cattle? Absurd.

"We'll make it," Teri whispered to the fertile land around her and the animals on it. "We don't have much time, but I know you won't let me down. I know it."

XII

A COP'S ADVICE—TERI VISITS THE VET—
SQUIRMING KITTENS—GOSSIP

Officer Donnelly rolled by the veterinarian clinic the next morning, her gun belt riding high.

"Did you get Jeff home okay?" Nedra asked.

"Yeah, no brutality charges pending." Joanne opened the back door and examined the lock in the daylight. "This door is so banged up, I can't tell what happened," she said. "Has it always been this way?"

"Probably not until I moved in," Nedra conceded. "Delivery folks have knocked it a lot with their dollies. I supposed Eppy will get after me when she sees it."

"Count on it." Joanne sighed and shut the door.

"I suppose Teri is upset," Nedra said.

"Yep. I hate it when the kids of good people screw up. Makes me wish for the old days when we could grab a punk by the collar and shake some sense into him. If we tried that these days, we'd get the stripes sued off us."

"Come on," Nedra said, "I'll get you some coffee." In the corner of the waiting room, Nedra poured a cup of dark roasted brew from her Mr. Coffee.

The officer accepted the mug with her large hands. "Steve checked out his story with his girlfriend. She verified what he told us—that he did visit her late at night on occasion, and that, yes," Joanne blew across the surface of the steaming coffee, "she was expecting him last night. Could be she's lying to help the kid or could be she's telling the truth."

"Which do you think?"

"It's not my job to judge. We didn't find a ski mask or flashlight on him. We checked the streets and alleys around where we found him, too. A big fat zero."

"So you think he's innocent."

"Like I said, it's not my job to judge, just round up the suspects." The officer sipped some of Maxwell House's finest. "I called the physician's clinic and the hospital first thing this morning and told them to watch their drugs."

"Why would they break in here instead of the clinic?"

"They've got a pretty good security system next door. From what I can tell, all you have is a boy and a dog with a broken leg."

"Touché," Nedra laughed.

"My feeling is that if someone's that desperate for junk, they'd take off for the Cities where they could get it by holding out their hand on Hennepin Avenue." The officer grunted. "Hell, they wouldn't need to go that far. We've got our own players right here in town—and more in Mankato. Junk is everywhere."

"So I hear."

"I've heard they've been having some problems out on the Thompson farm. Sick cows or something. That right?" The cop tried to make the question sound casual, but Nedra could tell by the way she studied her face that the answer was important.

"The cattle are healthy as far as I can tell. Their reproduction capacity is shot to hell."

"Know what's wrong?"

"I'm working on it."

"I suppose they're running up some pretty high bills."

"Not really. The U of M fees are mostly token—only thirty bucks per work up. If we were sending human tissue to some lab, we'd probably be looking at bills in the hundreds or thousands. And my fees..." Nedra placed her look down the hallway. "Well, when

I settled my dad's estate after he died, I found he had been carrying several accounts interest-free for over twenty years. It's the nature of the business. Maybe someday I'll get a dressed chicken or two out of it."

"It's not exactly Wall Street for you, is it?"

"No, it's not." Nedra paused a moment. It wasn't much of a street at all for Annie. "You know, the real problem for Teri is that no calves means no sales. And given the tiny profit margin that small herds have, those cattle are an expensive hobby. She'll probably have to reduce or sell off the herd. None of the options facing Teri is easy."

The cop drained her coffee mug. "I read in some magazine about spongy brain disease in cattle. Think that's the problem?"

Nedra's eyes softened with amusement. "Not here. That's over in Britain."

"Good. I was thinking maybe the kid caught it."

"No. I think his condition is called adolescence."

"I'd get a better lock on the doors, if I were you. Harvey's got some good ones," she said, referring to her husband, who owned the hardware store. "When you get a new set of keys, keep them to yourselves."

"Right."

"The kid still here?" the officer asked.

"Uh-huh. I'm letting him sleep in. I'll check his dog out this morning, feed them both, then give them a lift home. By the way, from what he's told me about the accident, it seems as though Lana Osborne ran over the dog. Can you do anything about it?"

"Dog on a leash at the time of the accident?"

"No."

"Can't help you, then," she said, opening the front door. "I could give the kid a citation for letting the dog run free. That's a violation of the city's animal control codes." The officer touched her eyebrow in an informal salute, then disappeared.

⌘

Later that morning after Tony left with his dog, Nedra declawed a couple of Siamese cats, then did another eyeball of her office. Everything looked in place. She was tempted to print the list of her entire inventory and check it against what was on the shelf. A veterinarian's office contained material that someone could want for a lot of twisted purposes —PCP, drugs used for euthanasia, even scalpels and syringes. But, like Joanne had said, the person who broke in didn't get a chance to take anything, so why bother?

The cows bells on the front door clattered to announce the arrival of Teri Thompson. Her blond hair was as messed up as a pitchfork of straw. She wore a perplexed expression. "I hear you had a disturbance here last night."

"Someone broke in." Nedra put her elbows on the high counter.

"Well, I about had a heart attack when the police came to the house with Jeff."

"Believe me, I was surprised myself when the cops drove up with him." Nedra felt Teri's haunted eyes rake over her, looking for duplicity. She gave the widow a confident, little smile. "I'm sure Jeff was just on his way to see Carolyn."

Teri scowled. "I don't know which would be worse, his being a thief or being involved with that Osborne girl."

"Why do you say that?"

"I'm not one to go saying bad things about people," Teri said, "even though I'm sure plenty bad has been said about me."

"Not that I've heard, Teri."

"You haven't been around long enough." Teri drummed her calloused fingers on the counter. "You know," she said, dropping her voice, "I probably shouldn't say anything, but that Carolyn thinks she's a royal princess. And why not, the way her mother caters to her—she won't even let the girl clean her own room. Says that house work is beneath her. She expects everything to be done for her. I pity the man who marries her. He'd better have a whole wagon of money to spoil her with. I don't know what she sees in my boy, poor as he is."

"Perhaps the mystery of hard work and diligence. Or his good looks."

Teri brightened. "God, he is a handsome kid, isn't he? Just like his dad. Of course, good looks can be another type of heartache altogether."

The cow bells clanked on the front door once more.

Teri leaned close to Nedra and whispered. "Believe me, if Jeff ever does any wrong by you, I'll see that it's set right."

Sadie Larson, one of the town beauticians, hauled a cardboard pet carrier full of mewing kittens into the clinic.

"Here they are, the whole pack of 'em!" Sadie cried, working a piece of gum around her mouth. Her bleached hair shot out in every direction from her head. Nedra guessed the woman to be in her late thirties. By her clothes—white stretch pants with a spangly red T-shirt down to her thighs, she looked sixteen. "You get 'em fixed up with shots, Doc, and I'll give you a couple. You, too, Teri. You could use a good mouser or two out on your place, couldn't you?"

"I don't think they're at the mousing stage," Teri said, peeking inside the box.

"Maybe the doc here could shoot 'em up with some of those steroids. Turn 'em into lions overnight. What do you say to that, Doc?"

"Are you selling swamp land in Florida, too?" Nedra asked as she prepared a combination of feline vaccines used for a kitten's first series of shots.

"You buying?" Sadie said. She snapped her gum and guffawed, then centered the box on the exam table. Dull thuds and tiny cries emanated from the carrier.

"Well, I see you have business to take care of," Teri said, turning to go.

"Don't worry about it, Teri. You have enough on your mind these days."

"By the way," Teri said, " did you send all the samples you took to the lab?"

"Only a few. I'm sending them up in batches, starting with the most likely ones for trouble. It's less expensive this way, if they find what the problem is early on."

"Good," she said. "Let me know, though, before you send out any more. I have to watch my expenses." With a final glance at the box of kittens, she slipped out the door with a jangle of bells.

⌘

As Nedra lifted the last of the kittens out of the carton, she saw Stitch Feldon waving a sheet of paper in the doorway of the exam room.

"Hey," he said, flapping the paper harder, "I wrote down those Gaussmeter readings like you asked. Here it is, all nice and official."

"Thanks," Nedra said. She had a piebald kitten in the crook of her arm. "I didn't mean for you to run over here with it. You could have dropped it in the mail." She reached out for the report with her free arm.

"No problem. I was in the neighborhood."

Nedra ran her eyes down the page. "Looks good."

"Why'd you want something like this, if you don't mind me asking?"

Nedra moved behind the front counter, the kitten cupped against her chest. "I want to keep it on file. The more information we have about the situation, the better." She slid the report into the in-basket, then headed back to the examination room.

"Cute little bugger you have there," Stitch said, nodding toward the kitten that was now trying to climb up Nedra's shoulder. He turned to the beautician who was busy batting the rest of the straying and tumbling kittens to the center of the exam table. "You giving any of these away?" he asked.

"Sorry, buster," Sadie said. "They're all spoken for."

"That so? I sure wouldn't mind a couple of them."

"They would mind it plenty." Sadie snapped her gum.

Stitch showed his yellow teeth. "Have a good day, ladies."

⌘

Nedra finished with the last of the immunizations as the front door closed behind Stitch. "Why didn't you want to give any kittens to him?" she asked, her eyes round with curiosity.

"I'd sooner you kill 'em that have that baboon put his paws on my babies. He'd torture them to death."

Nedra shot Sadie a sharp look. "Are you serious?"

"I may be a joker, but not when it comes to animals. My clients let me know what's going on. Stitch had a dog once. Half starved the thing to death, then beat it. Stupid thing just licked his hand. That's why I like cats. They got pride. You try that with a cat, and whoosh, out the door, adios bastardos."

"If you hear of anyone mistreating an animal, Sadie, I want to know about it. I won't tolerate that type of behavior."

"Glad to." Sadie peered at Nedra, then made a half circle around her. "Say, Doc," she said, "who's been cutting your hair?"

"No one special. I just get the ends trimmed."

Sadie lifted some blond strands by Nedra's ear and examined the ends. "This looks like one of Dee Dee's chop jobs." The beautician let the hair flop back down. "You paid her to do this?"

"Yep. I got change back on my dollar, too," Nedra deadpanned.

"Just between you and I, the state oughta flush her license right down the tiolah. She don't know which end of the scissors to hold."

"It's that bad, huh?"

"I'm not saying it don't look good. With a face like yours, you'd look good with an Army boot crammed on your head. I could do something really cute, though."

"Cute's not my style."

"Yeah? How about moderately stunning?"

Nedra laughed. "Closer."

Sadie squinted at Nedra's hair like she was about to take her shears to it. "Yeah, you could use a good trim. Maybe two inches. Better stop in for a clip this week. Ten percent off." She snapped her gum. "Professional courtesy."

XIII

CAROLYN'S VISIT—PENNED

"You never pay any attention to meeee," Carolyn Osborne whined. She lifted her long hair up off her back like she was airing it out. She knew such a pose accentuated her bust because she had practiced it lots in the bathroom mirror.

Jeff tossed a pitchfork of cattle droppings into a wheelbarrow. "Hang on." He withdrew the tines from the pile and scooped up another load.

"You'd think a woman could get a little more attention than a mountain of cow shit."

Jeff hesitated for a moment, then frowned. He tossed the pile into the wheelbarrow. Sweat glistened on his bare back. "You know I don't like rubbers. Why can't you just go on the pill so I can get everything out of what I put in."

Carolyn rolled her eyes skyward. "God, get off that, would you? You're not having any problems that I've noticed."

Jeff stabbed the pile of manure and straw again. "Yeah? Well, you wouldn't notice a thing like my pleasure, would you?"

"Hey, get real." Carolyn ran her nails lightly down Jeff's spine. "I'm aware of your every move, big guy. Like I've got radar coming out of every pore."

Jeff felt his skin erupt in goose bumps and a stirring in his Levis. "Yeah? So what's your radar telling you now?"

"That it was real stupid getting picked up like you did." Her nails dug deeper and her voice turned hard. "Now my mom knows about me sneaking out at night. You shoulda seen her when the cops stopped by. You know how Lana glories in her Super Bitch trip. She ragged on me 'til she got hoarse."

"You think it was fun for me, having the cops push me around like I'm some sort of punk, then taking me to mom like I was a two-year-old." Jeff stabbed the pitchfork into the manure.

Carolyn put on a mammoth pout. "Lana doesn't want me to, well, you know, see you any more..."

"Screw her. She thinks I'm beneath your family."

Carolyn watched Jeff toss a load of excrement into the wheelbarrow. How could anyone stand the smell? She wouldn't put up with his mucking around in the manure for the rest of his life. "So, who do you think is gonna take the fall for doing the vet's office?"

"Eppy Sinclair, for all I care."

Carolyn let out a mean hoot, while Jeff heaved another forkful into the wheelbarrow. She slid her hands across Jeff's shoulders. Jeff tossed the tool away, twirled around, grabbed Carolyn by the waist, and hoisted her off the ground.

"Come on, farm boy, let's party." Carolyn bit the top of his shoulder. She scrambled up the ladder to the loft with Jeff close behind.

⌘

"What's that?" Carolyn whispered.

Jeff ignored her.

"Hey, stop." Carolyn pushed against Jeff's bare shoulder and wiggled into a sitting position.

"Hey!" Jeff cried. "What are you doing!"

"Someone's here."

"No way." But Jeff cocked his head, listening. He heard a squawking noise just outside the barn and Samson's barks. "Shit." He jumped off the couch, rearranged his jeans, and climbed down the loft ladder.

"Aaack! Aaaack!" The cries came from the south side of the barn.

Resting a hand on the gate between the large south door and the pen that wrapped around the southwestern edge of the barn, Jeff peered around the corner. There, pinned against the barn wall, was Matt Jensen. A cow stood two feet in front of him, blinking at the shivering farmer like a bored sightseer.

"What the hell are you doing here?" Jeff asked. "Quiet," he said to Samson, who stopped barking immediately. The dog squirmed at Jeff's feet and growled in Matt's direction.

"Get this damn thing away from me!" Matt pleaded, his face as gray as the clouds overhead. A light mist had started up, shrouding the landscape with small beads of moisture. Betsy's back glistened with the fine drops. "It's going to kill me for God's sake! Help!"

"Only if she sits on you," Jeff grinned. "Old Betsy's about as dangerous as a boulder. Now Loco would be a different story."

"Shut up and get this beef away from me!"

The cow ground her cud like it was a fist-sized wad of chewing gum. Her tail flicked behind her in a long, lazy arc.

"Well, I don't know what to do," Jeff said. "Here I find you trespassing. Maybe I should just let old Bets take you down."

"I'm telling you, boy, if this cow so much as touches me, I'm suing you."

"Hey, Matt boy, I didn't put you in the pen. Seems to me that you must have climbed in yourself."

Matt took a sliding step to the left. The cow followed his movement.

"Damn it, she won't let me past."

"You think you're such a hotshot farmer," Jeff jeered. "You can't even handle a tame cow. Just walk over here, you idiot."

"I'm warning you..."

Jeff drew his lips inward, then let loose a shrill whistle. "Hey!" he called. "Hey!"

Betsy turned her thick neck toward the motioning boy. She blinked slowly, as if deciding which party was more engaging, then rotated the rest of her bulk toward Jeff. The mud squished under her hooves as she turned, and the flies buzzing around her eyes adjusted to the new position.

Jeff unlatched the gate leading into the barn and stepped toward the cow. "Come on, girl," he said, grabbing her halter. "Matt here is going to crap in his pants if you don't back off." He heard a giggle above him and caught the flash of Carolyn's head as she ducked back inside the open hay doors. Matt didn't seem to hear it.

Matt kept his eyes on the cow as Jeff lead her away. When the gap between the barn and the cow reached several feet, Matt marked the range of the fence, eyeing the weather-beaten boards like a high jumper measuring for height and distance. He took three shallow breaths—all the air that could fit into his terror-possessed body—and broke into a run.

Betsy tried to swing her head around to look at the commotion.

A loud, high-pitched scream tore out of Matt's throat.

"Run! Run!" Jeff cried. "Betsy's breaking free!" The boy dug his boots into the muddy ground as if the cow were trying to drag him. Betsy stood as still as a slab of rock, then flicked an ear against a fly. "You can do it! Hurry!"

Matt rushed to the fence and scrambled over the wooden slats. His back belt loop snagged on a nail.

"Shit!" Matt cried, trying to yank his pants off the fence. "I got my damn jeans caught!"

"For Christsakes, jump! I can't hold her back any longer." Jeff took his hand off Betsy's halter. The cow, standing in the mud like a Remington bronze, didn't flinch a muscle. "She's coming after you!"

"Damn!" Matt let his weight carry him to the ground. A sharp rip sounded over the rythmatic grinding of Betsy's teeth.

Jeff climbed the wooden slats and jumped to the other side of the fence. "Whew," he said after he landed. "I thought you were a goner for sure."

"Shut up." Matt twisted around, trying to assess the damage to his torn belt loop. "Damn. I paid forty bucks for these jeans."

"What's a belt loop when you have your life?"

"I told you to shut up." Matt swiped the Stetson off his head and rubbed his forehead with his arm. He fit his cowboy hat back on and adjusted it carefully.

"I didn't realize you were so scared of livestock."

Matt swatted the rear of his pants, knocking off the dirt. "You laugh now, boy, because you won't be laughing later."

"Maybe." Jeff patted Samson on the head. "Kind of silly to go into a pen when you're such a wimp about cattle."

"I'm telling you, leave it alone." Matt straightened up and adjusted his belt and silver buckle. "Besides, I didn't see the damn thing—I thought all the cattle were in the pasture. I was just cutting across to the back to see if I could find Teri, and around the corner that damn thing comes. You shouldn't have a wraparound pen like that."

"You shouldn't go crawling around where you don't belong."

Matt started to roll up the sleeves of his Western shirt. "Where's your mother?"

"In town. You could have figured that she wasn't here all on your own, Matt. Her truck isn't here."

Matt made his way toward his Ford, readjusting his cowboy hat. "Tell her I stopped by. I want to know about her intentions on payback."

"I'll tell you right now what it is: Get out of here. Get out of here before Loco gets out of his pen."

Matt kept on walking toward his truck, his legs a bit unsteady. The torn belt loop curled out from his jeans like a soft, tiny tail.

XIV

THE LOCAL CAFE—A COP CONFESSES

A strong brew percolated behind the counter of the Wildflower Cafe on Main Street. As Nedra walked past town folks taking an afternoon break, she gave one of the ex-farmers a pat on the back. "How's retirement, Charlie?"

"I'm so busy loafing, I'm going to have to hire help," the old man said.

"How much you paying?"

The retiree guffawed, along with the rest of the crew.

The cafe was the centerpiece of the town's social interaction, with people wandering in and out from early morning to ten at night, picking up snippets of gossip and leaving behind their fragments of information and opinions. The cafe was the only one remaining on Main Street. Thirty years earlier, three had dotted the street. This one was in a deep, narrow building that had been a grocery store through the Nixon years, then converted into a dining hall. It retained the high, tin ceiling and ceiling fans, and now was ringed by a mural of country scenes painted by an art class from the high school.

Nedra took a seat and ordered a medium Diet Coke while she plugged into the local gossip stream. Today, gossip was light, and concern about the crops heavy. The corn and beans were languishing. The farmers needed a stretch of sun to salvage their investment.

At three-fifteen the heavy front door screeched open and Officer Joanne Donnelly ambled in, her leather holster riding her midsection. She flashed her dimples at a couple of widows in the front booth.

Nedra excused herself from the table and motioned the cop into an isolated booth. Joanne followed her, alert and expectant.

"How's it going, Doc?" she asked, lowering her frame into the red vinyl seat.

"I wish I could pull a Dr. Doolittle sometimes," Nedra said, sliding into the booth. "It sure would make my job easier."

"You seem to speak cat pretty well. My little guys sure melt in your hands."

"They're sweethearts," Nedra said, referring to Joanne's two tabbies. One had been in a couple months before with a urinary tract infection.

The waitress slid a steaming mug of coffee in front of the officer. Joanne attempted to peel off the wrapping from a tiny slab of sugar, but her fingernails, clipped to the quick and beyond the rounded edges of her fingertips, were useless. "Harvey says you stopped in to get new locks. Got them installed?"

"Annie put them in. The same key opens the front and the back. We have the only keys."

"Good." Joanne manipulated the sugar between her fingers. "Used to be you could have sugar bowls in restaurants. Now folks think it's unsanitary. We're going to sterilize ourselves out of existence." The cube clunked to the table for the third time. In exasperation, Joanne dropped the still-wrapped sugar into the cup.

"Any news on the break-in?"

"Nope. We did another search of the area this morning. Zilch." She banged the spoon around the mug a few times, then fished out limp scraps of paper and scraped them onto a napkin. The cop blew over the rim and sucked in a bit of coffee. Nedra could tell she was sizing her up.

"What if you can't figure out what's happening to Teri's cattle?" Joanne took a bigger drink with purposeful nonchalance.

"Then I'll have to write it off as an anomaly." She stirred the ice in her drink with the straw.

"What does your gut say is going on?"

"I think they ingested chemicals. Who knows what, though. We usually have to know what we're testing for. It's driving me crazy."

"Why's that?" Joanne brought the brown mug up to her mouth again. Her eyes knifed over the ceramic edge.

Nedra thought for a moment. "Don't unsolved crimes drive you crazy? Same in my profession. I like to close my cases. It gives me a sense of completion."

Joanne smiled. "Yeah, I know what you mean. I still haven't figured out who tipped over all those gravestones at the cemetery two Halloweens ago. Bugs me to this day."

"See?" Nedra took a sip, then continued, her voice dropping. "This case gnaws on me, Joanne. And it goes beyond the diagnosis problem. Something just isn't right out there."

"Like what?"

"I don't know. Over the years, I've developed a sixth sense for animals in pain. I'm sensing a farm full of hurt." Nedra played with her straw. "How well do you know the Thompsons?"

"Pretty well. Teri and I were classmates." Joanne glanced at her watch. "Well, I should be pushing off," she said, digging into her pocket for a bill. "Want to ride around with me for a bit?"

The way Joanne locked her eyes on her, Nedra knew she wasn't asking a question. Joanne had something to say, and Nedra wanted to hear it.

⌘

"How do you like this town?" Joanne asked as she backed the car away from the curb.

"I like it." Nedra tried not to gawk at the dashboard and all the buttons and switches. She'd never been in a cop car before.

"Folks have been treating you all right, then?" She gave Nedra an I-know-everything look.

"It's taken most people a while to warm up, but everyone's been decent. Decent and polite."

"Oh, yeah, this is Minnesota. You can't forget polite."

At the west end of the business district, they turned south. When they reached the edge of town, Joanne steered the Ford into the town park. She slowed to a crawl as they began to circle the forty-acre area that abutted a nine-hole golf course. A few kids goofed around the soggy softball diamond playing a variation of five-hundred.

"You know, I hadn't been on the job but a couple of years when I got the call to go out to the Thompson farm. It wasn't easy for me back then, being the first female in uniform. Sorry to say, I had to crack a few heads before some of the young punks in this town took me seriously." She stopped the car by the bridge and cut the engine. "I used to be pretty tough back then."

"Really?" Nedra wondered where Joanne had softened up.

"Come on," the cop said, getting out of the unit. "I want to check the river. See how close she is to spilling her banks." Joanne led Nedra down a path under the bridge and along the Amelia River, the water running high.

As Nedra followed the solid, gun-toting figure, she wondered what the officer had in mind. She felt she was part of a conspiracy, that they were like kids climbing up to the tree house to whisper their secrets.

"I used to come down here all the time when I was a kid," Joanne said. "They had a rickety old bridge then, nothing like this steel and concrete monstrosity. I like to check out the area a few times a week. Never know what you'll find."

Nedra slapped at a few mosquitoes. The narrow dirt path wound back to a small rapids where the dropping water rushed over rocks and boulders. The rocks were placed so they could be used as stepping stones across the twenty-foot wide river. A cardinal called out overhead, and a pair of blackbirds lazily took flight from one bank to the other.

"My senior year in high school, my best friend Jenny Watkins and I would come here." She patted a tree behind them. "We made out like crazy under this old willow."

"That so?" Nedra said. She wasn't sure if it was the content of the revelation that surprised her, or that fact that it had been made.

"Yeah. Then she took off for college and got married. I did, too—married that is. College came later. It seemed the easiest thing to do, especially since I wanted to stay here."

Joanne leaned an arm against the trunk and absorbed the scene before her, the water breaking into a thousand sparkling pieces against the rocks, the trees across the way waving their leaves. A dozen different smells rose from the bank, from sweet grasses to rotting fish.

"Have any regrets?" Nedra asked.

"Before I had my kids, I would have said yes. Now, they make it worth it." She snapped a long blade of grass from under the tree and put the end in her mouth. "Still sometimes I wonder what could have been. Especially when I see you and Annie. I give you two credit. You've got guts."

"So do you, Joanne." A shy smile hooked the corners of Nedra's mouth. She patted Joanne lightly on the back.

"Sometimes I think I'm a coward when it comes to that part of my life."

"We all have to make choices. I think people usually make the right ones given the circumstances. It's some sort of instinct for survival."

"Think so? Maybe that's why I like my job so much. Compensation, you know. Wearing a stick and nine millimeter makes me feel in control." She surveyed the high river. "Much more rain and this baby's going to flood."

They heard the thud of footsteps and turned to see a freckled-faced teenage boy sauntering toward the rapids with a fishing pole and bucket.

"Hi-ya, Jimmy," Joanne said. "Got a license?"

The kid turned about six shades of scarlet. "I forgot it at home, ma'am."

"See to it that you have it next time."

"Yes, ma'am."

As the kid claimed a good-sized rock, the women stepped back the way they had come, but the air seemed to have freshened and the light intensified. Joanne turned to Nedra, her voice low. "Seems like I have the same conversation every time I meet that kid. Family's got money—his father runs the Amoco station and his mother works at the nursing home. One of these times I'm going to have to do more than talk." As they scrambled across the loose rock underneath the bridge, cars whined on the road overhead. Joanne bent down, picked up a rock, and sidearmed it into the river.

"Used to be great skipping stones here," she said. Her voice bounced off the bridge, making it loud and hollow. "When they put in the new bridge, they hauled in all this damn gravel. I tell you, kids' childhoods are being choked off. Sometimes it's done nice and slow like taking away a river bank. Sometimes it's quick, like kids seeing their father die. Choked the childhood right out of those Thompson kids. Saddest thing I ever saw in my life." Joanne flung a piece of gravel toward the water and watched it plink through the surface and disappear.

When they reached the car, Joanne unlocked the door and rolled down the window. She stood, one foot on the car frame, an arm resting on the open door, and gazed across the green playing fields to the north.

"It was the damnedest thing," she said. "I was the first on scene—got the call from 911. Ambulance came a few minutes later—seemed like hours. Christ, I never felt as all alone as when I wheeled up that driveway. It was my first real emergency. Everything else had been drunks and disorderlies, vandalism, usual pissant stuff that a small town has. But this was life and death. Before I even took two steps, I knew which one it was. It was my first on the job." She cocked an eye toward Nedra. "I suppose you took your first one hard—even though it was an animal."

"Yeah, it was during my first anesthesiology rotation at school. A five-year-old dalmatian had a rear leg amputated for cancer. I thought he was going to make it, but a blood clot killed him. I cried for two days."

"Hell of a thing, isn't it, losing a life?"

"Yeah, yeah it is." Nedra watched a red setter bound across the open field in the distance, chasing a yellow ball thrown by its owner.

"So what happened to Ed Thompson? All I've ever heard was that he died in a silo accident."

"Corn bin, actually. Nothing unusual about that. Farmers are always getting busted up or killed. He and Teri were filling the bin with shelled corn that afternoon. It was just the two of them." Joanne wiped a spot of perspiration from her forehead. "Jeff and Jessie were walking up the drive—the school bus had just let them off—when they heard their mother scream. They saw her up on the ladder, yelling to them to call 911. Jeff was able to turn off the machinery, but it was too late.

"When I reached the scene, there was this awful silence, the boy was white as a pail of primer, standing by the control box. He looked at me like I was the Man from Mars. 'My dad,' he said real soft. 'My dad.'

"Teri was standing at the top of the ladder, peering over the edge into the bin. She was like one of those marble statues you see in books. She starting yelping, 'Ed! Ed!' I flew up that ladder, grabbed her by the belt, and hauled her down. When I went back up and looked in, all I saw was a quicksand of corn and churning dust.

"'He's in there!' Teri was yelling. 'He's still alive. I know it!'"

"It didn't take a genuis to know that the guy was a goner. I tell you, Nedra, there wasn't a sign of him anywhere. The guy was buried completely. Even if we had found a hand or arm, we wouldn't have been able to pull him up. We could have died just as easy—gone under or gotten our lungs full of dust. Matt Jensen showed up then. He started praying and crying out to the Lord like he expected the Big Hand to come from the sky. It was a god-awful mess." Joanne sighed. "We couldn't find Ed's body. We had to empty out the bin before we had anything to bury."

"Was there an autopsy?" Nedra was sweating right along with Joanne now.

The cop nodded. "He suffocated to death. The weight of that corn crushed the air right out of him. Poor bastard. Worked like a fool and left his family with only tattered clothes, a few boards nailed over their heads, and a relatively new tractor."

"Ed's big toy."

"So if you think the family's a bit weird, they probably have every right to be. Teri never was the same afterwards. I can tell by the look in her eyes—sometimes I think I see a whole ringful of spirits wrestling behind them. Christ, they lost a good-hearted father in front of their eyes, then saw the farm roll over on its back. Hell of a life."

"Ed was an okay guy, then?"

Joanne turned her sharp eyes on Nedra. "Yeah. Quiet guy." She swung into the driver's seat and closed the door. Nedra followed her lead as Joanne started up the engine. "Ed was as nice as they come. Good looking, too. Everybody liked him. He liked the ladies a little too much, maybe, but he was a good guy." She clicked her tongue. "Careful, too. It still bothers me that he could have been so careless around that bin."

XV

A GROWING CONCERN—THE COUNSELOR IS IN

Annie stood at the kitchen door, hands on her hips, watching Nedra sample some beef stew. "Eating one of your patients?"

Nedra dipped the spoon back into the crock pot and fished out another mixture of meat, mushrooms, potatoes, carrots, and peas, rolling in red wine. She blew a cool stream of air across the stew, slurped it down, and made a great show of licking her lips. "Hope not." She fitted the cover back on top of the pot and gave Annie a playful smile.

"I'm next," Annie declared as she slipped into Nedra's arms for a welcome-home kiss. Annie stepped back and examined her partner. "What are you so pleased about? Surely not my cooking."

"Joanne Donnelly took me for a ride in her car."

"As a passenger or detainee?"

"Passenger. Don't worry, I didn't ask her to turn on the lights and siren."

"High class all the way, babe."

"You know how I told you once I thought she was a false positive?"

Annie grinned at Nedra's classification system. "Looks like a lesbian but isn't. Yeah, I remember."

"Well, she's an inconclusive. She told me she had a girlfriend in high school."

"A girlfriend girlfriend?"

"Yep. The kissing kind."

"Whew!" Annie trailed after Nedra into the living room. "But she's married."

"She just followed the conventional route."

"Why did she tell you this?"

"I don't know." Nedra scooped the orange cat off the couch and scooted under it. Copper stretched across Nedra's lap, dangled her paws over the cushion, and closed her green eyes in contentment. "Maybe I'm just the vet confessor."

"Dr. Nedra Wells, repository of the town secrets." Annie said, claiming the other cushion of the couch.

"It's great having a kindred spirit in this town. Especially one with a badge."

"She's probably felt pretty isolated over the years."

"She's tough. I don't think it's bothered her too much." Nedra buried her fingers in the cat's furry stomach. "She told me something else—about what happened out at the Thompsons when Ed died. She was the officer on duty." Nedra put her feet up on a coffee table that had been refinished to match the oak dining room table. A neat row of magazines, *Newsweek, English Teacher, The Journal of Veterinary Medicine, Star Trek: The Official Fan Club*, lined one end of the table. At the other end sat a crystal bowl filled with polished stones—pink quartz, amethysts, Brazilian agates, and a number of Lake Superior agates that Annie had found and polished herself. A Solberg print of caribou hung over the davenport, and a pair of smaller pictures of cardinals and finches decorated the adjacent wall.

Annie plucked up a Brazilian agate that her brother had sent from South America and listened closely as Nedra filled her in. She loved to hold polished stones in her hand. They helped her feel attached to the distant places of the world.

"That explains a lot about the kids," Annie said, setting the stone back in the bowl. "They must have been traumatized. They're probably still not over it yet. You know, I'm going to check with the school counselor tomorrow. She may have some insights into the Thompsons."

"I hope so. Jeff may have broken into my office; Jessie is identifying with a cow." Nedra felt a cold ball of apprehension between her shoulder blades. "The more I hear about that family..." She shuddered and dropped the subject.

⌘

"Lord, let this day be over," Betty Gaynor, the school guidance counselor, said the next day as she closed the top drawer of a file cabinet. The lock caught with a sharp click.

"What's up?" Annie asked.

Betty sighed and slid behind her metal frame desk. "All the end of the year stuff. It's too much to do, especially with so little support from the administration. They lay off half the clerical staff, then expect me to do all my copying and filing myself. I'm sure it's no different for you."

"It's crazy." Annie parted the vertical blinds to take in the sweep of the back lot of the school and the rise that ended in a two-lane black top. Beyond the road, clusters of trees and farm homes dotted the flat land. "Pretty soon we'll be assigned janitorial tasks."

"I draw the line at cleaning toilets," Betty said, crinkling up her nose. "If they ask me to do that, I'm collecting my paycheck and kissing public education good-bye." She blew a kiss toward the superintendent's office one flight up. "So long."

"And give up summer vacation?" Annie claimed a padded chair. The plaid cushion warped under her hips.

"Vacation? It's sanity reclamation."

Annie examined the school counselor. A few streaks of gold fanned through her short, moussed hair, which was the color of molasses. She wasn't beautiful, but she was good-looking in her own sort of way. While Annie hadn't had much interaction with her in the past, she had noticed her kindness when dealing with students. Nine months of being penned up with twelve- to eighteen-year-olds would have hardened even Mother Theresa, but Betty didn't have as much as a sharp edge when it came to kids.

"I got your note about wanting some background on Teri Thompson's kids," Betty continued. "Does this have anything to do with Jeff being picked up by the cops the other day?"

"Kind of. You know that the Thompsons have been having a hard time of it lately."

"Lately?" Betty's eyebrows rose. "The last five or six years are more like it. So what about Jeff? Did he break into Nedra's office?"

"He was in the area, that's all we know. Do you think he would do something like that?"

"It wouldn't surprise me. He used to be a pretty good kid, but like so many these days, he thinks the rules don't apply to him. He can't think beyond his own needs." Betty opened the first of two manila folders on her desk. "What do you want to know about him?"

"I understand that both he and Jessie were at the farm when their father died. Did anyone in the family go through counseling?"

"Not the kind they needed. I made arrangements with their teachers for their assignments, and I talked with them about their schedules and getting back into the swing of school. Usually I just let them talk when they wanted—which was about as often as a solar eclipse—but that's it. I think they talked with the Lutheran pastor, but maybe that was just for funeral arrangements. I don't know the specifics. I do know that both kids tried to put up a good front, but they must have suffered terribly. I mean, wouldn't you if you saw your dad die?"

Annie let her gaze drift to the fertile land outside the window. She wondered how her parents were doing on their latest political mission to El Salvador. A tractor inched along the highway, then turned on to a gravel road. "I would, yes," she said after a moment, "but I'm not them."

A half-hearted smile came across the counselor's face. "True. We never know what it's really like to be another person." She turned back to Jeff's file. "The boy's grades dropped off the world for a couple of quarters, then started to climb up. Same with his sister," Betty said, opening up Jessie's file. "Both of the kids are bright. Jeff especially. He's shown a lot of aptitude in the sciences. In fact, he won a blue ribbon at the State Science show. He designed a new type of windmill. He says he wants to build the real thing on the farm—he just can't afford the materials right now."

"Really? That's pretty ambitious."

"And practical. It would pay for itself in no time flat if he could generate enough electricity to sell back to the utility company."

"What about Jessie?"

The counselor shrugged. "Her strengths also seem to be in the sciences, but it's a little early to tell."

"You know, Betty, she said something rather peculiar to Nedra the other day. Nedra was out on the farm collecting samples—did you hear about the deformed calf?"

The counselor nodded. "Not the first one lost, either, I hear."

"Right. Well, Jessie put her arms around the neck of the cow that had aborted, and asked Nedra if she, Jessie, were to give birth to a dead baby without legs, if the doctors would try to save it."

Betty blew out a long stream of air. "What did Nedra say?"

"Wait, that's not all. Jessie went on to say that being the mother of a freak was as good as being a freak."

"I'm not a psychologist, but boy, that sounds like a red flag hoisted up a tall pole."

"Do you think Jessie wanting to be a freak relates to her father's death?"

"You mean she's acting out some unresolved issues? Could be. Then, again, it could just be her way of getting attention. Some kids do it by sticking rings through their noses."

"So, it could be something...or nothing."

The counselor nodded. "The Thompson kids stay pretty much to themselves, except for Jeff having a girlfriend. I don't know how serious the relationship is. The whole family's a bit reclusive. Odd, really, but small towns seem to have a healthy tolerance for eccentrics. I made a few trips to the farm to talk with Teri about the kids' hygiene. They were coming to school dirty and smelly. Jeff has straightened up—especially since he's interested in girls now. Jessie still looks bedraggled, but passable."

"Does anyone help them out?"

"The in-laws have written them off. I think the Sinclairs are the only relations who will stick their fingers in when needed."

"Eppy and Helen? They're related to the Thompsons?"

"Oh, sure." Betty frowned in thought "I think they're cousins of Teri. Something like that."

"Well, well. Small world."

"Small towns," Betty said, "are always full of inbreeding. When I first moved here ten years ago, I tried to draw a genealogy map of this town so I knew who was related to whom. It looked like a road map to broken chromosomes."

Annie laughed. "Good thing you and Don brought in fresh genes."

"We're keeping them to ourselves, thank you." Betty turned serious. "Boy, too bad it's summer break now. I'd love to get the Thompsons into my office for a little chat."

"Can you call up Teri and express concern about Jeff?"

"I'm afraid not. It happened outside of school. If I did call her, someone would be sure to complain that I had neither the authority nor training to be meddling with the psychology end of things. They'd be right, though I think I'm a damn good reader of people. I'd be slapped with a reprimand." Betty frowned. "Frankly, I don't know that I'd want to tangle with Teri."

"Why's that?"

"Let's just say she's not always on intimate terms with reality."

Annie started. "Are you talking mental illness?"

"No. It's more of a stubborn, willful disregard for anything that she doesn't want to hear."

"So if Nedra has to condemn her herd..."

"Plan on the National Guard to take them away."

XVI

JESSIE RIDES—A QUARREL

"Hi-ya, honey! What are you up to?" Helen Sinclair turned away from her patch of irises and poked the cultivating fork in the ground next to her knees.

Jessie Thompson, still astride her bicycle, planted one foot on the wide lawn of the Sinclair home. "Nothing. What are you doing?" The girl's cheeks had a wide smudge of pink from the exertion of the bike ride.

"Clearing out some weeds. They grow faster than Jack's beanstalk." Helen brushed the dirt from her gloves. "Say, your hair is cute. It's long enough to wear in a pony tail now."

"Yeah. Can I take Buttercup for a ride?"

Helen beamed at the request. She loved to help out the Thompson kids. And their requests were so minor. Nothing like a new Mustang or some three-hundred dollar leather jacket that so many kids demanded these days. "I don't see why not. Eppy's out in the tack shed. Let's go ask her."

The girl and Helen cut across the backyard to a small shed by a corral and barn. The door to the tack room was open.

"Ep!" Helen called as she approached the tiny shack.

"What?" the elder Sinclair said grumpily, glancing up from her work. She was adjusting the links of a heel chain on a spur.

"Jessie's here." Helen stuck her head in the door. "She's wants to take Buttercup for a ride."

"Just for a little while, Eppy. I'll be back in an hour. Promise." Jessie slipped around Helen and entered the tack room. Six elaborately tooled saddles lined two walls. Ornate bridles hung above the saddles, and over the door two upturned horseshoes brimmed with luck. A workbench no longer than a yardstick held a variety of leather-working tools.

"You want to go running off with the horses and you just got here? Why don't you keep us company for a few minutes?"

Jessie slid her eyes to Helen and sighed. She positioned her rear end sideways on a saw horse.

"That's more like it," Eppy said. "Now, tell me, what's this about Jeff being picked up by the police?"

"Oh, that was just something stupid. He didn't do anything wrong."

"Some people think he broke into the vet's office."

Jessie's small ponytail swung from side to side as she shook her head. "No way. He wouldn't do something like that."

"Well, that's what I think, too. He's must be pretty worked up about the Osborne girl to run to her place in the middle of the night."

"I don't know why. She's so dumb. She's always smiling and wears makeup about an inch thick. She's got this purple lipstick she wears sometimes. It's really gross."

"Well, Jeff seems to like her," Helen said.

Jessie shrugged. "He just likes to screw her."

"You don't say," Helen said. The small, dark tack room suddenly seemed quite hot to her.

"It's true. I hear them sometimes up in the hay loft."

Eppy snapped the chain into place. "Then that's where the incident should stay. In the hay loft. That's nobody's business and I don't want to hear another word about it. Now, tell me what happened when the cops brought Jeff home."

"Mom seemed kind of upset, but she didn't say much. She never does, you know." Jessie drew a line on the dusty floor with the toe of her sneaker. "Matt's trying to get her to sell the farm to him. I heard them fighting about it."

"Really?" Eppy put down her file.

"He's such a hypocrite, always going to church. But I don't think he's nice, under it all. I think he's mean."

"He's a glob of goose shit, that's what," Eppy said. "What about Jeff? He can't be too pleased about Matt's offer."

"He's not." Jessie jumped off the saw horse and reached for a bridle on the back wall. A little plaque with the name "Buttercup" was over the peg where the equipment hung. "I'm going to go ride now, okay?"

"Okay, honey," Helen said. "Where are you going?"

"Along the river."

"Are you coming back for a saddle?" Eppy asked.

"No. I'm riding bareback."

"Well, you be careful," Helen said. "When you come back, I'll fix a nice, hot bath for you and make your favorite dinner—hamburgers, tator tots, and baked beans."

As the girl picked her way through the grass of the long pasture toward a grazing pack of Palominos, the Sinclair sisters watched from the wooden fence of the corral.

"Poor kid." Eppy jangled the lone spur in her hand. "She's having a hard time of it."

Helen raised a hand to her brow to shield her eyes from the sun as she took in the receding figure of an awkward girl on the edge of womanhood. She felt protective of her, and wondered at the fierce tie that a mother has for a child when she felt such a strong bond for a cousin. "It's part of growing up."

"We've got to be careful with her," Eppy said. "I don't want to make a mistake like we did with her mother."

"We won't," Helen said, placing her hand over Eppy's on the fence and patting it. "We won't."

⌘

"Betty's parting comment, in so many words, was that Teri has a tenuous hold on reality. She could be major trouble." Annie plunged a white dish towel into a freshly washed tumbler.

"I've had a feeling that Teri wouldn't be open to bad news about either her herd or the farm. If she's losing money year after year, as the Sinclairs claim, and she's not changing any of her management practices, then she's living in a dream world."

"The crash is coming and she won't acknowledge it, not even when she's sitting with her possessions in a suitcase at the end of her driveway."

"God, it's sad to see." Nedra twisted the stopper in the sink. The sudsy water started to swirl down the drain. "After that last episode with Jessie, I don't know that I feel comfortable going out there myself."

Annie raised an eyebrow. "You want protection? I don't believe it!"

"No, it's more like having a witness."

"Ahhh. You have a point."

"If Teri looses the farm, what do you think will happen to her," Nedra asked as she turned on the cold water faucet.

"If she and Eppy can stop their fussing, I imagine the Sinclairs would take her in, seeing that she's a relative."

"I wondered why Eppy loaned her all that money, and why Teri called Helen about the latest calving fiasco. Funny, I never thought of them as being related." She squeezed a sponge, wiped the splash board behind the sink, and cleaned the basin.

Annie stacked the last of the plates in the cupboard and then came from behind and put her arms around Nedra.

"How you doing, cowgirl?" She gave Nedra a squeeze.

"Staying in the saddle." Nedra turned around and planted a kiss on her lips. "How about you?"

Annie put her forehead against Nedra's. "Working on it."

Nedra's good mood whirled down with the dishwater. "What's working and what's not?"

"We're working. The town's not. Sometimes I don't know that I can do this any more."

Nedra eased her head back. She saw the dark flecks in Annie's eyes deepen. "We have a major problem then."

"I guess so," Annie nodded. "I've been thinking, if I move back to Minneapolis, I could come down weekends. We'd still be together. Or, I could live here during the week and go up to the Cities on the weekend."

"Annie, that wouldn't be a life together."

"It could be. People commute across the country. A relationship is anything we say it is. We define its boundaries."

"We'd grow apart."

"No, I promise we wouldn't." Annie lightly traced Nedra's jaw line with a finger.

"Just like we promised our friends in the Cities that we wouldn't?"

"Shit," Annie said. She turned away.

"I'm just trying to be realistic." Nedra reached for a slip of hair that hung on Annie's neck, then thought better of it.

Annie turned to face Nedra. "If we let ninety-two miles..."

"Ninety-five."

"Ninety-five miles wreck our relationship, we don't have much of one to begin with."

"What does that mean?" Nedra said, caught between anger and terror.

"It means that we're stronger than a two-hour drive. Or at least *I* think we are. You seem to have doubts." Annie's face was splotched with anger.

"I want us to be together...and happy."

"I'm not happy here. I feel too closed in. I'm tired of missing out on everything in the Cities. I want more of a life than a small town can give."

"If you move back, when would it be?" Nedra's voice sounded tinny.

"I'll stay through the school year. I might as well since I have a contract."

"If you're as unhappy as you say you are, how will you last another year?" Nedra cut across the kitchen and entered the living room.

"I will, that's all." Annic followed Nedra and settled next to her on the couch. "Honey, I feel sometimes that our life together is your life, not mine, not ours. Yours."

"Because we moved here?"

"Partly. It seems that everything has to be your way—living here, having the job you want, spending our time the way you want to spend it. I feel like I'm doing all the giving in this relationship."

Nedra opened her mouth, then shut it. "Wow," she said at last. "I had no idea you felt that way."

"Am I way off base here? Can you see where I'd feel that?"

Nedra thought of everything Annie had done for her—Annie had been instrumental in the start up of her private practive, from relocating to setting up the computer software in her office, to painting the walls of the kennel. And what had she given Annie in return? Not a hell of a lot. "I feel so stupid and inconsiderate, Annie," Nedra said, her eyes moistening. "I'm so sorry."

"Honey," Annie said, taking her lover's hand, "I've been a part of all the decisions. I could have said 'no' at anytime. Now when I think of staying in this town until I die, I feel like I'm suffocating. I didn't feel that way at first. Probably because of my job. But my job isn't enough."

"And neither am I?"

"Nedra, I have only one life."

"We're committed to only five years."

"But what if you want to stay and I want to leave at the end of five years? What then?"

"We'll work it out."

"If I stay, I think I'm postponing the inevitable."

"Nothing is inevitable, Annie. Nothing." Nedra wanted desperately to believe it herself.

XVII

HELP FROM AFAR—NEDRA AND THE PROFESSOR—A PROFESSIONAL EXCHANGE—DEALING

Nedra spent Thursday morning testing a herd west of town for pseudorabies, a highly contagious disease found in swine. The state had set up a program trying to eradicate the disease, just as it had with hog cholera a few decades earlier. Nedra's grandfather had been part of that campaign. A new generation, a new disease. The kicker about this killer was that it could so easily spread to other livestock—cows, poultry, sheep—as well as dogs and cats. Horses couldn't catch it, though. Nor humans. At least not yet, Nedra thought as she opened the back door to her office. God knows what organisms could mutate into. Look at AIDS. It probably started as a disease in monkeys.

Nedra sucked in the familiar fragrance. The place smelled like a vet's joint again. The aroma of drugs, particularly the sulfa in fifty-five-gallon drums in the storage area downstairs, had subsumed the last vestiges of paint odor. It was a smell she had grown up with at her dad's office, which had been in the basement of their house. She believed that after all these years of breathing in the powder from the pharmaceutical companies, she was either going to be immune to every disease known and unknown or her double helix was already starting to unzip. The former she'd gladly embrace; the latter didn't matter that much—she didn't plan on having kids, and she owned a tidy insurance policy with Annie as the beneficiary.

Annie and Tony were in the kennel feeding a couple of piglets that they had let out of the cage. The little oinkers slobbered and slurped from bottles of milk. At birth, they'd been joined by a flap of skin at the hip. Nedra had sliced them apart two days earlier. In another day, they'd be able to survive the rough and tumble of litter life.

Annie left Tony to the pigs. "Randy called while you were out. He wants you to call him back."

Nedra saw the reassuring glow in Annie's eyes, the one that said, *I still care. We'll work this through.* Nedra pretended to grimace, then picked up the phone and punched Randy's number at the Diagnostic Lab. She got a recording. "Sure, Randy," she said as she hung up, "be out of the office."

"Pretty inconsiderate." Annie crinkled her nose. "Whew, want me to help you bury those clothes?"

"I suppose I smell like a pig pen."

"Uh-huh."

"I'll be back," Nedra said, heading toward the basement. She stuffed her clothes in the washing machine and took a quick shower.

Fifteen minutes later Nedra tried Randy again. This time he answered.

"No answers for you here, Needs," Randy said. "Everything came out negative."

"Damn."

"Now, look on the positive side, my dear. At this point, we can rule out disease. That means you won't have to deal with me any more."

"That's a blessing, for sure," Nedra said, a smile in her voice. "Are you going to hand me over to toxicology?"

"On a platter. Remember Don MacInnes?"

"Of course. Tox 5165. I was our group's designated note taker in his class, remember?

"Yeah. That's probably why you got an A and I didn't," Randy said. "I chatted with him about your case. He's the U's field vet these days. He'd love to pay you a visit."

"Terrific."

"No charge. The state will pick up his tab."

"Even better."

"He's leaving next week on vacation so he'd like to come down tomorrow morning. How about it?"

"Sure. I'll make arrangements out at the farm."

Randy gave Nedra the vet's number so they could finalize the visit, then rang off.

"No luck with the latest tests," Nedra said, smiling sadly at Annie, "but they're sending down a big gun."

"Something wrong, Nedra?" Tony stood at the open door, his brown eyes large with concern.

"I'm having a problem finding out what's wrong with some cows," Nedra said.

"A mystery sickness?"

"Yeah."

"Maybe a priest can come to say prayers. He can sprinkle the cows with holy water. My grandmother in Texas did this with a burro she had."

"Did it help?"

"The burro didn't die."

"Maybe I should call the parish," Nedra said. She examined the bright, open face of Tony. She'd become quite fond of him in the short time he had been around. "You know, old buddy, you're almost half way through our work agreement."

"Yeah, I know." Tony's lower lip swelled out.

"You've been a big help," Nedra rushed on.

"I like to help you."

"You like to clean up poop and pee, huh?"

"Nooo," he laughed. "I like to play with the animals. They're fun."

"Yeah? Well, I'll tell you what. Would you like to come in for about half an hour every day—except Sunday—and clean up around here? Take care of the animals. Feed them. Wash the floors on Saturday morning?"

Tony's eyes popped wide open.

"I'll pay you." Nedra quoted something around the minimum wage. "But you can put in only four hours a week at most. Some weeks it may be less, maybe only two or three hours if I don't have any animals in the kennel."

"Hey, man, it's a deal!" Tony clapped his hand into Nedra's.

"I'll talk to your mom about getting you a social security number."

Tony looked from Nedra to Annie, then back again. "You guys are really cool!"

"You'd better check with your mom first," Annie said.

"I take it back," Tony teased. "You're almost cool."

⌘

Nedra fit in a spay job and a neutering on a dog and a cat respectively first thing Friday morning. As she waited for Dr. MacInnes from the University to arrive, she leafed through a couple of drug and equipment catalogues. An advertisement for an x-ray machine, as shiny and sexy as a new car, made her linger. "Dream on," she said out loud. She made a mental note to talk to the town physician about when he planned to replace his x-ray machine. She wanted first dibs on the used stuff.

At ten-thirty, Dr. MacInnes ambled through the front door. In his late fifties, the six-foot doctor carried twenty more pounds since Nedra had last seen him. His black hair was now gray, and his mustache had faded to white.

After a few formalities and sharing of the case file, Nedra locked the front door and hung a clock in front of the window. Across the top it said, "We Will Be Back at..." and underneath the hands of the clock fingered one-thirty. After securing the back door, Nedra and her former professor climbed in the Ranger and took off.

Clover and rich grass covered the grazing land at the edge of town. Teri Thompson's small herd bunched together, as cattle are apt to do, at one end of the pasture. The corn in the east fields still seemed sickly. From the main road, the farm looked abandoned, and a bit sad. A few peeling shutters hung askew on the house, and the fence posts continued to weather into driftwood.

As the truck lurched from pothole to pothole on the dirt drive, MacInnes said, "I take it that this is a poor family."

"Yes. Teri has pride and is about as willful as they come. She's very defensive about her cattle."

"Emotional?"

"Yeah."

"That's good to know."

Nedra circled around the drive and stopped the Ford when it pointed back to the main road. When she and MacInnes stepped from the truck, Samson bolted up from the barn, yelping and carrying on like they were an invading army.

"Now why are you making such a fuss?" MacInnes asked the animal in a soothing voice. He offered his hand, palm up, to the dog, who jigged around a bit more before decorating a tire with a yellow stream.

"That's Samson," Nedra said.

"You're a very good guard, aren't you?" the vet continued. The dog leaned in for a quick sniff. Liking what he smelled, he sniffed some more, then rolled over to offer the professor his belly for tickling.

The back door of the house creaked open and Teri approached them.

"Hi, Teri," Nedra said, raising a hand in greeting. "This is Dr. Don MacInnes from the University. Doctor, this is Teri Thompson."

The soft-spoken vet nodded to the farmer and took her hand. "I hope we can figure out what the problem is here." The wind ruffled through his longish hair.

"I do, too," Teri said. "We're sure stumped."

After a stop in the barn, the trio made its way to the pasture. Dr. MacInnes asked Teri about the history of the cattle, which he had already read in Nedra's file.

"This batch is from stock I bought a few years ago. I...uh...lost my original herd thanks to the bankers and my husband. I haven't had a bit of trouble until this spring."

"Who were the sires?"

"We have a bull in the herd. The last cow, we took to a nearby farm for mating."

When they reached the herd of grazing cattle, Dr. MacInnes took a close look at the three cows that had aborted. He checked their mouths, their eyes, their ears, their hide, and their gait.

"They seem to be pretty healthy cattle," he said. He swept his eyes over the total herd, then patted the nearest cow. "They seem to be eating properly. How's their drinking?"

"Fine," Teri said. "We haven't noticed any change." She gave Nedra a questioning look, knowing that she had already answered these questions for Nedra.

The University vet asked her more questions about feed and water, as well as chemical use on the farm.

They walked along the western perimeter of the pasture. "Is this fence electrified?" the vet asked, looking at the barbed wires strung along poles."

"Yes, but we haven't had the electricity going for years. The barbs seem enough to keep the cattle inside. We've had only one break out in seven years."

"How about the low land over there?" MacInnes asked. He pointed at the small pond at the northwestern part of the farm. "Is there always water there?"

"Yeah. It's fed by a spring, so we don't rely on the rain to keep up its level. Even in the drought a few years ago, we had water. Of course, now we have too much."

"And you said you've had the water checked?"

"Yes," Nedra said. "The worst that can be said about it is that it's hard."

"Nothing wrong with that," MacInnes said. "It's another way for livestock to get minerals."

They turned back toward the barn.

"Do you have an answer?" Teri asked.

"The truth of the matter is," Dr. MacInnes began, "many times we don't find the cause for spontaneous bovine abortions. Nationally, the success rate is only thirty to thirty-five percent. The rest of the cases are chalked up as unknowns."

"But I need to know what's happening," Teri said. "This can't go on. If I don't get calves out of this herd, I'm going to lose money."

Nedra wondered at the conviction she heard in Teri's voice. *Going to lose money?* It was as if she weren't tens of thousands in the hole already and about to lose her farm to Matt Jensen.

"I understand," MacInnes said. "If it were one cow that couldn't come to term, you could ship it to market. But if you're looking at multiple cows with the same problem, we have an interesting situation. One solution would be to sell off the entire herd and buy a few new cattle. Start fresh. Or give up that portion of your operation. It's tough to make a go of it on a small herd these days, as you know."

"I know that," Teri said, her lips pinching together. "But I have no intention of selling the herd, at least not all of it."

"My best guess at this point is that you have a sire problem. Some animals have chromosomal problems—they're never quite right, and usually their offspring aren't either. It's something that we usually don't look for, but given the situation here, I'd say it's the mostly likely bet."

"Even though there were two sires?" Nedra asked.

"We don't know that for sure. With pasture mating, anything can happen. The bull here may have gotten to the dam before the neighbor's bull did." MacInnes turned to Teri. "Is that possible?"

"I don't know. We separated the bull from the herd when the last cow went into season." Teri ran a hand through her windblown hair. "What can we do about it?"

"You've mated this bull in previous years, right?"

"Right. No problems, then."

"Hmmm. Normally, I'd recommend genetic testing of the bull, but the easiest thing to do would be to get rid of him."

"Just the bull?" Teri seemed to brighten.

"For now. If you continue to have problems, you might as well get rid of the herd."

"That won't happen," Teri said, "no matter what."

"Well, that's your decision of course. The state can't force you to do it since we're not looking at any sort of parasite or disease."

The three stepped into the roundabout by the house.

"Is there anything else you need to see, Dr. MacInnes?" Nedra asked.

"No. Teri, I thank you for your time. It seems that Dr. Wells here is keeping on top of the situation." He turned back to look at the herd in the distance. "It's one of those cases that may keep us wondering for a long time to come. Are any of the other cows pregnant?"

"A few are still *post partum*," Nedra said, "and the others?" She turned to Teri.

"I keep the bull separate from them. Bossie and Lucky have been in season a few times, but I'm not mating them until I find out what's going on."

"The next time they're in estrus, why don't you let them mate," MacInnes said. "Once they breed, we'll see if the problem is throughout the herd." The professor looked to Nedra for confirmation.

"Sounds like a plan to me."

"My only suggestion is to observe the cows carefully and let Dr. Wells know of any peculiarities." Dr. MacInnes started toward the truck. "I wish you success," the vet said. "Let's hope the saying 'three times and out' applies here."

⌘

As soon as Nedra and MacInnes were at the bottom of the Thompson driveway heading back into town, MacInnes turned to Nedra. "What do you think about genetic problems?" he asked.

"Too many holes. If all three abortions were caused by genetic problems, why did the cows abort so late in their pregnancy? Normally, they would abort in the first five or six weeks. Then, given that the sire has produced viable offspring, why is the problem occurring now?"

The professor brushed away a buzzing fly. "I concur. I find the overall good health of the herd the real thorn in this case. If we were looking at an environmental problem, the whole herd would be affected, not just three or four cattle. Or, if the herd was getting hit by electromagnetic fields—as Randy suggested—they'd all be jittery and off their feed."

"I know. It doesn't make sense."

"Exactly. We can run a series of tests looking for specific toxins if you want, but personally, I think it would be a waste of time and money. The herd is sound."

Nedra's face tightened. "Except that they can't reproduce worth a damn."

⌘

"That University guy have any ideas?" Matt Jensen asked. He chewed on a long stem of grass as he leaned on the Thompson's tractor. Jeff had stopped across the road from Matt's house in the late afternoon. He was cultivating the driest parcel of the Thompson property.

"What's it to you?" Jeff shut off the motor. The sounds of the field rose as the engine cut out: the busy whine of flies, the wind playing on the green tongues of corn stalks, the creak of boots against the steel of the tractor.

"Just curious. Time's ticking away, son. Really, the cattle aren't important any more. You know that. Even if your mother sold them at premium prices, she wouldn't have enough to pay me off. And there's nobody on this earth who's going to lend her another dime."

"We'll pull it off," Jeff said. He hated hearing those words roll out of his mouth. They sounded as ridiculous as his mother's *good times are due*.

Matt let his eyes linger on the land behind Jeff's plow. "Another rain and your fields are going to be water logged into August. Or should I say, my fields."

Jeff felt his gut burning away. He hated the way Matt looked at their family farm like he owned it already. He loathed the curl of his neighbor's lip, the arrogance of his eyes. Jeff tightened his grip on the steering wheel to keep his hands from trembling.

"I'll tell you why your farm is failing," Matt continued. "Your mother's possessed. She can't even see that those stillbirths are a sign from the Lord Almighty that she should give up farming."

"I don't believe in that religious crap," Jeff said. "Besides, those calves are dying because...because that's the best thing." Jeff felt his face redden under Matt scrutiny. "Mom won't keep a herd around that can't produce. She'll give in. Eventually."

"Eventually's not soon enough," Matt said. "That herd and your farm will be long gone by the time your mother relents."

"We'll see," Jeff said, reaching for the tractor's ignition.

"Too bad you're not old enough to run the place. Maybe your family would have had a chance."

"I'm ready to run it any time."

"Sure you are." Matt ran a hand along his clean-shaven chin. "I plan to tile that acreage there," he said, nodding toward the south end of the Thompson farm. "If I could have done it last year, my fields would be sitting pretty now, with all that water running off into the river."

"You wouldn't even have access to the river if my dad hadn't sold you that land."

"Yep." Matt slipped the Stetson off his head and adjusted the dusty black band. "Boy, his ashes are going to smoulder when I pick up the rest of your land."

Jeff stomped on the gas pedal and chugged away. "It'll never happen!" he yelled over his shoulder. "Never!"

Matt watched the boy bump along the fields. "You're as full of cockeyed dreams as your mother," he called out. "The Lord help you all!"

XVIII

MEETING WITH THE PREACHER—EPPY BENDS AN EAR

The Reverend Gustavus Olson ran a palm down the front of his yellow and red Hawaiian shirt, the one he had bought in the Radisson lobby on Maui the year before when he and his wife had celebrated their fortieth anniversary. It was his favorite shirt and while not exactly the kind of cloth associated with his profession, he was on the short side of a year before retirement and figured the Lord would forgive him if his flock would not.

As perplexed as he was about his congregant C. Mather Jensen, Olson refused to let the self-righteous so-and-so, the strongest epithet he could muster, taint his day. "Can you help me out a little more, Matt. I just don't understand what it is that you need."

Matt let out a dry little cough, then placed the tip of his tongue in thc middlc of his uppcr lip. "Wc'vc known cach othcr for a fcw years, Gus."

Too many, Olson thought; immediately he retracted his uncharitable thought, and wondered if the closeness of retirement, like the closeness of heaven, emboldened truth to step forward. If it would keep its mouth shut for the next twelve months, he'd survive.

"Something like five or six," the pastor said.

"That's right. I'm a no-nonsense Christian, wouldn't you say?"

"I could, yes."

"After all, I was named after God-fearing Cotton Mather himself, you know." Matt's self-satisfied smile spread across his face. "I only want the best for others."

"Frankly, I fail to understand how calling in your note to the Thompsons is for the good of Teri and her family." The Lutheran minister pressed himself deeper into the cushions of his worn leather chair. Olson loved the dim office that had been his home for nearly twenty years. The smell of burnt wicks and melted wax, brass polish and brewing coffee, filled the inner sanctum like a homey cloud. The walls, lined with hardcover books that had nicks and tears in their faded jackets, provided a cozy wrap of theology. Not that the minister clung to the dogma with a scowl and condemning eye. No, that he left to his younger brethren Matt, the most conservative Lutheran who had ever stepped across his plush burgundy carpet. Olson believed in the benign Norwegian trinity of love, lefsa, and smooth waters: a religion for those who want to get along quietly on a full stomach.

"I think Teri isn't right, if you know what I mean."

The minister rubbed his bald crown fringed with short, white hair. "I'm afraid you'll have to spell things out for me."

"It's no secret that Teri worships those cows of hers."

"Worships may be putting it a little strongly."

"I don't think so. She's willing to risk her family for them. It's not sane."

"There are some people who say anyone who goes into farming in this day and age is insane. There's nothing wrong with pursuing a dream. Teri's a strong lady. If she falls short, she'll find a way to come through it. She's faced hardship before."

"The thing is," Matt said, "I don't know that she treats those kids of hers right."

"Why do you say that?"

"She works them half to death. I was just talking to Jeff the other day. He bears most of the load, and he won't say a word of complaint, I'm sure, but I'd be surprised if those kids are even eating right. He was looking peeked and unkempt."

"More so than what's fashionable these days?"

"Unhealthy like. I figure that by calling Teri's hand, by forcing her to sell, I'm saving the kids."

"Hmmm, that sounds rather self-serving," the pastor ventured.

"Maybe it does, but it's the truth. I don't see why people should be making me into a bad guy when I'm just saving Teri from herself."

"Well, there's more than one way to save Teri." The pastor steepled his fingers in front of him, his elbows resting on the armrests of the chair. "You have quite a bit of land now, Matt, and I imagine a fairly decent income."

"Sure do. I've been blessed, I'll grant you that. My grandfather was very generous to my brother and me. Aaron got his land and I got money to invest in a farm of my own. I've got a nice spread of land, as you know—160 bushels of corn to the acre last year, and a 120 back a few years ago during the drought. Getting access to the creek was a Godsend, and I thanked the Lord every day of that drought for His goodness."

Pastor Olson had little patience with piousness. He thought it peculiar that this conservative sheep had stayed with such a mild flock for so long. Some folks had speculated that he was interested in Teri Thompson, but Gus felt that the age and maturity difference was too great a leap. "Have you considered a little neighborly charity?"

"You mean give them money?" Matt gasped.

"Or food and clothing. It would be a neighborly thing to do. You could even donate some paint for the buildings—they're pretty weather worn."

"I wasn't thinking along those lines, Gus. I'm talking about saving the kids from an unfit mother."

"That's quite a charge."

"I don't like to hurt anybody. You know that. It's just that...well, I can't as a good Christian sit by and let people suffer, especially children."

"Don't you think they'll suffer if you took their home away?"

"Only in the short term. Long term, they'd come to appreciate what I did."

"I saw Teri last Sunday in church. She seemed fine to me." Pastor Olson swiveled in his chair to look out the office window. On the west end of Main Street—kittycorner from a row of expensive homes that fronted nearby Lake Amelia—the lush lawn of the church undulated in the strong morning breeze. "She may be a bit eccentric, but small towns are pretty good about tolerating individualists like Teri. If you're talking about a land grab, Matt, that's one thing. If you're talking about abuse or some such thing, that's a different thing all together."

Matt fingered the rim of his cowboy hat nervously.

"Is that what you're suggesting? Abuse? Because if it is, I need to tell the authorities."

"I wouldn't go that far yet."

"Not every family is a happy one, Matt. Not every family has money. The Thompsons are not the poorest members of my congregation, but like all whose lives I touch, I'll pray for them. In this case, I'll give them special attention." Olson frowned. "Meanwhile, I suggest you look into your own soul and see if you can find the charity and compassion to act in the wisest way possible."

⌘

Matt stepped into the overcast Wednesday morning, leaving behind the cool, large spaces of the church. Charity and compassion! Hell, he'd given the Thompsons a five-year ride already. That was charity enough.

He crunched across the small gravel parking lot behind the sandstone structure, to his Ford pickup, the only vehicle there except for the dark Taurus owned by Helen Sinclair, the church treasurer. As he approached his vehicle, his black Lab, Midnight, jigged around the front seat, stuck his long nose out the open driver's window, and barked a wild greeting.

"Hey, boy," he said as he opened the door and pushed the dog back across to the passenger side. He slid onto the cracked vinyl of the seat. "That was a close call," he said, ruffling the crown of the Lab's head. "I don't need a Sinclair on a good day like this? Right?"

The lab licked his master's face in agreement.

"Hello, Matt," a voice said.

With a sinking feeling, Matt turned from his dog to the open window. "Helen," he nodded and touched the brim of his cowboy hat. It could be worse, he thought. That could be Eppy standing outside his cab. Not that she would ever show up here. She wasn't into religion, and frankly, he couldn't understand why Helen even bothered.

"How are the crops?"

Matt fussed a moment with the dog. "Some replanting to do. But I'll survive."

A form lumbered from the alley leading into the parking lot. Quickly, Matt jammed the key into the starter.

"Well, Matt Jensen!" Eppy cried as she approached the vehicle. She sidled up to the truck window and showed a wide, malevolent grin. "Stopping by for a confession?"

Matt started the engine. "Wrong denomination, Mizz Sinclair. If you'd attend church more, you'd know that."

"Hah!" Eppy cried.

"I don't know why you bother hanging around the church," Matt said. "You certainly don't believe in any of its teachings."

"If you want to stack your good deeds up against mine," Eppy said, "I'll wager God'll snap open the pearly gates in record time for me."

"Good deeds..." Matt began.

"Oh, stuff your damn Bible quotes. I didn't stop you to have you recite Scripture to me. I have something to say to you about Teri."

The chirp of birds and the soft whoosh of the breeze through a row of nearby pines filled the sudden silence.

"Go on," he said with a sigh.

"I know you've been hanging out at her place, badgering her to sell. And now I hear you're tightening the screws on her to pay off that debt. You can take your money and go to hell for all I care."

"Eppy," Helen admonished.

"Teri's had a lot of heartbreak in her life. You know that. You were there that day her husband died."

"You don't need to remind me," Matt said. His insides had started to twist up again, worse than they had been when he was talking with the pastor.

"She had it hard as a child and hard as a young mother. She's getting into her middle years, and it's time she had a good life."

"She'd have a good life if she'd get off the farm. She's working herself to death and everyone knows it. She's got some equity in the place. Once she sells, she'll have a nice little income."

"With the emphasis on little," Eppy said. "Have you ever thought that maybe the farm is what gives her a purpose?"

Matt took his foot off the brake. The pickup jerked backwards.

"Listen," Eppy cried as the Ford churned up the gravel, "you're not buying her out. You're not forcing her out. Period. I'll buy that patch of land if I have to and, by God, I'll turn it back into wild prairie! You sure as hell will never have it! That's a promise!"

XIX

FURTHER EXAMINATION—A GRUMPY SON—IN THE BARN—TERI'S CONJECTURE—A SON'S ANGER—STITCH'S WISDOM

"I don't understand why you need more samples," Teri complained.

"To see if there are any changes in the blood chemistry. This is strictly on my own, Teri. I won't charge you anything." Nedra wrote the number from the cow's ear tag on the test tube filled with blood and slipped it into a wire tray. The three cows that had aborted were in their stalls. Jessie was fetching the two others from the pasture, but leaving the bull in his corral.

Teri turned to Annie, who stood on the other side of the cow. "Will you spend your summer helping Nedra out?"

"A bit. If nothing else, it's fun to take a ride in the country."

Jessie came through the wide doors, two cows in tow. "Here are the others!" she said. "Lucky and Bossie were half way across the state!"

"Thanks, Jess," Nedra said. "I'm finished with these three. You can let them go back to the pasture if you'd like."

"What about Loco?"

"Just the cows this time," Nedra said.

Jessie peeked at Annie, self-conscious at seeing her teacher outside of the school setting. She backed the cows out of their stalls and led them through the barn door while Nedra readied another test tube for a blood sample.

"We've got some chores to do back at the house," Teri said. "Let us know when you're done. If Jeff comes along, send him up to the house. He should be back from town sometime soon."

"So why aren't you testing the bull?" Annie asked moving into the stall with Nedra.

"I'm no fool. I'd rather be fed fully conscious into a meat grinder than tangle with that animal. Besides," Nedra said, patting Bossie on the rear, "these are the two cows I really want to examine." She quickly took blood samples from both, then slipped on a rubber glove that went all the way to her right arm pit. She squirted some lubricant on the glove, then patted the rear end of Lucky. "All right, girl, I'm doing a little pelvic exam," she droned. Slowly and gently, she inserted her hand, then her entire arm into the cow.

"Golly, honey," Annie said, batting her eyes, "why don't you ever do that to me?"

"That would be a new way to get a throat tickle, wouldn't it?" Nedra's smile dissolved as she concentrated on palpitating the cow.

"What are you looking for?" Annie asked.

The side door of the barn crashed open. "Hey!" Jeff called out. "What's going on?"

Nedra withdrew her arm from the Hereford. "Follow-up exams."

"Follow-up exams? There's nothing wrong with these cows."

Nedra dipped her gloved hand into a pail of warm, soapy water. "I'm exploring every avenue I can, Jeff," she said as she scrubbed the length of the glove.

"You're running up the bill, that's what."

Nedra rolled the top of the glove down her arms. "You know that's not true."

"Jeff," Annie said, stepping forward, "your mother told us to send you up to the house if you came back. I suggest you go and let Nedra finish her work."

"No!" Jeff said, balling his hands into fists. "I want you off the farm!"

"I don't work for you, Jeff," Nedra said. "I work for your mother, who happens to be a good woman. I hope some day you'll come to appreciate her."

Jeff's face grew motley with anger. "Get out of here!" He stepped between Nedra and Lucky. "Now!"

"Not before I talk with your mother," Nedra said, snapping the glove off her hand, one finger at a time.

"What about the last cow?" Annie asked.

"Forget her," Nedra said, keeping her eyes steady on the angry boy. She absorbed the defiant look on his face, the one that said to her *you'll never catch me*. "I'm beginning to see how things really are."

⌘

"He's been out of sorts lately," Teri said to Nedra and Annie as they settled in the kitchen. "Don't let him bother you."

"I know it's frustrating for everyone," Nedra said, "but we need to work together."

"Maybe it's better if we let things cool for a bit," Teri said. "All this uncertainty is hard on everyone."

Through the back screen door, they heard the banging of metal.

"They're your cattle," Nedra said at last.

Jessie turned from the kitchen window. "Jeff says you're going to condemn the herd. Is that true?"

"No, it's not," Nedra said.

"Why not?"

"Jessie," Teri snapped, "you shut that mouth of yours."

"I just want to know," Jessie pouted.

"You get to your room. That's all the knowing you need."

"Mom, come on."

"Enough, I said!" Teri's hand flashed out at Jessie in a short, violent arc. The girl jumped to the side at the last moment to avoid the swipe. A strange, squawking sound burst from her.

Nedra leapt up from the kitchen table and grabbed Teri's arm, stopping her from going after the girl. "Teri!" she cried. "Don't!"

Jessie slid along the kitchen counter toward the door, her eyes huge with panic. "Mom!" she cried.

Nedra hung on tightly as Teri tried to jerk away.

Jessie escaped through the door. She stumbled toward the barn, her legs pumping, her sobs lingering in the air.

"You stay with Teri," Annie said to Nedra. "I'm going after Jessie."

⌘

At first, Annie couldn't tell where the sounds were coming from. They were short, little noises, more whimpers than cries. She cocked her head toward the hay loft, then walked slowly past the stalls.

"Jessie?" Annie called out. "Jessie? Where are you?"

The sound stopped. Annie listened hard. She heard the clanging of metal in the distance where Jeff was working on the tractor, and the rush of the wind through the large doors that opened to the pasture. Swallows chirped and Samson padded toward the bales of hay in the southwest corner. He lowered his head, sniffed, then trotted forward, his tail giving a tiny wag. Annie followed the dog.

"What's up, Jessie?" she asked, sitting on a bale. The rough hay dug into her skin through her jeans. "Come and talk with me, would you?"

The dog plunked down behind a bale across from Annie. She heard the slurping sound of canine licks.

"Cut it out, Samson," Jessie said. She sat up. Her hair was messy and decorated with stray, yellow spikes. Her eyes were red and swollen, and her cheeks as pink as a prize rose.

Annie moved across the aisle and sat on the bale of hay next to Jessie. "What happened back there?" she asked, fingering the twine around the bale.

"I don't know. I didn't say anything," Jessie said. She started to cry again.

"Does your mother get angry at you often?"

"Not much."

"What does she do when she gets angry?"

"Yells." Jessie sniffed. "I know what you're thinking, but it's not true. She doesn't hit me. She's been getting kind of riled up lately, but she never hits—raises her arm sometimes, but never hits."

Annie nodded, keeping her eyes fixed on the girl.

"You won't tell anyone about this, will you?" Jessie asked. "I don't want my mom to get into trouble. She's good to me. She really is."

"I know that, Jess," Annie said. "But I'm worried about her. And you."

Jessie's eyes filled with tears again.

"Sometimes you all seem very sad here. Why is that?" Annie picked a piece of straw from the girl's hair.

"I don't know." The girl ruffled the crown of Samson's head. "Sometimes things are so hard. Sometimes I get lonely, like no one pays any attention to me."

"Is that why you think it would be neat to be a freak—so people will pay attention to you?"

Tears slid down Jessie's face. "Nobody loves me like I am now."

"Oh, honey," Annie said softly. "People love you. Sometimes they just forget to show it. They get busy and..."

Jessie's eyes grew round. Annie realized that Jessie was focusing on something behind her.

"Hey," came a low voice, as Jeff strode toward Annie. "What are you doing to my sister?"

Annie turned and locked eyes with Jeff's. She didn't move. "Your sister is upset," she said.

"I can see that," Jeff said. "I don't want you touching her."

Annie felt a flush on her cheeks and a sudden coldness in her stomach. She knew what he was insinuating. "Grow up, Jeff," she said sharply. "You don't know a thing about what's just happened."

Jeff stopped, taken aback by Annie's commanding voice.

"Leave me alone," Jessie whined. She hugged the dog closer to her chest.

Jeff approached his sister carefully, like he would a skittish horse. He nudged her foot with the toe of his boot. "What happened?"

"Mom got mad at me," Jessie said.

"What did you do?"

"Nothing." Jessie started to cry again. "She tried to hit me."

"No shit?" Jeff rubbed the top of his cap and let out a low whistle. "Boy, you must have really pissed her off. I get picked up by the cops and she doesn't lay a finger on me."

"All I did was ask Nedra if she was going to condemn the herd."

"Yeah?"

Jessie nodded. "I didn't say anything bad."

"She's right, Jeff," Annie said. "Your mom seemed to explode over nothing."

"She explodes sometimes," Jeff said, "but it's never over nothing. It's always over those goddamn cattle."

Jessie continued to sniffle.

"Come on," Annie said, reaching out a hand to the girl, "let's go back and talk with your mom."

"No," Jessie pouted.

"Let's go, kid," Jeff said, pulling his sister to her feet. "Get it over with."

⌘

"I didn't mean for that to happen," Teri said. She and Nedra had moved outside to the weather-beaten picnic table. A hawk floated on a wind current high above the corn field.

"I know," Nedra said, thinking that she really didn't know a thing.

"Things sometimes just happen."

Nedra noticed that Teri's hands, folded on the table, were shaking. Nedra reached across and patted them. "I know," she repeated.

"Don't go thinking I'm some sort of child beater. I'm not, and I'll swear to that on a truckload of Bibles. Sure, I spanked them now and again when they were little, but I don't hit them."

"I'm sure you don't," Nedra said.

"That was stupid of me to pop off like that." Teri's fingers raked through her hair.

"Why did you?"

"I guess I'm just scared of what's going to happen to my herd," Teri said. "I'm afraid that you're going to make me destroy them."

"I've told you, I have no grounds to condemn the cattle." Nedra paused. "What do you think is wrong with them, Teri?"

Teri played with a splinter in the table for a moment. "I know it sounds crazy, but I think maybe somebody's trying to hurt me."

"How?" Nedra felt at last that the truth was peeking out of its shell.

"By hurting my cattle." Teri's eyes tightened with pain. "Everyone knows how much they mean to me. I've even thought sometimes that you were doing something to them, that you were in on it."

"Why me?"

"Just scared I guess. I thought maybe somebody had put you up to it so you'd have an excuse to condemn them." Teri waved her hand. "I'm sounding crazy, aren't I?"

"Teri," Nedra said, placing a hand on the woman's forearm, "I'm not your enemy. It's my job to help you succeed. If I don't help my clients become better producers, then I'm not going to make it in my practice." Nedra let her words sink in, then continued. "That said, I need to point out to you, that you can't let your herd destroy your farm. They're a drain on the balance sheet. That's why there aren't small herds around anymore. You have to be realistic. You need to think beyond your cattle to your whole farm and family."

Teri shrank from Nedra's touch. "I want my cows. I need them."

"What makes the cattle worth sacrificing your farm for? What's going to happen to Jessie and Jeff?"

"I'm not sacrificing my farm—or my kids. You watch. Good times are coming, I can feel them. I just have to weather out this set back."

"Teri, in a couple of weeks, Matt Jensen is going to start legal proceedings against you to get the money you owe him."

"That was my husband's debt. I shouldn't be responsible for it."

"But you are."

"We'll see." Teri turned to look at her herd grazing in the pasture to the west. "Look at them out there," she said, "chomping on the grass without a care in the world. Lucky thing they're so dumb, huh?"

"Yes, it is. Teri, tell me..."

"Sure, I sell the young ones, but never directly to market...though I know that's where they eventually wind up. I usually make believe that they don't." Teri fingered a thread on her top. "I don't like to think about Matt and my troubles. I'm limiting the herd to five females and a bull, and I'll have them as long as I can. I give them a good life. Just a calf a year from each is all I ask. To pay for their keep."

A squirrel scurried up the oak tree next to the table, its claws scratching on the bark. A southerly breeze swept over the long rows of corn as Annie, Jeff, and Jessie emerged from the barn.

"They're coming back," Teri said, her gaze fixed on the barn. "Oh, God, what will I say?"

"An apology would be a good place to start."

"They just don't understand." Teri dug the palms of her hands into her eyes, then looked at the stoney faces of the group approaching the picnic table. "I'm sorry, baby," she said to Jessie. "I didn't mean to scare you."

"I know," Jessie said, keeping her distance. She hung back at the far edge of the table.

"What the hell is wrong with you?" Jeff barked.

"I lost my head. I was just telling Nedra here that I never hit my kids."

"That's right," Jeff said, turning his angry eyes on Nedra. "I don't want you two to blow this thing up and make it into something it's not. Now I think it's time you left us alone."

"If that's what you want," Nedra said, rising from the bench.

"It is. I don't want you coming back here. Ever."

⌘

The moment Nedra's Ranger disappeared down the drive, Teri turned on her son. "How dare you order anyone off my farm!"

"I'll do what I want." Jeff picked up the bench and flung it across the yard. "You're frigging crazy. You're cow crazy, and now you go hitting Jessie in front of people. By evening, they're gonna have social workers crawling all over this place. By tomorrow, you won't have a farm, and you won't have kids. Not that you deserve any of it."

"The one thing I don't deserve is your mouth. I own this farm. It's mine. Not yours. My name is on the mortgage and on every legal paper there is."

"You may own this farm, but you're not going to run it any more!"

"You'll have to kill me first!"

"I'll do something even better than that. I'll sell your damn cattle."

"I've heard that before," Teri said. "You're too much of a coward—like your father."

"Dad was never a coward," Jeff cried.

"You don't know everything, Jeff Thompson, though you sure as hell think you do. And I'll tell you one thing else, I'm so blasted tired of your complaining and surly face, that by God, if you don't like it here, then get the hell out. There's the road any time you want to go down it."

"You'll see," Jeff said, a supercilious tone creeping into his voice as he headed to the house. "Just wait."

⌘

"Sure you've got the smarts to run the farm," Stitch said as he and Jeff walked along the western perimeter of the pasture. "You've been playing it cool so far."

"A lot of good it's all going to do me. I never thought that Matt Jensen would call in his note." Jeff scrutinized the steel fence post to make sure that the barbed wires were attached firmly. He started toward the next post.

"Well, that is a kink in the scheme of things, ain't it? It's a damn shame. So close, now this." Stitch kicked at a patch of tall grass. "Pissing bad luck."

"I don't want to give up now. There must be something I can do." Jeff grabbed the upper wire of the fence with his gloved hand to test the tension.

"You're in a tough spot, kid. Your mother ain't willing to sell the cattle..."

"Yet."

"Yet? That don't count no more. We're not talking about getting some of the blood off the balance sheet. We're talking about losing the farm right down the piss hole, whether or not the cattle get sold this week or next. Unless you sell the damn herd three times over, you're still gonna be short of cash to pay off Matt."

"There's not a soul on this earth who'll lend my mom one dime. Even Eppy is dried up."

"Shit, yes. What you had before was time: Get rid of the cattle, strengthen the bottom line, and in few years, you'd get the farm humming like she was coming."

"Weather permitting," Jeff said impatiently. Stitch didn't know squat about farming. He had no idea what it took to run a successful operation, even a small one.

Stitch laid a thick hand on his greasy cap and screwed it around his head a bit. "You know, people might not like giving money to your mother, but maybe they'd be willing to take a chance with you."

"I couldn't go around asking for a loan. My mom would find out. I'm not old enough anyway."

"I ain't talking 'bout normal channels, if you know what I mean."

Jeff pulled up short. "I don't think I do."

"I'm speaking of a private party..."

"Not Eppy. I told you..."

"No. I was thinking of me."

Jeff's eyes went wide. "You?"

"Sure." Stitch hitched up his sagging pants. "I've got money put away. How much you need?"

"After I sell the cattle, probably twelve thousand."

"Twelve? No problem."

"Stitch, do you mean it?"

Stitch held up his hand to cut off the boy. "Hell, you're the closest thing to a son I got. I know how much you deserve the farm. We've run short of time for Plan A. Plan B says I put my money where my flapping lips are."

"Really? I mean, you're serious?"

"Hell, yes. I'll work something out with my cousin to help you sell the cattle right away. Once you get the cattle sold, I'll know how much to pull out of my account." Stitch hesitated. "Of course, I'd need some sort of promisory note myself."

"I don't think I can sign it while I'm a minor."

"Sure you can! We can just date it after your birthday. We can have everything sorted out by then. I'll have my lawyer draw up the papers. He won't blab either—confidential business."

"Wow," Jeff said, his face bright. "It's really going to happen isn't it."

"You betcha. In fact, let's shake on it right now." Stitch held out his hand to his only nephew, who grabbed it and pumped it.

"It's a deal!" Jeff turned to the land of his dreams. "This will be mine. At last!"

"I've got some work to do," Stitch said. "I'd better be on my way."

"Thanks, Stitch!" Jeff cried. "You're terrific. Really. I mean it."

Stitch grinned at his gullible fool of a nephew. He didn't have a lawyer. As for the money, well, he had about enough to make a decent rattle in a tin cup.

XX

THE INTERGALACTIC SALES REP—HELEN AND THE MINISTER—AN UNHAPPY SISTER—AN UGLY MEMORY

Nedra fit a slide into the empty slot midway through the tray and lifted the next specimen out. Randy Bell had sent the prepared slides from the second Thompson abortion case down from the Diagnostic Lab at Nedra's request. She selected the first rectangle of glass and read the description on the white label next to the iodine-stained spot to the left. Starting the magnification at one hundred, she adjusted the power until she had multiplied the view another threefold. She fine-tuned the focus, then stared at a group of liver cells, round and red. The plasma and nucleus membrane seemed strong and even, and the internal structure sound. These cells, like all the others she'd examined, appeared normal.

Microbiology had been one of Nedra's least favorite subjects in vet school. She preferred dealing with the whole animal, one that she could lay a stethoscope against, not some tiny one-celled entity that squiggled under a glass or stared back at her like a fried egg.

With a sigh, Nedra slipped the glass from under the clips of the microscope, then carefully wrote her observations in a notebook. She placed the slide back in the tray and reached for the next. She heard the front door open.

"Hey-yah, Doc, you here?"

"Be with you in a minute," Nedra called out. She placed her microscope back in its protective container and fastened the small metal hook to hold the cover in place. After she washed her hands, she moved into the waiting room.

"I thought that was you," Nedra said, breaking into a grin when she saw Dick Lancaster of Diamond Laboratories. "I'd recognize that baritone anywhere." Of all the vet supply reps who swept through on their quarterly pitches, Nedra found the rotund guy with the Grecian formula hair the most likable. He made his home in Fort Dodge, Iowa, and spent most of his time on the road. He loved it all. The motel rooms, the cafe dinners, and most of all, he had confided once, the road whizzing by under his wheels and the big sky above him that he could keep an eye on.

"What do you have for me this time?" Nedra asked as she settled into a chair.

"Well, let's start with the usual." Dick began to run down the list of supplies as Nedra ordered what she needed.

"The best thing I have for you is a new treatment for fleas and ticks. You don't have to dip the dogs any more. Makes everyone happier—owner and pet." He handed over a sample and let Nedra run her eye down it.

"Oh, good. I've been reading about it."

"Second week it's available. We're gonna clean up with this one. The pet stores are going crazy." He pulled out a handful of brochures from his steel briefcase, which was the size of a small trunk, and fanned them on the coffee table. "I'll leave a few for your clients," he said, as he handed Nedra a brochure and a data sheet.

"This stuff is selling faster than we can make it," Dick continued as Nedra read the specs. "Even if I place your order today, it's going to take three weeks minimum to get here. I tell you, Nedra, we've got a real winner. I'll leave a few samples with you." He placed three boxes on the table next to the brochures.

"Thanks," Nedra said. "Let me try these out, then I'll see about ordering some next time you come through."

"Believe me, you won't want to wait. But feel free to call in your order. No problem with that. Be sure to give them my name though." The salesman went through a list of up and coming products, then brought the focus back to current needs. "Anything else you need? Syringes? Gloves? Teat tubes? Vacs for pink eye? Staph? Lepto?"

"Leptospirosis," Nedra mused. "Now that's something I wish I'd seen today." She thought back to the Thompson slides. Not one slender, spiral-shaped organism had popped up on the Thompson slides.

"What do you mean?"

"I'm just having a hell of a time with a diagnosis. Spontaneous bovine abortions. Wish I'd seen a little lepto critter under the scope so I could blame it on him and close the case."

"Localized outbreak?"

"Yeah, the problem's in one herd. We've run lots of tests but nothing is clicking into place."

Dick turned back to his catalog. "How're you fixed for rabies serum?"

"Fine. I could use some more formalin."

"Yeah? You drinking the stuff?"

"I've been preserving a number of bovine fetuses."

"I'll put you down for what...?"

"Four gallons. That should hold me for a while."

Dick scribbled on his order pad. "Say, this may sound kinda funny, but have you thought of UFOs?"

"Can't say that I have, Dick."

"That's been happening a lot out west. Cattle being butchered right out in the pasture, sometimes with odd shapes being left in the ground, sometimes radioactive readings. Body organs taken right of out the cattle, so these aliens weren't looking for meat."

"Maybe the aliens eat organs, not muscle," Nedra said. She suspected that Dick's sole source of news came from the tabloids in supermarkets.

"Organ eaters," he said. "Say, there's a thought."

"The calves I'm talking about, though, were aborted, and one deformed; they weren't butchered."

"Sure, but you know there are supposed to be all sorts of magnetic waves coming off UFOs. They can disrupt a town's power grid. No reason they couldn't cause a fetus to go haywire."

"That's an interesting theory you have there."

"Sure. There've been a few sightings in southern Minnesota recently." A row of sweat droplets appeared on Dick's forehead. "In fact, just this past weekend a calf was sliced up in the field just outside of Blue Earth. We're talking less than sixty miles away. When the farmer went to bed Saturday night, he had a thousand head. Sunday morning, nine-hundred ninety-nine and one missing its insides." Dick tipped his head significantly.

"The authorities are blaming it on a UFO?"

"Oh, no," the sales rep said, his voice hushed with conspiracy. "They'd never say anything like that. The cops say it's a bunch of kids on some voodoo prank."

"You're kidding."

"I'm not. I was through there on Monday. The town's buzzing."

"I haven't read anything about it."

"I'm not surprised. These things are hushed up, you know."

"Well, Dick, I appreciate your thoughts."

"Glad to help." He turned back to his catalogue and finished taking Nedra's order. "Been back to the Cities lately?" he asked as he clicked shut his briefcase and reached into his jacket pocket.

"Only a quick trip up and back. We just don't get around to a long weekend like we keep talking about. I've been pretty caught up in my practice," Nedra said apologetically.

"Oh, sure. It's tough hanging out your own shingle. Tougher to be married, I'd think. That's why I'll always be a bachelor—I want things to be my way. I'm too selfish."

The words nearly dropped Nedra's heart to the floor. She watched Dick play with a small envelope. Had she herself been too selfish with Annie? Of course she had. If Annie had been doing all the giving, Nedra must have been doing all the taking.

"I'd never think that of you," Nedra said, trying to turn her thoughts back to the sales rep. He seemed as pleased with himself as always, unaware of how his confession sounded, or how it impacted Nedra.

"Well, here, maybe these will help you out." He guided the small envelope across the coffee table with a forefinger.

"What's that?" Nedra asked.

"A couple of tickets to the next Star Trek convention in Minneapolis. Mid-July. Can you use them?"

"You bet! Thanks, Dick."

"My pleasure, Doc. Here, you can have this, too." He handed over a pen with the Diamond Laboratories logo. "Well, if that does it, I'll push on. Give my regards to Annie, and remember, keep your eye to the sky."

⌘

Hula girls. Colorful rum drinks with pastel umbrellas. Golf year-round. Pastor Gus Olson made a mental note to talk to his wife about moving to Maui after he retired. Even Oahu would do.

"Do you have a moment?" Helen Sinclair stuck her head into the private office of the Lutheran minister.

"Of course, of course! Come in, Helen!" Reverend Olson rose to usher her into the chair occupied by Matt Jensen two days earlier. "What can I do for you?"

"I'm concerned about Teri Thompson," Helen said.

"Are you?" A knot of apprehension blossomed in the minister's stomach. He might have a serious problem on his hands.

"She's going through hard times, what with Jeff acting up and the crops in danger and the problems with the cattle. Now Matt is getting greedy for her land."

"So I've heard. Teri does have quite a load these days. I have been praying for her, and I mean to pull her aside after church next Sunday for a little chat."

"Well, that's a start," Helen said cheerfully.

"What would you like me to do, Helen?" Gus Olson asked quietly. One part of him tried not to think of how happy he would be sitting under a coconut tree listening to Don Ho. The other, stronger part, the good minister of over forty years, zeroed in on his parishioner.

"Well, she doesn't seem to want to talk to anyone, but she's suffering. I can see it in her eyes."

"Yes?"

"Well, it's the farm and those cows. She's a little...touched when it comes to them. She's just not facing reality."

"I know she's fond of her cows."

"Obsessed is a closer word. She called me. Said that her boy is threatening to sell them to pay off some debts on the farm. And Matt won't listen to reason."

"Is that so?"

"Yes. I don't know what to do. Eppy threatened Matt with buying the land herself, but she never would. She's had it with Teri and her stubborness. She won't hear of pouring any more money into that farm."

The pastor nodded. While some congregants, like the Sinclairs, knew the meaning of charity, they also realized its practical limits.

"I think she needs more help than what we're able to give her, Gus. Her miserable childhood has probably scarred her for life, and now she has had year after year of trouble. Is there anything you can do about Jeff—talk to him to get him to settle down? And maybe Matt. I don't know how such a Christian man can be so hard-hearted."

"Uh-huh."

"Then there's Teri herself. She needs something more than anyone's been able to give her. I'm talking spiritual comfort. When she loses the farm, she's going to go right over the edge, I'm afraid."

"I think I'm due for a little visit to the Thompson farm," the minister said.

A huge smile swept across Helen's face. "You're a prince, Gus. A real one."

⌘

"Why was Uncle Stitch here last night?" Jessie asked.

"What do you mean?" Jeff threw a bundle of straw into a stall and spread it out like frosting on a cake.

"Well, I saw him out here in the pasture, talking to you."

Jeff pressed the tines of the pitchfork into the floor and rested an elbow on the triangular handle. He examined Jessie standing across from him, twirling a piece of straw in her hand, a pout pushing out her mouth. "I don't know. Stuff. The farm, the windmill I'm thinking of building."

"I don't like him. I think he's mean."

A bat swooped through the barn and out into the night sky, visible through the open doors. The crickets rubbed their tunes, and the cattle, in for the night, snorted deeply.

"He's an all right guy. In fact, he's nicer than you think. He cares for us, Jess. He really does. Unlike mom."

"You don't think she cares about us?"

Jeff continued with his shoveling. "No. You have to have four legs and mooo to get noticed by Mom."

"I don't like Stitch. He's like Grandpa Winthrop," Jessie said. "He's mean just to be mean." The girl stepped on a slat of wood and set her elbows on the top plank of the stall. Her T-shirt, caked with dust, took on another streak from the wood. "Aunt Eppy said once that Grandpa wasn't very nice to mom."

"Yeah?" Jeff gave a bunch of straw a final shove into the corner and set the pitchfork aside. He tugged his T-shirt out of his pants and wiped his face with the front. His bare stomach was tan and muscular.

"Helen wouldn't let her say anything more. I never liked Grandpa. He was always so grouchy. I didn't even feel sorry when he died."

"Well, he probably had worries of his own," Jeff said. He picked up a hose and carried it to a watering barrel. "Before you go, turn the water on for me, would you?"

"Was he ever mean to you?" Jessie plodded over to the faucet and gave it a quick turn.

"I can't remember," Jeff said. He felt the cold water surge through the rubber hose.

⌘

Grandpa Winthrop. That was not a topic that Jeff let himself think about much.

He remembered running up to his grandpa's farm to tell him about the accident at the farm, about how his father had died. He was afraid to go, but his mother insisted. It was about like what he expected: fury in his grandpa's eyes that exploded into a whollop-ing. Jeff had tried to escape from his grasp, but Grandpa had a hold of his belt, and as Jeff tried to run, Grandpa struck him again and again on his backside, hitting him as if he were to blame for his father's death. Jeff felt humilitated and enraged. If he could have, he would have smacked his grandfather to show him how it felt to be hit.

But it wasn't just the beating. Jeff remembered his father's funeral, walking behind his mother as the casket was carried down the burgundy carpet of the church. Grandpa was to her right, holding out his arm for his daughter. It was the only time he had ever seen them touch, but he hadn't really thought of it then. He was too busy trying to plug up the tears that wanted to spill down his face, and holding his lips rigid when all they wanted to do was swell up and twist around as he gulped down his sobs.

Afterwards, in the church basement, when all the people gath-ered to eat the casseroles and brownies that the Circle had made, people would come up to him and say they were sorry like they really were. All he knew was that he didn't want to be there. His father was dead and the last thing he wanted to be doing was stand in a basement having people tell him how sorry they were. It wouldn't bring him back. He searched for his mother to tell her he'd walk home. He'd had enough. She wasn't sitting at a table nor was she huddled in a group. She wasn't in the kitchen, either. She was...

"You're about as deep in thought as a man can be," a voice said.

Jeff jerked his head up. Reverend Olson stood before him, dressed in his collar and a kindly smile. "My mom's in town," he grumbled.

"So Jessie said. I met her coming to the barn." The pastor stepped across a soft pile of manure. "I haven't seen you in church in a while. I thought I'd drop in and see how things are."

"Fine."

Gus Olson held the boy's gaze for a moment. "What were you thinking, just now?"

"I was thinking about my dad's funeral." Jeff turned off the water.

"What about it?"

"I don't know." He started to wind the hose around his arm. "You wouldn't understand."

"Maybe not. But would you give me a shot?"

Jeff finished looping the hose around his arm, then hung it over a bracket by the faucet. "There was a lot that happened then that I didn't understand. I've always tried to make sense out of it."

"Like what?"

"This is just between you and me, right?"

The minister nodded. "It sure is, Jeff."

"Well, you know, after the service, when everybody was downstairs in the basement eating, I found my mother in the foyer. She was with Matt Jensen. He kept repeating something, like *tell me...tell me*."

"Go on."

"Grandpa Winthrop walked in then through the side door. He'd probably been taking a few snorts of Jack Daniel from his hip flask." Jeff chuckled unhappily. "You should have seen how purple his face got when he saw my mom and Matt. 'Have you no decency?' He hissed it. Really hissed it. I'd never heard a voice like that, not even from him. And him talking about decency, like it was fine to be drunk at my father's funeral, like it was fine to hit people and scare them."

"He was a difficult man," the reverend said.

"Yeah. There he was, blowing up, and all I wanted was for Dad not to be dead." Jeff turned his wide, blurry eyes on the minister. "Were my mom and dad, you know, unhappy with each other?"

"Why do you ask?"

"I always felt there was something going on—Dad, Matt, Mom. They were mad at each other. Maybe it was money or the land. I never knew exactly what. But it was like there was a storm blowing in, then suddenly it was gone and my Dad dropped into a grave. Nothing's been right since."

"Were they right before?"

"No," Jeff said, surprised at his quick response. "No. Not before either."

"Every parent has a complicated life, Jeff," Gus Olson said quietly. "I don't think either of your folks ever pretended to be perfect."

"I never expected them to be perfect."

"What did you expect?"

"I don't know." Jeff watched the water collect at the downward mouth of the hose. "To love me more, maybe." The last drop fell to the floor and hit with a muted ping.

XXI

COP TOUR

Nedra listened to the sound of water splashing into a bucket. She stepped quietly down the basement stairs of her office.

"Are you snoopervising me or what?" Tony stood at the large basin sink, working the spigots like they were valves at Grand Coulee Dam.

"Or what," Nedra laughed. "I thought you might like some help carrying that bucket up the stairs."

Tony turned off the faucets and lifted the pail, which had a crown of popping suds, from the sink. "I have it completely under control, boss lady." He carried the full bucket between his legs, with two hands gripping the metal handle.

Nedra tried not to look askance. "Okay."

"Hey, it's my job, you know," he said, setting his burden on the bottom step as he took a breather. "Unless you want to work for me now."

"You'd be too tough a boss."

Tony's laugh reverberated off the cement block walls. "I see you took my advice," he said when he reach the top of the steps.

"About what?"

"Blessing the cattle at the Thompsons. I was at the cemetery last night with my mother, and I saw the minister over at their farm."

"The Thompsons did that on their own, then," Nedra said. "Hope it works."

"It will." Tony grunted as he set his burden down by the back door. "I believe in miracles."

He picked up the pail just as the oak door swung open, barely missing the bucket. "See?" he grinned.

Joanne Donnelly stuck her head through the doorway. "Have a few minutes?" she asked.

"Come on in," Nedra said warmly.

The cop shut the door behind her and made a point of inspecting the lock. "I see you got the kind of dead bolts where you don't need a key to get out—you have a knob that you can twist."

"I thought it safer this way," Nedra said. "If I have to evacuate the clinic, I want exits where we don't fumble with keys."

"You have a point," Joanne conceded. "You're still susceptible to a break-in, though."

"It's an imperfect solution, I admit, but one I'm willing to live with." Nedra motioned the cop toward the waiting room, leaving Tony to clean out the kennel room. "Any developments about the break-in?"

"Zip. I try not to take this stuff personally," the officer sank into a chair. "That's what they taught me in all those Criminal Justice classes I took at Mankato State years ago. Make it personal, you make mistakes. It's starting to bug the shit out of me, though. Like Teri's cows for you, I suppose."

Tony trudged into the waiting room, mop in hand.

"You know," Joanne said, "I never have had a tour of this place. Show me the downstairs."

"Gladly." Together the women went down the rear steps, Joanne in front, Nedra a close second. The steps creaked with their weight. "Wow," Joanne said as soon as she reached the basement floor.

The refrigerator hummed to life. Joanne scanned the room. One wall was lined with barrels, large and small, with labels from the Diamond Laboratories, and an antique Cold Spot refrigerator. On the opposite wall, an enclosure held a small bathroom, and next to it, a large double sink with stacks of trays filled with test tubes. A washer and dryer were tucked under the staircase. "This is one hell of an outfit you have here," she said.

"Dirt cheap, too, " Nedra said. "I picked up the refrigerator for ten bucks at an estate sale. The washer and dryer are from my mom's old house when she moved into an apartment."

"Nice."

"These babies," Nedra said, patting the washing machine and dryer, "saved my relationship with Annie."

"How's that?"

"She couldn't stand the smelly clothes I'd bring home to wash. They get pretty mucked up—manure, urine, and blood."

"So you decided to wash clothes at the office."

"I didn't go to college for nothing, you know."

Joanne let out a low laugh as she walked the perimeter of the basement and then settled on a step. The dehumidifier rattled to life. "I keep wondering why someone would want to break in here."

Nedra hopped on top of the closest barrel. The backs of her sneakers bumped the thick cardboard. "Me, too."

"You know, there was a break-in last year here, before you moved to town," Joanne placed a hand on the railing.

"Really? Who was involved?"

"Rumor had it that it was Stitch Feldon's doing, but we had zero evidence. I didn't think it was related to this incident at first, but I'll consider anything at this point."

"Stitch? What could he want in this office?"

"Back then, probably gold, petty cash, or laughing gas. Now, who knows?"

"Nitrous oxide might improve his disposition."

"Fat chance. Stitch is a Grade-A jerk. If there's trouble to be stirred up, he'll be there with a spoon and a smile."

"Has he been involved with anything serious?"

"He's been a suspect in a number of minor incidents around town. We caught him once and were able to pin a petty theft on him. He didn't serve any jail time for it." Joanne adjusted her service belt. "He used to be an electrician, but no one would let him into their house after his conviction. Jake at the utility company finally hired him out of pity, but he only lets Stitch do line work, nothing indoors."

"What can you do?"

"Talk to him, for whatever that's worth. Damn. I should have pressed him harder a year ago. I hate it when people screw up. I hate it worse when I do." Joanne eyed the barrel under Nedra and motioned a hand toward it. "What's inside your stool?"

"Sulfa drugs. Want a look?"

"Yeah." Joanne got up and lifted the tops off each barrel and looked inside at the giant plastic bag holding yellowish powder.

"I had a lot of fun with these barrels as a kid," Nedra said. "When my dad emptied one out, my sister and I would take it to a hill in our backyard and roll down."

"You had a good childhood, huh?"

"Yeah. I was one of the lucky ones."

"You were." The cop tapped down the lid of the last container. "I hope this episode doesn't sour you on small town life."

"Having come from the big city, Joanne, let me tell you, there's no comparison. I don't know that I could ever go back."

"You're not thinking about that, are you?" Joanne started up the stairs.

"Well, we're here on a trial basis. If it works out, we'll stay. If not, we move. Or at least Annie will."

Joanne turned to face Nedra. "Tell me what it will take to make it work. I want you to stay. Both of you."

XXII

A QUESTION FOR THE PROFESSOR—DOWN TIME

Nedra called Professor Don MacInnes at the University of Minnesota on Saturday morning from her office.

"I have a question for you about the Thompson cattle," Nedra began. "Do you think someone could be tampering with the herd?"

"What on earth for?" Dr. MacInnes said.

Nedra wanted to back off when she heard the shock in his voice, but she pressed on. "I haven't figured that part out. But it's a possibility, isn't it?"

"I suppose so," MacInnes said slowly. "I was hoping for something a little less...dramatic."

"And a little more scientific?" Nedra smiled into the receiver. "If someone really wanted to destroy the herd, how would they do it?"

"They'd have to use a bacteria, virus, or chemical that we don't normally test for. To find out the substance, we'd have to know what it was in order to test for it. Hell, for that matter, we could be looking at more than one method, or some physically induced harm."

"Especially given that two fetuses were normal and one deformed," Nedra added.

"Right. Or someone could even do a combination of methods on one cow. Pour antifreeze down the cow's mouth, say, then beat on her abdomen to induce labor. Or electricity—maybe rig up a dampened electrical flow to agitate her into an abortion."

"It would take some finesse, whatever the method. Otherwise you'd end up with a dead cow."

"Then the question is, why not kill the dams outright, if you want to get rid of the herd? Why kill the fetuses only?"

"That's a question that's tormenting me at three o'clock in the morning."

"I have to warn you, Nedra," MacInnes said, "that you're thinking along dangerous lines, and I wouldn't suggest sharing your ideas with anyone at this point. It's something you want to be sure of. If you level a charge like that and it turns out to be unfounded, not only is your reputation ruined, but somebody is apt to sue you for defamation of character, if not malpractice."

"And we still wouldn't be any closer to knowing what the hell is happening on the Thompson farm."

⌘

No matter how Nedra tried to hide it, Annie always knew. They never spoke of it, nor of how Annie sensed it. It was not something Nedra ever wanted to talk about, though she felt that Annie was just waiting her out. Maybe someday, in the bright sunshine, Nedra could say to Annie, *How do you always know when I've had to put an animal down?* It was not a matter she would ever bring up in the dark, in bed.

Nedra felt Annie's hand caress the plane of her back. The touch was light and precious, like a little cat spirit. It was filled with comfort and sympathy.

"Hey, baby," Annie said softly.

Nedra turned on her back and drew Annie close. "Hey."

Annie nibbled on Nedra's neck.

Today it had been a geriatric cat. Nearly twenty-four years old. She had lost most of her kidney functions and had started to have grand mal seizures, possibly the result of a brain tumor. Putting her down was the kindest thing to do, and Nedra did it while the owner watched, sobbing. It wasn't something she had been taught in vet school, how to deal with death and a client's grief. She had gotten more detached over the years, but not enough never to care. She would always feel the loss. That's one of the things, she hoped, that made her a good vet.

They kissed, slowly and tenderly, then blended in each other's arms. At the foot of the bed, two felines breathed quietly, observing the night. After a few minutes, Nedra felt Annie's breathing grow regular as she seeped into unconsciousness. Nedra lay still with a thousand thoughts bumping around her skull.

There were the questions relating to her practice: What did she do with the quarterly tax forms? If Tony stayed on, how would she start making social security payments? Then there were the case questions: Could Jeff really be to blame for the Thompson cows aborting? Why would he do it? All these questions dimmed for a while as Nedra considered the biggest one, the one lying next to her.

Why did everything have to work so well with Annie, except for geography? If Nedra were to create a companion for herself, she could not have made a better model than the one the Callahan clan had given birth to. She had sensed it from their first meeting.

Nedra had been helping her friend Sandy, a big-boned softball player, move from her apartment into one that she'd be sharing with her lover of six months. Nedra had hauled the first boxes into the apartment. The brightest green eyes she'd ever seen met her in the living room.

"Hi," Nedra said. "These are kitchen things." She felt a beam of electrons burst directly from her stomach to the nerves between her legs.

"Kitchen's that way," the woman with the dark red hair said. She pointed a freckled arm to the left.

Nedra trooped to the back of the apartment, wondering who the redhead was and what the connection was with her friend who was moving in here. By the time Nedra got back to the living room, Sandy was coming through the door. "Nedra," Sandy said, "this is Annie Callahan. Annie, Nedra."

"So you're the vet," Annie said. Her voice was neutral, but her eyes livened with curiosity.

"That's me," Nedra said. "And you're..."

"A friend of mine," Sandy said, making her way toward the bedroom with a load of clothes.

"I know Sandy through work," Annie explained. "We're both at Central High."

"Ah," Nedra said. She shifted her weight, knowing she should continue unloading the U-Haul, but she was reluctant to leave. "What did you mean by the 'so you're the vet' remark?"

Annie's face broke into a wide, fabulous smile. "Sandy's mentioned you. I have a cat. I'm looking for a good vet."

"Oh." Nedra felt her heart shrivel to a walnut. A patient referral.

"Well, that's delicate," Sandy said as she reentered the room. "I recall mentioning that Nedra was the hottest catch north of the Caribbean, a decent person deserving a wonderful mate, and an all-around nice gal."

"I don't remember all that," Annie said, a blush spreading across her cheeks.

"I'm surprised, Sandy," Nedra teased, trying to cover her embarrassment and pleasure, "that you forgot to mention my extraordinary wealth and mythical beauty."

"She knew that wouldn't impress me," Annie said, smiling. "Come on, I'll help carry up the next load."

The beginning was that simple. What could have been clumsy and mortifying flowed, instead, into a smooth, comfortable interchange. By the end of the moving-in party, Nedra and Annie had set their first date: the Star Trek convention the following weekend. It felt like compatibility squared.

If they were living three centuries ahead in the fictional future of Star Trek, the distance would be nothing. Nedra could beam to work from a hundred miles away, then beam back in plenty of time to help make dinner. But this was the real world, Nedra thought, staring at a thin crack in the bedroom ceiling. Annie rearranged herself and murmured in her sleep. Nedra felt caught in a dilemma common to so many: giving your lover freedom, yet keeping the relationship intact.

Dick Lancaster's words haunted her: *I'm too selfish.* Nedra turned on her side and plumped her pillow. Had the pursuit of her dream of a small town practice made her unsuitable for Annie? Was she worthy of a relationship, especially with a jewel like Annie? How could she meet Annie halfway without diminishing either her career or their relationship? Was it even possible?

It had to be possible. Nedra vowed silently to do everything in her power to make it so.

XXIII

TRAIL RIDE—QUESTIONS

Eppy rode point on a string of Palominos heading out from the Sinclair farm. Nedra, Annie, and Helen followed behind at a leisurely pace through the ditches along the gravel road to a narrow dirt trail by the swollen river. The waters were four feet above their normal height and spilling over the banks at some turns.

The rain from the morning had cleared, leaving a bright, turquoise sky, and a soft path. The horses clicked along, going upstream in a westerly direction, under a spread of cottonwoods and white oaks. They followed the bend of the river northward where it would eventually emerge from its source, Lake Amelia, at the western edge of town. The western side of the lake retained its wildness because Eppy owned the land and believed that the rest of the lake shore was overdeveloped.

Nedra listened to the water splash and felt the warm breeze against her face. The rhythm of her mount, a large gelding that matched Eppy's, was steady; the saddle rubbed lazily against her inner thighs. She hadn't been on a horse since the previous fall and found the pressure points pleasantly familiar.

Half an hour into the ride, Eppy swung her horse around into a small lush clearing where the river and lake met. "Who wants to take a break?"

"Me-me-me!" Annie said, waving a hand over her head. "I'm getting sore."

They dismounted and tied the animals to scrub bushes. Eppy loosened a blanket roll from the back of her worn saddle and shook it open on a patch of foot-high grass. Helen untied a thermal pack from her horse, set it on the blanket, and pulled out apricot and curried chicken pita sandwiches, a Tupperware container filled with a vegetable-ham-artichoke salad, and a bottle of chilled chardonnay. Each woman claimed a corner of the large plaid square and faced the feast in the middle of the blanket.

Eppy uncorked the wine and splashed it into small plastic glasses. "This hasn't breathed properly, but who cares." The breeze picked up slightly, and the branches overhead dipped in response. The elder Sinclair's graying hair stirred back from her face as she handed glasses to everyone.

Annie took a sip of wine. "Why do you have so many Palominos?"

"Always had a thing about Roy Rogers," Eppy said. "I think we were twins separated at birth."

"But he's not nearly so handsome," Helen said. "Or young."

"True, but his Trigger was a helluva sight smarter than these old yellows." Eppy waved a sandwich at the cluster of horses nearby tearing mouthfuls of long grass from the bank. "I used to raise them for show. Had fourteen of them at one time. Sold them all except for a handful. These I'm going to let die off."

"Great food," Nedra said after she had tasted the curried chicken.

"Thank you, honey," Helen said. "I just love to cook."

"I heard recently that you two are related to Teri Thompson," Nedra said to no one in particular.

"Took you nine months to find that out?" Eppy roared. "By God, the grapevine must be withering."

"My dear," Helen said, as she finished chewing a bit of ham, "my mother was a Yaeger. Teri's mother was her baby sister, making Teri my first cousin."

"Not mine," Eppy huffed.

"What do you mean?" Annie's eyes darkened to a shadowy green. "If you're sisters..."

"I'm related by marriage only," Eppy said, squinting as the sun burst between the tree branches overhead. "I married Helen's brother, Homer."

"But everyone calls you the Sinclair sisters," Nedra said.

"Well, it's been more than thirty-five years since Homer died," Eppy said. "People tend to forget, especially when the alliteration works so well. The Sinclair sisters. It sounds better than the Sinclair sisters-in-law, don't you think?"

Nedra and Annie exchanged a look.

"Sooo," Annie said, "you two have been living together for how long?"

"Since I married Homer. That was in 1950." Eppy examined the flow of the river to her left. "I know what you're thinking," she said, turning back. "That we're as queer as Gerty and Alice B." The elder Sinclair showed a row of expensive teeth. "Well, you're right. We are."

"Why didn't you say anything before?" Nedra asked.

"Oh," Eppy said, "I wanted to see how long it took you to figure it out."

"All right, you two," Annie said, "spill it. I want to know everything, from the beginning."

"Well, I met Homer in college—in an economics class." Eppy said. "I was majoring in econ; he needed the class for his ag degree. He was about as bright as the new moon when it came to numbers, so I helped him with the assignments. Anyway, he had this piece of land here that he worked with his father. He wanted a wife." Eppy tasted her wine. "I didn't pretend with him. Told him I wasn't interested in men, much less making a bunch of squawking babies and washing smelly diapers. I didn't know anything about women, though. Not then. I told him if he wanted good cooking, I'd marry him. If he wanted good sex, he'd better find somebody else. The old fart settled for the bargain, saying that sex was overrated anyway. He must have believed it. I never heard a word of complaint from him in the seven years we were together."

"How did Helen come into the picture?" Nedra asked.

"I met his baby sister that first summer before we were engaged. Homer took me to the family for an inspection."

"I was home from Iowa State," Helen said. "Homer kept sending me letters all winter and spring about this great gal he'd met, a girl who wanted to be a stockbroker on Wall Street, of all things. I thought she was pretty great, too. First time I saw Eppy, she had on this gray linen suit—you know, it was just a few years after the war and those form fitting two piece suits were the rage—and more waves in her hair than the Pacific Ocean. I got all worked up, but I just couldn't understand it."

Eppy's eyes brightened with memories. "Believe me, I wanted to ditch Homer right then and run off with this beauty to New York. But to get her, I knew I'd have to marry her brother. The courtship and marriage were pretty much a sham. After we married, Homer and I moved in—his folks built this house right next to the old homestead. We tore the old place down after the folks died and replaced it with a machine shed. When Helen finished college, she moved in with us here. There were three bedrooms, one for each of us. But Homer knew where I slept."

"We didn't rub his face in it," Helen said. "He was always as pleasant as could be. I did feel a mite guilty..."

"Not me," Eppy said.

"I did, but then, you know, when he was dying, he said to me how happy he'd been to have two such fine women look after him." Helen's eyes teared, and she brushed a knuckle across her cheek. "And he told Eppy here to take good care of me. She has."

"Back then," Eppy said, examining them, "people didn't think anything of it, the two of us living together. We had a marriage to cover it. But they knew we were attached. No suitors ever came knocking on our door."

"Male ones, at least," Helen said dryly.

"Now I may like to flirt sometimes," Eppy confessed, "but I always know where my heart is."

"I know you do," Helen said, patting Eppy's knee. "Anyway, no one ever crossed us for being together all these years. That's God's truth. The people in this town have been good to us."

"They've been good," Eppy said, "because we own half the goddamn town."

"Now, Epiphany..."

"Don't now me." Eppy swung her eyes around to the younger women. "When Homer died, he owned the homestead. He left it to us. Plus, he'd taken out a couple of insurance policies I never knew about."

"Eppy invested wisely..."

"Finally got some use out of that college degree. I own quite a bit of property here in town and in Mankato—mostly commercial and rental holdings these days. I dumped most of our farm land in the early eighties. When prices were on their way to the moon, I knew it was time to hit the eject button. Most of the proceeds went into the stock market. God, I made a killing. I earned thirty-eight percent in '87 when others were choking in the ashes. Sold my stock six weeks before the bottom fell out. Put it into cash, then later into utilities. I have enough utilities to keep us in light and water to the year 6000—then I reinvested in the stock market only 50 points above its low. Face it, we're a couple of rich old biddies, and this town knows it."

"So you say. People like us here. Maybe not you," Helen teased Eppy. "Most people would rather face a dragon."

"I don't give a dried cow pie about what people think. If they find me offensive, to hell with them. I don't want them wasting my time." A couple of chipmunks bickered overhead and a fish jumped out of the stream and slapped back through the water.

"Then you two have been together..." Annie looked expectantly at Helen.

"More than forty years."

⌘

Back at the Sinclair farm several hours and many stories later, Nedra stroked the back of her Palomino with short, firm motions.

All the horses, now in halters tied to the fence, were receiving a rub down from their riders. "What's going on with Teri these days?" Nedra asked Helen, who stood on the other side of her horse.

"What do you mean, dear?"

"I'm wondering if her obsession with her herd is clouding her thinking. She doesn't seem to realize that she's about to lose her farm."

"She hears what she wants to hear," Helen said.

Eppy patted her Palomino's neck. "I don't know how she came to choose a cow for a pet. They all look as dumb as a tree stump to me. At least with a dog or cat, they have a certain look, you know, an intelligence about them. I read somewhere that eyes are protuberances of the brain. If that's true, when I look a cow in the eye, all I see are brains made out of Styrofoam packing peanuts."

Everyone except Eppy laughed.

"I think it's pitiful," she continued. "That boy of hers belongs in college. He can make something of himself, but he's buried up to his neck in that farm. He's getting as obsessed about the land as Teri is about the godforsaken cattle. It's a damn good patch of acreage, like all the land around here."

Eppy stopped the stroke across her horse's back for a moment. Her Palomino snorted and stamped the ground. "Hey there, boy, you settle down," Eppy commanded. "Teri's as stubborn as that bull of hers. I've told her a million times to turn that walking beef into hamburger and shoe leather. Stocks, livestock, and men are alike—loyalty to losers will only break you. She won't hear of it."

"She's as stubborn as you are, Ep," Helen said.

"Stubborn and smart is one thing. Stubborn and stupid is another."

XXIV

A CONFUSED STATE OF MIND—EMERGENCY—
LOTTIE SHARP AND HER CHIHUAHUA

"Eppy and Helen," Nedra cackled as she pulled on the cords to the living room drapes with a crisp motion. The beige linen whooshed shut across the picture window and blocked out the glowing street lamps. The cats sniffed at the horse smell on Nedra's jeans and flared their tiny nostrils. "Who would have thought?"

"It scares me a little," Annie said.

"Really? Why?"

"I'm not sure." Annie squatted down to check the VCR. "First they tell us that they saved our jobs. Now they tell us that they're dykes, too. It all seems just a little weird, even manipulative."

Nedra picked up Kettle, the black tabby. "I didn't get that impression."

"I've known people like Eppy. They love power and control," Annie said. "Oh, good, *Star Trek* taped okay."

"Meaning?"

Annie hit the rewind button. The machine clicked, then whirred to life. "Meaning that we're fine as long as we stay on her good side. The moment we slip, she's going to turn on us. Just don't sign me up for Eppy's fan club."

"I don't get it," Nedra said, plopping down on the sofa. "Here we spend a fun day with them, and they practically bare their souls to us. It's as if you don't want friends in this town."

"What does that mean?"

"It may mean that maybe you don't want friends so you'll have an excuse to leave." Nedra hated how that sounded.

"Whoa," Annie said, standing up and facing Nedra. "Where's that coming from?"

"I don't know." Nedra pressed her lips together as she examined her feelings. "I guess I'm afraid that one day I'm going to wake up and you'll be gone, or I'll come home from work and all I've have is a note from you."

"You know I'd never do anything like that. We're going to work this through together."

"I want to believe that, but I don't know if I can—or should."

"It sounds like you don't trust me." She straddled Nedra on the couch. "Ouch! God, I have saddle sores."

Nedra gave Annie a quick, sad smile. "I trust you, but I still get scared."

Annie put her forehead against Nedra's. "Then you don't trust me."

Nedra felt tears springing from her eyes. "I do. But everything is so screwed up."

"What is, honey?"

The whine in the VCR went up half an octave as the internal mechanisms shut down.

"Things with us. Being in this town, trying to have a small practice like my dad, only the world's changed. I have to advertise in the Mankato paper to get enough pet business; I have to board animals; I have to keep track of everything—all the invoicing and inventory because I don't have a support staff. I don't have other vets like I did at the clinic in the Cities where I can chat about the practice—I have to call the University if I want to talk to anybody."

"Sounds like you're the one who wants to move."

Nedra put her head against Annie's shoulder and started to cry. "I don't want to," she said. "I really don't. I just feel so all alone sometimes, and guilty about you, and about Dad. I've been so selfish."

Now Annie's tears came. "Oh, baby."

"You know, I did feel guilty at first that you'd given up so much to be here with me, but then I sort of got used to it. I thought everything would be okay. But you've given up a lot. I just don't know how to meet you halfway."

Annie kissed Nedra's cheek. "You're stepping in the right direction. Now I'm starting to feel like an ogre."

"You're not. You never could be."

Annie cradled Nedra in her arms and rocked her for several minutes. "I'm sorry that you've been feeling bad about your father," Annie said at last. "Can you tell me more about it?"

Nedra ran a hand up and down Annie's arm.

"I realize that I was selfish with him, too. I always felt guilty knowing that I didn't go and practice with my dad in the last years that he was alive. He handled everything by himself. He wanted me to come back and set up shop with him, but I couldn't. Maybe if I had—if I hadn't have been so self-centered—he wouldn't have worked so hard, and he wouldn't have had that heart attack."

"Stop it, Nedra," Annie said softly. "Stop it. You can't blame yourself for his heart attack. You couldn't go back to your home town to live. You know why. And you know that a town of 1,200 could never support two vets."

"I know," Nedra said, wiping her face with the back of her hands.

"Your dad was barely breaking even the last few years of his life."

"I know." Nedra let out a ragged sigh. "If only he were here. He'd know what to do about...everything. Even those damn Thompson cows."

"You're doing all you can."

"I'm not sure." Nedra played with a button on Annie's shirt. "I called Dr. MacInnes at the U this morning. I asked him if someone could be aborting the cows on purpose."

"Your Jeff theory?"

"Yeah."

Annie began to undo Nedra's pony tail. "What did MacInnes say."

"To drop that line of thinking. Period."

Annie stroked Nedra's hair for a few moments. "Are you willing to do that?"

Nedra examined Copper's tail flicking from under the drapes. "No. Damn, I hope I'm wrong."

"The world won't end if Teri looses the farm."

"It will for her." Nedra closed her eyes. "That feels good."

"You're becoming as obsessed as Teri."

"Passionately inquisitive," Nedra countered.

"We can't solve anything now and we're both filthy dirty. How about a shower?"

"Together?"

"Yeah." Annie leaned in and kissed Nedra.

Nedra felt a small pressure on her chest from Annie's weight. It was a signal that things might get serious. In the first year of their relationship, any kiss led automatically to a pile of clothes on the floor and a scene of rolling, heated lovemaking. After six years, a kiss could end with a smile, a hug, a brief make out session, or a hot time between the sheets. The road to the bedroom had become filled with subtleties and unspoken questions and answers: Is this just a kiss? Do we want to get down?

Recently, it had taken on a special, raw edge. Every time they made love, Nedra wondered if it would be the last time. Nedra kissed Annie hard, imprinting the texture of her mouth in her memory.

With one hand, Annie unbuttoned Nedra's shirt to the waist and undid the front bra closure. There was no question now where this encounter would end.

"What about your saddle sores?" Nedra asked, unzipping Annie's jeans.

"Were you planning on wearing a saddle?" Annie asked.

Nedra laughed and twirled Annie under her. To hell with tomorrow. She had Annie now, and a deep and urgent desire.

⌘

Two hours later the phone rang. As Nedra fit the receiver to her ear, she pinched the bridge of her nose and squinted to clear her head of sleep. "Dr. Wells," she said.

"I JUST FOUND A FLEA ON MY DOG!!!" a crackly voice shouted. The caller sounded like an elderly woman.

"Who is this?"

"Lottie Sharp!"

"Mrs. Sharp, why don't you call me Monday morning?"

"I won't have fleas in my house! You need to take care of it RIGHT NOW!"

"How many fleas did you find?"

"One. But where there's one, there're more!"

"Maybe not. Your dog could have picked up a stray in the grass."

"I'm not taking any chances! I won't have them in the house! I need that flea shampoo RIGHT NOW!"

"It's 10:30 at night."

"I know! All the stores are closed! You live right next door to your office. It shouldn't be any problem to open up your shop. I'll be there in ten minutes!!" The line clicked into a dial tone.

Nedra stared at the receiver, then rolled her eyes at Annie, who had propped herself up to enjoy the show.

"Don't tell me," Annie said as she snuggled back down, "I heard every word. You know, you're spoiling the people in this town rotten."

"I've had great practice with you, honey." Nedra patted her lover's rear as she reached for a T-shirt.

⌘

"I can't find any other fleas, Mrs. Sharp," Nedra said. She dropped one crushed black dot in the garbage, then positioned the Chihuahua in the center of the examining table.

"Well, I want that shampoo that you have. I'm not going to bed until my baby is clean and I know every flea is dead. Once they get in your home, you might as well dynamite the house to get rid of them!"

Nedra reached for the new brand of shampoo left by the sales rep Dick Lancaster, then thought she'd better stay with the brand familiar to her for this client. She read the directions to the seventy-eight-year-old woman. Mrs. Sharp nodded at every word.

"I suppose I should get one of those collars, too."

"I'd wait a bit for that. You don't want to overdo it with the shampoo and a flea collar. That can be too much toxin for a small animal like this."

Nedra felt the dog's underside. It was firm and distended. Gently, she lifted the dog to take a closer look. The teats were slightly swollen.

"She's gained a little these past weeks," Mrs. Sharp said. "I need to put her on a diet."

"That's not the problem," Nedra said. "She's pregnant."

Mrs. Sharp's eyes bulged out behind her glasses. "Not my little Muffin!"

"'Fraid so."

"How could you?" Mrs. Sharp snapped at her dog. The wag in the Chihuahua's tail dropped perceptively and her eyes took on a confused look.

"How old is she?"

"A year and a half. A neighbor gave her to me for my birthday."

"Do you know who the sire could have been?"

Mrs. Sharp patted her tightly waved white hair. "She always goes out on a leash."

"Does she ever sneak outside?"

"Once in a while. She hasn't gotten out for, oh, maybe in late April I think it was. She ran over to the neighbor..." Mrs. Sharp's eyes narrowed. "They have one of those Snoopy dogs!"

"The Hoffman beagle? Hmmm..." Nedra felt the dog's underside again. "I think we can assume that's the sire, which is bad news. It's a mismate."

"What do you mean?"

"A tiny dog like this can't carry the pups of a breed that's so much bigger. Your dog is probably six weeks along in its pregnancy and she already looks full term. It'll kill her."

Mrs. Sharp's eyes welled with tears and her hand went over her mouth. "Oh, Lord, Lord. Muffin's been misused!" As if sensing her companion's distress, the Chihuahua wagged her tail with more vigor and licked the old lady's bony hand.

Nedra petted the small dog. "I'd like you to bring Muffin in Monday morning. I'll terminate the pregnancy and spay her at the same time."

"I won't have you put her under. My last dog died from the anesthesia. I dropped off my poor little Daisy—she was a toy poodle, the cutest thing you ever saw. I left her to be spayed and the next thing you know, that Dr. Gunderson was on the phone telling me how sorry he was. He could just as well have ripped my heart out. I wouldn't be a bit surprised if he wasn't a vet at all. He was a quack, I'm sure of it!"

"Now, Mrs. Sharp..."

"I don't care what anyone says. I'm not taking any chances with Muffin."

"I understand your..."

"I don't want any arguments from a young thing like you, either. You're not putting this dog under! Period!"

"Then we'll have to use drugs." Nedra leveled her eyes at the old woman. "That's not going to solve the problem for future encounters with the neighborhood dogs."

"The drugs won't knock her out, will they?"

"No. She'll be fully conscious. But there's always a risk with their use."

"It can't be worse than putting her under."

"Animals have been known to die from this."

"They die from anesthesia, that's for sure." Mrs. Sharp's eyes narrowed to accusatory slits. "What kind of drug would you use?"

"Something called a prostaglandin or dinoprost. It doesn't have as many side effects as other drugs because it's a chemical that's produced naturally by animals," Nedra said, successfully avoiding the word testosterone.

"Have you used it before?" Mrs. Sharp picked up the Chihuahua and hugged it. She seemed to have forgotten all about fleas and Muffin's indiscretion.

"Sure. We use it mainly on horses, cows, and show dogs. Owners don't want a mating accident to ruin a special breeding line."

"I like the sound of this drug more and more." Mrs. Sharp crossed her arms. "I'll take my chances with it."

"Okay." Nedra slid back the glass front of a cabinet and reached for a red and white box. "I should have three bottles," she muttered when she saw only the bottle in her hand and the box containing the second one on the shelf. She opened the carton and pulled out a thirty milliliter vial.

"I want you to do it right now. Give her the shot and get it over with."

"It's not that simple. For dogs it takes two to three injections a day over three to six days."

"Three to six days! Child, you'd better get started!"

"You'll have to leave her here because I need to keep her under close observation."

Mrs. Sharp's face sank. "Leave her here? Overnight?"

"Probably for several days."

"Can't I just take her home? I live only..."

"I'm sorry. It would be increasing the risk of harm."

"You're young to be so hard." Lottie made a sad, sighing sound. "I'll stop by three times a day then. I'll feed her, too."

"Muffin would appreciate it." Nedra checked the label for the dosage for dogs. Oh, man, she thought, the prescribed overall dosage was high, although the individual injections were small. Twenty-five micrograms per kilogram of body weight. She set Muffin on the scale. Five kilos. She did the arithmetic quickly in her head, then confirmed it with a calculator. "I'm going to start her out with a low dosage so I can monitor the side effects, then increase it based on her tolerance." She positioned the dog back in the middle of the exam table. "It's your unlucky night, Muffin. Fleas *and* a shot." Nedra prepared a syringe and gave the Chihuahua an intramuscular injection. The dog yipped, then snapped at Nedra, almost nipping her thumb. It was going to be a fun few days.

"Now what?"

"I'm going to watch her for a while."

"How long?"

"It could take anywhere from five minutes to two hours for a reaction to occur."

"Oh, my!"

"You may as well go home." Nedra tucked the unhappy dog under one arm and took the elderly woman by the other. She guided her to the front door.

Mrs. Sharp halted at the entrance. "Don't I pay you now?"

"No. Why don't you wait until we finish next week. After Muffin recuperates, I think you should probably think again about getting her spayed. Probably within a year or two, I'll be using a new procedure that can be done under a local anesthesia. They may be doing it already at a clinic in Mankato. I can check for you."

"Well, I don't know. It all seems like such a bother." Without so much as a thank you, Mrs. Sharp disappeared out the front door clutching the flea shampoo. Nedra locked the door behind her.

The moment the door shut, Nedra hustled behind the front counter and turned on her computer. The usual humming noise of the fan seemed especially loud now that Nedra was alone in the office so late at night. As the PC went through its startup routine, Nedra petted the frightened, panting dog. She carried Muffin back to the kennel and placed her in a cage. "I'll be back in a few minutes," she said.

Nedra checked the back door to make sure that it too was secure. Standing at the rear entrance, she peered down the dark basement steps and thought about going to check the windows. But the basement seemed too spooky now.

At the front desk, she accessed her inventory spreadsheet. She searched for the order for the prostaglandin. Dick Lancaster, the sales rep from Diamond Labs, had stopped by in early October, she remembered, because it had been his first call on her as an independent vet, not as her father's child. He had given her a bottle of champagne. They had toasted the practice, the memory of her father, and the latest UFO sighting in Dick's sales territory.

Nedra concentrated on her October order. She had been filling the gaps in her inventory. She had asked Dick about prostaglandins because one of her new clients had mentioned artificial insemination. Dick said his company carried only a synthetically made product. Since she preferred natural products to synthetic ones, she had ordered the naturally made one through another pharmaceutical distributor.

Nedra initiated a name search for *Lutalyse*, the product name. The entry appeared after a moment. She tabbed across the columns until she came to the record of her last purchase. Four thirty-milliliter bottles of *Lutalyse*.

Nedra clearly remembered using one bottle on the Miller cattle operation. That left three bottles—the two in her cabinet and one missing.

"That's it!" Nedra said. But proving it would be a different matter.

XXV

SUNDAY MORNING AT THE OFFICE—
A VISIT TO TERI—A BOY'S DEMANDS

"Okay," Joanne Donnelly said as she leaned forward on the wooden side chair in Nedra's office, "you're missing a bottle of this stuff. What does that mean?" The police officer frowned. She was dressed in her civilian clothes, jeans and a burgundy polo shirt. A canvas belt looped around her waist.

Nedra glanced at Annie, who was standing in the doorway. In the background, Muffin yipped like a windup doll. "It means that a potent drug that can induce abortions has been stolen."

"God, doesn't that dog ever stop?" Joanne complained. "We can't go tearing up the Thompson farm looking for the missing bottle."

"Why not?" Nedra asked. "Don't you just need a search warrant."

"I need something more solid than 'I think' or 'I believe' to obtain one," the cop said. She lifted the bottle up and ran her eyes over the red and white label of the vial. "Tell me more about what this drug does. I can't understand a word on here."

"It's a prostaglandin, which has several uses. It's used to regulate a heat period in breeding animals, often in conjunction with artificial insemination. Farmers want to make sure their livestock is in cycle to get pregnant, otherwise they'd be wasting a lot of bucks on sperm that had no one to party with. It's also used to induce delivery and to induce abortion in instances of mismates."

"Is this used only with cattle?"

"No, with lots of animals. I use this brand because it works with a wide variety—cattle, horses, swine, and unlabeled use with dogs and cats. Some brands don't work with as many animals."

"Would vets be the only people who have this?"

"Most likely. A large cattle operation might order some directly from a vet supply shop, but they'd probably have a vet in on a consulting basis. You don't want to fool around with this stuff."

"Can humans use it?"

Nedra opened a copy of the *Veterinary Drug Handbook*. "According to the pharmacology bible, a cousin of this product is approved for human use. Chances are, this would probably work, too, though you didn't hear it from me."

"Humans, huh?" Joanne shook the bottle. The clear liquid sloshed around.

A warm breeze lifted the sheer curtains from a small window in Nedra's office. Paeans from the bells of the nearby Presbyterian Church announced the end of the service.

"How does it work?"

"It affects the hormone level in the animal. If you give a cow five milliliters of the drug intramuscularly, for instance, the cow would expel uterine contents in about seventy-two hours. With a dog, it takes a much lower dosage—depending on the phase of pregnancy—but several injections over a few days."

"That's why you have that obnoxious dog here?"

Nedra nodded. "The poor thing is scared and not feeling well, and she misses her mom." She reached for the bottle from Joanne. "This has got to be what's finding its way into the bloodstream of the Thompson cattle. I'll bet my practice that Jeff has been using this stuff on his mother's herd."

"But why abort the cows? Why not just infect them with something?"

"If Jeff had infected the herd with a disease, then I would have had to condemn the cattle. They'd go to the rendering plant, where the Thompsons would get about a tenth of what the livestock market would bring for healthy cattle. But if there's nothing wrong—no disease—then I can't condemn the herd. Teri wouldn't be able to afford to keep the cattle. She'd be forced to sell them."

"At full market price," Annie added.

Joanne eyed the bottle again. "Is there any way you could test for this drug in the Thompson cows?"

"It wouldn't do much good. All cows have testosterone. We wouldn't be able to tell if what we found was from the cow or an injection."

"Would this drug cause deformities?" Joanne lifted an ankle and set it on her knee. "Like the ones that occurred with that last calf?"

"Only one out of three was deformed. A prostaglandin wouldn't be responsible for the deformity we saw. The fetuses were already well along in their development before the dams encountered this drug."

"Given your theory," Joanne said, "answer this question for me: Why did the break in—I assume it was the second one—occur after Teri's cow aborted?"

"Maybe to get another bottle," Nedra said, "or to return the first one."

"Take back what he had stolen?" Joanne said. "Why?"

Nedra held the bottle up and examined the clear liquid inside. "I mentioned to Carolyn that I was setting up an inventory system. Jeff could have been returning the bottle filled with water so I wouldn't notice that it was missing."

"God, that's a thought alright," Joanne said. "Would he be that clever?"

"He's a bright boy," Annie said.

The cop clicked her pen and fit it into the notebook's spiral wire. "Nedra, I'll pick you up tomorrow morning at eight. I want to chat with Teri. She may know more than she thinks she knows. Or is willing to tell."

⌘

"What do you want with my mom?" Jeff Thompson asked, spitting out the words like venom. He stood behind the back screen door of his house and scanned the faces of Nedra and Officer Donnelly.

"We've had a development regarding the break-in at Nedra's clinic," Joanne said. "We want to talk to her."

"She's in the garden," Jeff said, opening the door and stepping outside. He started down the steps.

"We prefer to talk to her alone," Joanne said.

The women made their way around the two-story house, across the muddy mixture of dirt and splashes of grass that the Thompsons called a yard. Teri was kneeling, her backside toward the house, between rows of carrots. The fine, green heads of the vegetables, as delicate as lace, bounced in the warm air currents.

"Have a minute?" Joanne called out.

Teri glanced around and rose to her feet. "Hi, there," she smiled. She rubbed a spot on her lower back. "I can't bend over like I used to, that's for sure." Her hair, caught up in a navy bandanna, was covered further by a broad-brimmed straw hat. She wore jeans and an oversized long-sleeved T-shirt. "What's up?"

"Nedra here has discovered some drugs missing from her office."

Teri crinkled her eyes at Nedra. "Yes?"

"It's a drug, Teri," Nedra explained, "that can be used to abort animals."

Teri glanced up at the house.

Nedra followed Teri's line of vision. She saw Jeff duck behind a back bedroom curtain. "I've discovered a bottle of a prostaglandin missing from my office, and I've confirmed with my supplier the amount shipped to me. It's possible that someone used this drug on your cattle." Nedra held up a box. "It comes in a box like this," she said, holding out a carton and pointing to the Upjohn design. "Inside," she said, shaking out the insides, "is a bottle like this."

"Have you seen anything looks like that?" Joanne asked.

Teri stared at the box for a few moments, then shook her head. “Can’t say that I have.” She looked directly at the cop. “Do you think someone used this on my cattle?”

“It’s a possibility. You suggested the other day that someone might be harming your cows.”

“I know. I hoped it was just crazy talk.”

Joanne’s salt and pepper hair stirred in the warm easterly breeze. As she squinted into the sun, her eyebrows pinched together. “Why would someone do this?”

“Well,” Teri said, “it seems to me that just about everyone thinks I should get rid of my herd. I can’t imagine anyone doing something like this, though.” For a moment, Teri took in the expanse of the dilapidated farmhouse, the long slats of weathered, wood siding, the overhanging eaves. “Well, what’s done is done.”

Joanne examined her old friend. “What are you saying, Teri?”

Teri pounded the flat end of the hoe into the rich, black dirt. “We don’t have to have answers to everything. Maybe we should let this matter rest.”

Nedra’s jaw ached suddenly from joint to joint. This all seemed so wrong. Throughout her career, every client wanted to know what happened. Why is my dog sick? What’s this lump on my cat? Why did my horse go lame? What can you do about it? There was a tenacity in animal owners to discover the truth, for it helped absolve them of the guilt they felt over a distressed creature in their care. To know the specifics was to answer the deeper questions, Did I do something wrong? Could this have been prevented? And now Teri, of all people, not wanting to know what was happening to her beloved cows? It didn’t make sense.

Nedra felt Teri withdrawing from them, her thoughts moving from their conversation to the boy who stood behind the bedroom curtains.

⌘

It was more than a person could take, Jeff thought to himself as he watched the squad car pull away. He had a right to know. It was his house, too, and his land. He had worked it since he was four feet high.

"What did they want?" Jeff asked when he reached the garden. He towered over Teri, who had returned to cultivating.

Teri set her trowel down, then straightened her knees as she assumed her full height. When she lifted her eyes to meet her boy's, they were hard, flat circles.

"What did they..." Jeff stopped. "What are you looking at me like that for?"

"How am I looking?" Teri snapped off her gardening gloves and clapped them together. Little dirt balls flew off the white cotton decorated with a print of tiny rose buds.

"Like you could..." Jeff stopped again. He didn't want to say "kill" for fear that it would put an idea into her head, but that's what she looked like. He'd read stories about how people's eyes would go shark-like when they lost control. "Damn it, what did they say? I have a right to know. I'm family."

There was a little tug at the side of Teri's mouth. "There's that," Teri said. She snatched the trowel from the ground and then stalked toward the shed.

"Just what's going on?" Jeff demanded, keeping pace with his mother.

Teri jerked open the doors of the building. She slammed the tool on its hook and threw her gloves to the far side of the building.

"Lady, get a grip," Jeff said.

Teri turned to him. "What Joanne and the vet told me is private. Don't ask me again."

"But..."

"Go back to the house," Teri demanded. "I don't want you to mention this incident ever again, or to tell anyone about it."

"But.."

"I mean it, Jeff. Now go."

Jeff puffed out his lips, then did a one-eighty, but instead of going to the house, he cut across the yard to the barn.

Teri slid shut the door to the shed and clicked on the chain to the low-watt bulb overhead. She separated stacks of flower pots from each other, slid a saw horse away from a wall, emptied a box of wood scraps, and dipped her hand into a bag of fertilizer. Section by section, away from the prying eyes of her son, Teri searched.

XXVI

AN ELDER SPEAKS—CONVERSATION AT A SWING SET

"There you are, honey," Helen Sinclair said as she stepped around the back of Nedra and Annie's house. "I knew you had to be around someplace. Your car is in the drive."

Annie, who was crouching at the outdoor faucet, glanced at the voice. "Hi there," she said. "I'm just finishing up." For a moment longer, she let the water splash over a plastic colander filled with agates, then shut off the faucet. Rays of the early afternoon sun danced on the stones and set them sparkling.

"What are you doing?" Helen moved closer and peered into the container.

"I'm polishing some agates that I found last year. I didn't get my tumbler unpacked until recently."

"May I?" Helen asked, poised to pluck a wet stone from the pile.

"Sure."

The Sinclair woman selected a red iron-oxide rock decorated with concentric white bands. "Eppy has a small box of stones she's picked up over the years when we've been out birdwatching. I tease her about pointing her binoculars in the wrong direction."

Annie laughed. "All of these stones are Lake Superior agates. I found the one that you're holding about fifty miles north of Duluth."

"Is it finished?"

"No," Annie smiled. "This is just the first grind. I have one or two more cycles, then I add the polish. It's shiny right now because it's wet."

"What do you do with them?"

"Keep some here in the house or at school. Or I give them to friends or my brother, sometimes. He makes jewelry as a hobby."

"Oh, my," Helen said. "Do you?"

"Not yet. I keep telling myself that someday I'll get a band saw and start making jewelry myself, but I never get around to it."

"You let me know when you do, honey, and I'll be your first customer." Helen dropped the agate back into the colander. Her eyes caught the peony bushes in full bloom. "Would you like some horse manure for your flowers, dear? I'll bring some in next time, if you'd like."

"Thanks," Annie said, rattling the stones around. "What brings you here?"

"I was looking for some good company," Helen said. "Do you have a few minutes to chat? Maybe inside?"

"Sure." Annie tapped the side of the colander to hurry the drainage, then led Helen in through the back door. After Annie offered her guest refreshments, which the younger Sinclair declined, the women settled in the living room.

"You know," Helen said, "Eppy can be a handful."

Annie's eyes softened in sympathy at the understatement.

"She's often headstrong, arrogant, and childish."

Annie wanted to say, I've noticed, but she just nodded.

"And it hasn't always be easy living in a small town. Now I can't imagine living in a big city, but when we were young, we thought sometimes of moving to Minneapolis or New York or L.A. Anything had to be more exciting than a town like this."

"You'll get no argument from me."

"And the isolation! Just Eppy and me wondering what people thought, and not having anyone like us to share the inner rooms of our lives with. It's been hard at times, but we've stayed."

"Why? What kept you here?"

"The community. Sounds silly, doesn't it? I think everyone wants to feel that they belong to a group. I feel I belong to this town, to my Circle, to the old folks I visit in the nursing home, to the pockets of close friends I have. Up to now, my sense of community has never included other...you know, people like ourselves." Helen bent over to stroke a wandering cat. "You'll have to excuse me. There are some words I'm not used to saying out loud. Anyway, I suppose where you come from, your community was mostly made up of...people like yourself."

"Yeah. I had a pretty tight circle of friends."

"You haven't found that community here, have you?"

Annie felt tears warm her eyes. "No. Has Nedra been talking to you?"

"No. Should she?" It wasn't a lie. Joanne Donnelly was Helen's source.

Annie shook her head. "I'm thinking of moving back, but I don't want to leave Nedra. We've been going around and around with this."

"I thought you might be thinking that, especially with school out. It gives you time to brood."

"I'm not a moper."

"I want you to know, honey, that you and Nedra mean a lot to Eppy and me. She'd never admit it, but I'll say it for both of us. You two are like the sun shining. You pick our spirits right up. We'd hate to lose you, and we'd hate to see you dispirited or hurt. Either one of you."

"That's awfully kind, Helen. I appreciate it."

"You know, there are some activities over in Mankato every once in a while. Even dances. I think the four of us should go sometime. What do you say? We'd save you from being the oldest there."

"I don't know that a dance would do it, Helen."

"It would be a start. We weren't born with friends, you know. You build up a circle over the years. Now granted, we don't have as many...gays...as you're used to, but we have plenty of good people. That's what counts, you know. What's inside, not which gender you love."

"Are you saying that I'm being narrow-minded?"

"Not at all. I'm saying that you're a good girl, honey. Sometimes it's easy to overlook the riches right in front of you when you think of sparkling cities in the distance. Lake Amelia is a wonderful town with wonderful people.

"But I want friends I can really share my life with. I miss all the things a big city offers."

"If you moved back to the Cities and left Nedra behind, do you think you'd really be happy?"

"I don't know. Maybe in the long term."

"This world is full of big cities. I've been in a lot of them. But it has only one Eppy, bless her impossible heart. And there's only one Nedra."

"I know it. That's what makes it so difficult."

"No, honey," Helen said, giving Annie's knee a pat. "That's what makes it so easy."

⌘

Joanne tapped down on the gas pedal as she pulled out of the Thompson driveway. "I'm going to swing by the park. I want to check on the level of the river. Want to come along or go back to the office?"

"I'll tag along. I need to get back to the office by ten, though. My favorite patient is due for an injection." Nedra observed the cattle bunched in the pasture behind the barn. A stray ventured toward the far northern end where the boulders dotted the fields by the low land covered with standing water.

"No problem. I'll have you back in plenty of time." Joanne rolled down the window and readjusted her seat. "Jeff knows what's going on, doesn't he?"

"Yep." Nedra lowered the window on her side of the car. The breeze that rushed in ruffled a pad of paper sitting on the dashboard. "How can you tell?"

"Cop instinct. How about you?"

"Animal instinct."

Joanne swung the car along the old highway that looped around the southern edge of town past the high school, which had only a few cars in the parking lot.

Nedra pulled the bottle of prostaglandin out of her shirt pocket and examined the familiar label. "Both Teri and Eppy Sinclair mentioned an episode with Teri taking a cow to the State Fair. Do you remember anything about it?"

Joanne wagged her head. "Nah. I never paid much attention to the farm stuff. I was a town kid."

"Eppy said they kept the animal for Teri because her father refused to have it on his farm."

"Now that I would believe. Her old man was about as civil as a cornered skunk. Slapped the kids around, even in public. Makes me wonder what he did in private. Of course, in those days, we didn't think much about it. Nowadays, I'd be knocking on his door with my night stick, if you know what I mean."

"He's dead now isn't he?" Nedra asked.

"Oh, yeah. Old Man Winthrop died a couple of years ago. The doctor said it was heart failure. I never believed it. You gotta have a heart for that to happen."

Joanne steered the cruiser into the town park. She made a pass around the perimeter road at five miles per hour and checked the licenses for expired tabs on three cars lined up in the camping area. Finding everyone legal, she rounded the curve by the playground near the river. A woman sat all alone in a swing near a picnic table, making feeble little arcs across a sand pit.

"That's Lana Osborne," Nedra said, pointing at the School Board President.

"So it is. Mind if we stop?"

Joanne angled the squad car off the road and shut off the engine.

"Don't tell me you have to be under forty to swing on this set?" Lana said as she saw the women approach.

"No, ma'am." Joanne smiled as she adjusted her service belt. "Got a few minutes?"

"Sure. Have a seat." Lana nodded to the swing next to her. She held her sunglasses in one hand.

"Better not when I'm on duty. I can see the headline: COP SPENDS SHIFT SWINGING IN PARK."

Nedra laughed. Lana didn't. Nedra aligned her spine up against a fat metal pole. She noticed that Lana's eyes didn't have their usual haughtiness; they looked puffy and a bit red.

"How's Chip?" Nedra asked, referring to Carolyn's budgie.

"Fine, I guess. The feather is growing back."

"That's good."

Mrs. Osborne squinted into the sun. "Did you ever find out who broke into your office?"

"No."

"Probably kids. They're so out of control these days." Lana focused on the riverbank, distracted.

"Is everything okay?" Nedra asked. She shifted the weight on her feet. The deep sand swallowed the soles of her shoes. She felt several grains spill through the eyes in her shoes.

"Oh," Lana said, "I needed to get out of the house."

The radio in the cop car cackled. Joanne cocked her head to listen, thinking at the same time that if she had a swanky house like Lana's, she'd never leave it. When Joanne decided the call was not for her, she turned her attention back to Mrs. Osborne.

"Joanne," she said, "when a boy turns eighteen and he's been having relations with a seventeen-year-old, can he be charged with statutory rape?"

"We'd never be able to make it stick." Joanne slipped her thumbs under her belt. "You talking about the Thompson boy?"

"Yes, of course I am. By now everyone in town knows that Jeff and Carolyn are having relations."

"Well, Jeff is a good looking boy. Like his dad. You can't blame a girl for falling."

Lana picked at a thread on her stretch pants. "A boy shouldn't be going after someone as innocent as my daughter. She has her whole future ahead of her. She wasn't meant to stay in a small town. I want her to experience life at its best." Lana's gaze hardened and swept across the expanse of the playing fields in the distance. "I won't have her rotting in a town like this. Especially not for a boy like Jeff."

"What do you mean?" Joanne said.

"He's lowlife, that's what, hanging around with that despicable Stitch. The man can't put two civil words together. I tell you, if Jeff doesn't leave Carolyn alone, I'll...I'll..." Lana sensed the sudden official interest of the cop. "I'll be seeing you, that's what."

XXVII

MUFFIN PREVAILS—A LOFTY SEARCH—
OFFICE VISITS

Lottie Sharp's Muffin lay on the examination table, lifting her head, trying to see what was happening at her other end. With barely a grunt the Chihuahua expelled four pink, curled fetuses about the size of baby shrimp. Nedra kept the dog down and quickly scooped all tissue into a plastic bag and sealed it.

"Tony!" she called.

The boy popped in from the kennel, closing the door behind him. He wore a sea green lab coat bearing his name stitched in russet thread, courtesy of Annie. Underneath he wore shorts and an orange T-shirt.

"Here," Nedra said, holding out the bag. "Take this in the back. We don't want Muffin to be worrying over it."

"Are you about done?" He stood back from the table, waiting for permission to touch the dog.

"Just a few more minutes."

"Want me to clean up?"

"A little later."

Tony held the bag in front of him by a thumb and forefinger and reached for the doorknob.

"Don't let Mrs. Sharp see that," Nedra cautioned as the boy opened the door.

"Got it," he said and disappeared down the hall.

The little dog sniffed around trying to catch a scent of her offspring. She let out a couple of yelps, then settled back down as Nedra ran her hand along the animal's side. "I know the big guys can be tempting sometimes, Muffin," Nedra said in a low, soothing voice, "but you'd best find a boyfriend your own size. Got it?" The Chihuahua's tiny pink tongue flicked out.

"How's it going?" Lottie cried. She sat in the waiting room, wearing a sweater over a summer dress filled with bright peonies. She was knitting yellow booties for her neighbor's grandchild in this, her second hour of Muffin watch.

"Fine, Mrs. Sharp. We're almost done." Nedra checked the heart rate of the Chihuahua and found it normal. With a wet paper towel, she cleaned the rear of the dog, then took a final swipe at the smooth, shiny surface of the surgery table. "You can come in now," she said.

Lottie Sharp hustled into the room and laid a wrinkly hand on her dog's head. "That's a good girl," she said. "Is she going to be all right?"

"Fine," Nedra said. "For the next couple of days I want you to watch her closely."

They heard the front door open.

"Anyone here?"

Lottie Sharp wheeled around and stuck her head out the examination room. "You wait your turn, Stitch," she said, then turned back and closed the door. "That Stitch Feldon is here." Lottie dropped her voice to a raspy whisper. "He's a nasty character."

"That right?"

"He and his brother Ed were terrors when they were little. I had them both in second grade. It was like trying to hitch up tornadoes. Ed turned out okay...he's gone now...but Stitch, he's a different story. He's a regular potty mouth."

"I can't say that I know him well," Nedra said, adding a tone of encouragement to her voice.

Lottie glanced at the closed door as though she expected Stitch's ear to be glued to the other side. "He got stuck on that Teri

Thompson, oh I bet it was twenty-five years ago, and he's been a bitter fool about it ever since."

"How so?"

"He always has a nasty word about the Thompsons. When they almost lost their farm, you'd never seen a happier man. He thought they'd go broke and he'd buy the farm at rock bottom prices. He always thought it should be his, he being the older boy and all. But he was only his father's stepson. Some folks put a lot of stock in pure blood, you know. Silly, isn't it?"

⌘

Teri Thompson climbed the wooden slats up to the hayloft in her deserted barn. The cattle were out in the pasture, Jeff was in town sulking, and Jessie was...well, being Jessie, off somewhere.

Teri tried to recall the last time she had made the ascent to the wide platform spanning the south side of the barn. The doors where the bales came through via conveyor belt were shut to the afternoon sun. The loft was hot and possessed that fragrant, earthy smell of hay, even if it was the low quality ditch grass. Probably one of the reasons she hadn't visited lately was that she knew what went on up here. Jeff and that snooty Carolyn spent time alone here, probably making out like crazy. And even more. Teri considered the love den a moment. Better here, she once would have thought, than some motel that Jeff couldn't afford, or a parking spot on a country road waiting to get hit by passing cars. Now she thought only of the heartache he had caused, turning on her as he had and on her cattle. Her own flesh betraying her.

When Teri reached the top, she hoisted herself over the small ridge that ran across the open end of the loft. While a three-inch rise would not prevent anyone from tumbling over the edge, it would at least warn them where the ledge ended and to take care. Teri took a moment to orient herself to the space. She looked over the side to the wide barn beneath. No wonder the kids loved to play up here when they were little. It would be easy to pretend that they were lords of their universe.

There were about thirty bales stacked against the west wall. In a few weeks, Jeff would have a good portion of the loft filled from the first haying. They needed every stem they could get to tide them through winter, given the lousy weather that promised only pathetic yields.

A battered old davenport with threadbare cushions sat in a far corner. The burgundy and black monstrosity was a throwaway from Eppy and Helen back when the kids were youngsters. Eppy had even helped Ed hoist the thing up to the loft. Teri's work boots stirred the dust and the thin layer of hay.

Teri turned to sit on the couch, then thought better of it, imagining what her son did there with Carolyn. As much as she preached abstenance to him, she knew it was like telling Loco to be sweet and kind. Teri tossed the cushions to the floor, then dug her hands into the seams of the sofa. She didn't find so much as a nickel. She hated every moment she spent looking for that damn bottle of prostaglandin—she dreaded finding it, yet she yearned to find it.

She patted the cushions and found nothing solid. With sweat rolling down her face and the air thick with heat, Teri slid the couch away from the wall. Waves of dust rose from the disturbance. When the roiling clouds cleared, Teri saw nothing, nothing except a back cloth that bulged slightly in the center.

Teri edged the couch further from the wall, then pried away the upholstery tacks one-by-one in the suspicious area. She lowered the burgundy strip of cloth to reveal a small red toolbox wedged in the frame of the furniture.

Teri grabbed the box from its mooring. She'd never seen it before. Given the dusty but unmarred surface, she gathered that it had been hidden shortly after its purchase. A steel gauge, key-operated padlock was clamped over the latch.

"God damn you to hell!" Teri cried, staring at the box. She dropped the container to the floor, then bent over, hands braced against her knees, to catch her breath. All the while she kept her eyes on the squat, red evil. After a moment's calm, she swung her leg like a placekicker and sent the box crashing into the wall timbers. The metal held. She scooped up the box, held it over her head like Moses' tablets of stone and with a ferocious cry, hurled it to the floor below.

⌘

"Where'd you get the dog?" Nedra asked Stitch Feldon as she ushered him into the examination room.

"Answered an ad in the Mankato paper. Got him for free. He's ugly as shit, ain't he? But I don't need nothing special, not with my mug."

"Plenty of pit bull in him, I'd say." Nedra ran her hands on the dog's oddly colored coat, mottled with splashes of black and brown. The dog's face had a punched-in look. "Some bulldog, too. Maybe a little Doberman. How old is he?"

"Ten months. The last of the litter. The owners couldn't find a taker."

The dog licked Nedra's hand as she examined the hips. She peered in his ears and observed the clear, bright eyes.

"How's he looking?" Stitch asked.

"Healthy. He has a good disposition."

"I'll fix that quick enough."

Nedra placed her thumbs along the dog spine and wrapped her fingers lightly around his chest. She felt the rapid beat of the heart and the lungs busy with puppy breaths. It was this feeling of living tissue in her hands, the squirmy canine eagerness for life, and the trusting nature of the species, that prompted a speech that was never easy to deliver, but one she felt was her responsibility.

"Stitch," Nedra began, catching the man's eyes, "I want you to be good to this dog."

The lineman's face hardened. "Oh, yeah. I'm good to animals."

"That's not what I've heard."

Stitch flushed to a cherry color.

"I heard you beat your last dog. Is that true?"

"The hell! Who said that?"

"Who doesn't matter." Nedra patted the dog's head. She kept her gaze fixed on Stitch, whose eyes squirted around like water bugs. "What matters is that people treat animals with kindness. Your dog was not placed on this earth to be hit, kicked, punched, unreasonably confined, starved, or abused in any way. There are laws concerning the humane treatment of animals. I take those laws very seriously. I suggest you do the same, Stitch, and if you can't, you walk out of this office right now and leave this boy here with me."

Stitch's ears flamed red. "Jesus, all I want is you to give the little pisser his damn shots. I don't need no lecture."

"You need to know where I stand. I won't tolerate abuse of *any* kind, and this dog is going to have my *special* attention." As Nedra prepared a syringe with rabies and distemper vaccine, the only sound in the room was the thump of the puppy's tail against Stitch's stomach. "Before I vaccinate him, Stitch, I want to know if this dog goes with you or stays with me."

"Well, shit, lady," Stitch said, swiping the cap off his head and wiping his forehead, "I'll be good to it. Hell, a man's got to have a little company, you know."

"Okay, Stitch. Just remember that I'll be watching you." As Nedra finished with the vaccination, the cow bells on the front door rang out. Nedra stuck her head out the examination door to see Eppy Sinclair.

"I'm just finishing up here, Eppy," Nedra called out. "Give me a couple of minutes."

Eppy grunted, picked up a magazine, and began to wander through the pages. When Stitch carried his dog into the waiting room a few minutes later, Eppy tossed the reading material back on the coffee table. "Oh, Christ," she said, giving the dog a look of pity, "is that yours?"

"What the hell's the problem in that?" Stitch said, avoiding her eyes.

"Stitch," Nedra said, as she slipped behind the counter, "I'll ring you up here. Do you want to pay now or put it on credit?"

"Send me the bill." Stitch tipped down and let the puppy loose. He leaned on the counter with one elbow, and pivoted away from Eppy. The puppy caught the cuff of Stitch's jeans in his jaws and settled down for a good chew. Stitch eyed Nedra, busy recording the visit, and ignored the irritation at the bottom of his leg.

"Jessie tells me you've been spending some time at the Thompson farm," Eppy said. "I thought Teri didn't want you out there."

"What Teri wants and what Teri gets are two different things," Stitch said.

Eppy snorted. "That's the story of her life."

"It's not my fault. I gave her her chance."

"You gave her shit, just like every other man in her life."

Stitch leaned over and picked up his puppy. "That's what some women like, but then you wouldn't know anything about that." He pounded past the elder Sinclair and out the door with his mongrel tucked under his arm.

"The man's a walking screw-up," Eppy said to Nedra. "Stitch rewired my horse barn several years ago. Jesus, electricians and plumbers—takes ten of them to tighten a bolt, with enough ruckus to pop every coffin lid in the cemetery three miles away. I couldn't have anything disturbing my Palominos, you know. If a show horse gets the jitters, you might as well send him off to the glue factory. I finally ordered him off my place. Why the hell are you letting him keep a dog?"

Nedra came from around the counter carrying a roll of masking tape. "It's a free country. But I did warn him about cruelty to animals."

"You'll need to hammer it in with a two-by-four, I guarantee."

"What brings you in today?" Nedra tore off a strip of tape and joined the ends in a circle.

"Helen and I would like you and Annie to come to dinner this weekend."

Nedra started dabbing her lab coat with the tape, removing the dog hairs shed by her last two patients.

"If you're still together, that is," Eppy added.

"What does that mean?" Nedra's hand stopped mid-dab. She felt a hollowness inside her, cold in the middle, but radiating a heat that burned her face.

"It means that you'd better pay attention to your woman if you want to keep her."

"My private life is not open for discussion...or for your amusement."

"You find this amusing? I don't. And if you don't want to be gossiped about, don't live in a small town."

Nedra balled up the hair-strewn tape and flung it over the counter in the direction of a trash can. "Maybe it's time I started packing."

The wrinkles in Eppy's face flattened, and her complexion turned to paste. "Hold on, now."

"No, I won't hold on."

Eppy grabbed Nedra's arm. "You'd better hold on, girl. That Annie's a treasure, and if you let her go because of your silly pride and some stupid notion of letting her do her own thing, or whatever the hell the saying is, you're about the sorriest thing I've ever seen."

"Damn it, Eppy..."

Eppy's grip tightened. "Don't swear at me, child. I almost left Helen years ago because I couldn't stand a small town. I wanted to play the Big Board in New York. I never would have found happiness if I had. You may think you're doing Annie a favor by letting her do what she wants, but a lover fights to keep her woman. How else will Annie know how much you love her?"

"I can't decide what's right for her."

"What the hell are you? One of those animals you work on? You want to know what Helen did to make me stay?"

Nedra opened her mouth to answer.

"She told me if I walked out the door, there'd be no coming back in for me. No visits, no letters, no kisses, no nothing."

"That sounds like blackmail."

"Maybe it was. But it sure made me look at what I was choosing. I was focusing on the limitations of a small town, not on what I had—peace of mind, a community of decent people—but, for godssake, don't tell anyone I said that—and the only woman in the world for me. You're a smart lady, Nedra. Don't act as dumb as your patients."

XXVIII

A RAINY NIGHT AT THE SINCLAIRS—A DOUBLE BLANK—
EPPY PLOTS—A MOTHER'S DISCOVERY

"Well, hi-ya, honey! Come in out of the rain!" Helen Sinclair cried. She swung open the front screen door of her home. "What brings you here on a night like this?"

Teri Thompson stepped onto the tiled area in the Sinclair living room and stood for a moment, unsure of what to do. Her arms were wrapped around the tool box as if it were a baby.

"What on earth do you have there?" Helen said, not waiting for an answer to her first question.

"Is Eppy around?"

"I'm here in the kitchen!" a voice rang out. "Come on back. Take your shoes off or Helen will be up half the night cleaning up your tracks."

Planting the sole of one shoe against the heel of the other, Teri slipped out of her sneakers. The toes of her cotton socks looked like thick white scabs from darning. The heels were worn thin.

Teri rounded the corner of the front entry and crossed the dining area. Eppy was sitting at the breakfast counter, facing her direction.

"Coming to do some repairs?" Eppy asked, eying the red toolbox.

"Coming to get some advice," Teri said. She set the box on the counter.

"That I have plenty of," Eppy said. "Looks like a combine ran over that case of yours."

Helen moved around by Eppy. "Are you feeling all right, Teri? You're looking a bit peaked." Helen placed a hand across Teri's brow. "Why you're colder than a stone," she said.

"I'll live."

"Don't you think she looks under the weather?" Helen gave Eppy a significant look.

"Who wouldn't be in this type of weather. My rheumatism is kicking like a strapped bronco." Eppy fingered the break in the metal. "What happened to the lock?" she asked. The lid was kept in place by an old leather belt wound twice around the box.

"Took a crow bar to it," Teri said. "I had to get inside to see what was in it."

"Whose is it?"

"I don't know. I found it in the hay loft." Teri started to sniffle. "I should never have married Ed, never had a family. I thought maybe I could love him, but I couldn't. I thought maybe after he was gone, I could get everything right again on the farm, but I can't."

"Oh, honey," Helen said, sliding an arm around Teri's waist.

Teri struggled to even out her breathing. "Somebody's always got to wreck it."

Eppy squirmed in her chair, eyeing the beaten red metal in front of her. "For Christsakes, Teri, open up the box or I'll do it myself!"

Teri wiped her eyes, then uncinched the belt and slid it out from the underside. She grabbed the black handle on the top and flipped back the lid. Eppy and Helen peered inside like two girls peeking into a wishing well.

"Whooo-eee!" Eppy cried, snatching up a copy of *Hustler* magazine.

Helen playfully slapped her hand. "You put that down."

Eppy jutted her elbows out and twisted away from Helen. "Might learn something, you never know," she said with an evil grin. She opened the magazine to a layout of a naked woman. "Now isn't that the most ridiculous pose you've ever seen in your life?"

she asked of no one in particular. "Her butt's so high in the air she could paint the ceiling with it. And look at those lips. If she were pouting any more she'd need one of those branch props we use with our apple trees. She must need a ten-foot tooth brush just to reach her molars."

"Now, Eppy, be kind," Helen chided.

"Never." Eppy turned the page and let out a chuckle.

"Are these Jeff's?" Helen asked, her face soft with sympathy.

"I think they're Ed's. All the issues are at least five years old." Teri paused. "It's not the smut that bothers me so much."

"Really? Why, I'm very proud of you, Teri," Eppy said. "Perhaps we are blood relations after all."

Teri dipped her hands into the red case, shoveled the magazines together, and lifted them out of the box. She let the magazines drop to the floor. "That," she said, pointing inside, "is what bothers me."

The Sinclairs leaned over for a closer look.

"My heavens!" Helen exclaimed, blinking hard at the thin, neat rows of bundled twenty dollar bills.

"There's ten thousand dollars there," Teri said evenly, her glassy eyes focused on nothing. "I counted."

⌘

"Eppy stopped by the office today," Nedra said as she selected a domino from the pile. Their orange cat sniffed at the hem of her jeans, then wandered away, his tail as straight as a flagpole. Outside, a summer shower splashed against the windows. David Lanz's New Age music filled the evening with the upbeat melody from a piano and flute.

Annie gave the bones a final shove. "What now?" She slid seven of the nearest pieces toward her and began to set them on edge.

Nedra placed the seventh domino in the quarter moon arc in front of her. She arranged the tiles with blanks, fives and tens on the left side. Those were the ones to watch for special scoring possibilities. "She thinks I ought to give you an ultimatum."

"Does she?" Annie picked up a yellow pencil and quickly created a score card on the back of a utility bill envelope. The names of the two women, capped and underlined, stretched across the short end of the paper.

"Yeah. She says that I should tell you that if you go back to the Cities, you're out of my life forever."

Annie took a sip of her grapefruit juice in crushed ice. "Any doubles?"

"Nuh-uh."

"Twelve? Eleven?" Annie smiled weakly. "Double ten." She picked the tile from her arch and positioned it in the middle of the table, then scratched her score on the envelope. "So, are you giving me an ultimatum?"

Nedra joined a ten and blank tile to the middle of the double ten. "That's not our style, is it?"

Annie shook her head. The soft light from the chandelier overhead highlighted her copper strands.

"It may work for Eppy and Helen—in fact, it may take an ultimatum to get through to Eppy."

"Four more points for me," Annie said as she crossed the blank end of Nedra's tile with a bare bone.

"A double blank! Now that's pathetic, Annie. Scoring off nothing."

Annie stared at the new piece on the table, both halves of the domino without dots. The surface was as black as a starless night. "Is that what we're doing now? Just counting the days, while our relationship is a double blank, just a slab of nothing?"

"Not for me." Nedra's eyes teared. "We have something that's true and alive. I believe that with all my heart, Annie. That's what makes the chance of your leaving hurt so much."

Annie smiled weakly. "The Sinclairs must have planned a one-two punch. Helen stopped by to see me. She told me I'd be a damn fool if I left you, that your being here made life in a small town worthwhile."

"And?"

"I'm thinking about it." Annie reached across the table for Nedra's hand.

Nedra sprang out of her chair and moved to Annie's side. "Please," she said as she wrapped her arms around her, "I don't want to lose you. Let's find a way to make it work."

"I need to spend time in the Cities—with or without you. Maybe a weekend a month would do. But I have to have it."

It sounded like such a small request—some weekends away—some with the two of them together. "Would that be enough?"

"I can't promise that it will. We'll just have to see."

"No more planning weekends away, then staying home," Nedra said. "When we decide to go, we go, no matter what. Okay?"

"Okay."

"And a good place to start will be with the Star Trek convention the weekend after next."

"Really?"

"Really. It'll be like our first date."

Annie squeezed Nedra against her chest, stroking her as they wept together.

⌘

"Is it real?" Helen asked, reaching for a bundle.

Now it was Eppy's turn to slap her hand, only this time without humor. "Real or not," she said, "we'd better not touch it. Fingerprints, you know."

"I've done a good job touching them already," Teri said. "It probably won't hurt."

"Those bills have never seen the inside of a wallet. They're as wrinkle free as the day they rolled off the presses. Any idea what this is doing in your hayloft?"

"I don't know."

"I'll be double-damned," Eppy muttered.

"I don't know. I don't, really."

"Who all knows about this?" Eppy said.

"Just the three of us. I haven't told the cops. I want to know what's going on before I do that..." Teri's voice trailed off.

Helen patted Teri's hand. "Maybe you should spend the night here, Teri. You and Jessie. It's been a hard time for you. You could use a little mothering."

"I don't know what to do," Teri said. "I did drop Jessie off at one of her friend's for the night, though. I want her out of the way for what ever is going on."

"All right, all right," Eppy said. "Stay or go as you like, but enough sentiment. We've got to work out a plan here."

"A plan for what?" Helen asked.

"To find out who owns this money, of course!" Eppy shouted. She knew just what advice to give its owner: International stocks.

⌘

"So, like, you've got this place all to yourself tonight." Carolyn Osborne sniffed at the poverty of the Thompson farm house.

"Yeah. Mom's at Eppy's for a while and Jessie is staying in town with a friend."

"No kid sister. No mom. You've got it made to get laid. Come on. Let's go upstairs."

"Can't," Jeff said. "I've got things to do."

Carolyn's dark eyes tracked Jeff as he crossed the kitchen. He tore a sheet of paper from a pad by the phone and scribbled something on it. "What are you up to?"

"Running the farm, in case you haven't noticed."

"Since when is the farm more important than me!"

"Give me a break," Jeff said.

"Screw you!" Carolyn leapt toward her boyfriend, hands ready for slapping, just as the screen door jerked open.

"Carolyn!" Mrs. Osborne cried. "What are you doing here?"

"One guess, Lana." Carolyn's face was flushed with anger. She backed toward Jeff.

"Who invited you here?" Jeff said.

"I didn't need an invitation," Mrs. Osborne said. "Carolyn, get in the car. I'm taking you home."

"You can't make me."

Jeff gave Carolyn a little push. "Go on. I'll talk to you later.

"Je-effffff," the girl whined.

"Carolyn. Out. Now." Lana Osborne's eyes looked like stars ready to go nova.

"So blow a gasket. I don't care." Carolyn tramped past her mother, threw open the door, and huffed down the steps to the white Lincoln.

"I'm sorry that happened," Jeff said sheepishly.

"You think you can charm your way out of everything." Mrs. Osborne's small, red mouth grew tighter.

"Yep."

"God, you sound just like your father."

"Don't you say anything about my dad."

"Why? Afraid I'll tell the truth about him?"

"Shut up about my dad."

"I say what I want, sonny." Mrs. Osborne stepped toward the boy and aimed a manicured hand at his face. "And I get what I want."

XXIX

A BARREN LAND—A CALL FOR EPPY

"You're a real pal, coming along with me," Nedra said to Annie. Her truck rattled across the overpass above the highway east of town.

"I know, you just want some extra muscle in case Teri throws you off the farm."

"Extra muscle never hurt," Nedra smiled. "I think we'll be okay, especially if Jeff isn't around. Besides, we're not going to touch the cows, only ask Teri if she found a bottle of prostaglandin."

"Sure you are. You could've called."

"So, it's a tad transparent. They may not notice my wandering eyes." Nedra glanced at the Thompson's pasture. "That's odd. The cattle aren't grazing. At ten in the morning, they should be munching away."

"Maybe they're in the barn."

"Yeah, but why? It's peculiar."

At the top of the roundabout, Nedra turned off the engine of the Ranger. Right away, she noticed the silence. "Where's Samson?" she muttered. This was the first time that the farm dog had failed to greet her and water a wheel.

Nedra and Annie checked the house. No answer. Making her way toward the barn, Nedra called out both Jeff and the dog's name.

Still no answer. Uneasiness crept like an icy spider up Nedra's spine.

The wind had picked up since early morning, and the sun, still lost behind thick clouds, couldn't warm the land. Patches of sickly corn and oats undulated like flying carpets, and the smell of manure wafted up from the cattle pens. Nedra, drenched in the sweat of anxiety, swiped at her forehead with a blue bandanna as she reached the barn. She grabbed the handle of the side door and threw open the door.

When Nedra entered the musty interior, she paused to adjust her eyes to the shadows. The barn was as deserted as a ghost town.

Nedra placed a hand on the plank of an empty stall and absorbed the hollowness of the cavernous building. The stalls and dirt aisles contained only a scattering of straw, clumps of manure, and squadrons of busy flies. Old harnesses still decorated the walls, as did ropes and hoses and halters.

As Nedra stood alone in the empty barn, she thought of how animals made the world so alive and compelling. They gave the world its drone of life, the warmth of blood. All that was missing from the Thompson farm.

Leaving Annie to check the machine shed, Nedra walked behind the barn and found the bull, shut in his special pen, laboring his jaws on a clump of grass. "Loco, where'd everyone go?" she asked the animal. The bull lifted his head, fastened his ornery-looking eyes on Nedra, and snorted.

⌘

Eppy Sinclair was monitoring her portfolio on her computer link. A graphic of the Big Board ran across the bottom of her screen. IBM stock had taken another tick downward. "I'm taking a beating from you incompetent boobs!" she cried. "The entire executive level in your joke of a company should be..." The phone rang. "Get that, would you!" she called out as she made a note to herself on a scratch pad. "I'm busy losing money in here."

After a few moments, Helen called out from the living room. "Pick up the phone! It's Nedra!"

"Damn!" Eppy grabbed the extension, but kept her eyes on the ribbon marching across her monitor. "What is it?" she asked crossly.

"Annie and I are at Teri's place. No one's here, and the cows are missing. Do you know what's going on?"

"Well, Teri's here," Helen said, still on the line. "And I know Jessie was staying with a friend in town. Jeff should be there, though."

"Those bloody cows, too," Eppy said, beginning to back out of her program. "Did they break out?"

"I didn't see any part of the fence down, and there aren't any cattle wandering the roads that I've spotted. I called Matt Jensen. He hasn't seen the cows, either."

"Oh, my," Helen said. "Teri's going to be upset. Maybe we'd better come right over."

"Something sure the hell is wrong out there," Eppy said, thinking now of a toolbox with ten grand in it. "We're on our way."

After Eppy tossed the receiver back on the phone, she rushed into the living room.

"Oh, Lord," Helen murmured, "now what."

"There's no time to mope!" Eppy cried. "It's action time! You call Jeff's girlfriend. See if she's seen him. I'm going to the basement."

"What for?" Helen asked, reaching for the phone book.

"To get my truth teller."

XXX

A GATHERING FORCE

Nedra bit into a Nestles Crunch bar as she leaned against the passenger door of her Ranger. Perhaps she and Annie should leave and let the Sinclairs and Teri figure out what to do, but she felt an obligation to stay to see this thing, whatever it was, to the end. She was as baffled as everyone else seemed to be.

A distant sound drew Nedra and Annie's attention to the county road running north of the Thompson farm. Matt Jensen's truck rolled into view and bounced up the driveway. He parked the Ford behind Nedra's vehicle and hopped out.

"So, did you figure out what's going on?" Matt asked.

Nedra balled up the candy bar wrapper and stuffed it into a pocket. "Not yet."

"I can't believe that Teri would sell the cattle," he said.

As they waited, a Swainson's hawk circled high above them, the dark band at the end of its tail barely visible. The clouds parted, showing a patch of startling blue sky, then closed again. The wind rolled in from the fields, and the smell of fertilizer lingered in the air.

Another truck appeared, this one green, with a small trailer attached it to. Nedra didn't have to look twice. It was Stitch in his utility truck. The truck hesitated halfway up the drive, then labored on. Stitch swung the vehicle around so the trailer pointed toward the barn. Slowly the truck and trailer bumped over the earth and came to a stop a few yards short of the fence.

"Picking up the bull?" Nedra asked as Stitch clamored out of the cab.

"What no-brain wants to know?"

"Try me."

Stitch gave Nedra and Annie the thrice over. "None of your piss-pot business."

A third vehicle whisked up the Thompson drive. "Here comes Eppy," Nedra said with relief. Now they'd get some help. "Looks like Teri is with her."

Eppy drove the navy Taurus right up to the group and rolled down her window. "What the hell is this, Grand Central Station?" she cried. "Who the hell asked all these people here?"

Teri leapt from the car. "Where are my cattle?" She took a step toward Stitch.

"You stay back," he said.

"Where are they?"

"Too late," Stitch said. "They're done cooked."

"Tell me where they are."

"Why should I? I'm dealing with the boy."

"I think you'd better tell her," Eppy's voice rang out.

Nedra turned to see Eppy Sinclair standing by her car, pointing a twelve-gauge shotgun at them.

"Step back ladies," Eppy said. "I want a clear shot of this bastard."

"Put that damn goose gun away," Stitch ordered.

"It's got some business to do first." Eppy waved the shotgun at him.

"Leave me the hell alone."

"Eppy," Annie said, stepping forward, "think about what you're doing. Helen, you too." Helen Sinclair just shook her head.

"I don't have to think. I know exactly what I'm doing." Eppy made little thrusting motions toward Stitch. "Now you tell me what I want to know, or I'm going to blow so much shot into you, they'll be picking lead out of you until Christmas. If you're still alive." Eppy took another step closer.

Stitch shimmied along the side of the utility truck until he ran into the bumper. "Shit, Eppy, don't do it," he said, holding up his arms, as though his hands could stop all the metal pellets that threatened to explode in his face. "I was only helping out my nephew. So help me God."

"You wouldn't know God if you slept with Him," Eppy snorted. "Now, where's Jeff?"

Stitch lowered his arms. "He's a grown boy. I don't keep track of him."

"Where is he?" Eppy said.

Stitch's eyes wavered. "Don't know. Don't care."

"I'm counting to one," the Sinclair said. "I get an answer or you're going to be blind for the rest of your life. One."

"Okay, okay. He's down the road at my cousin's place."

"Tommy Feldon?"

Stitch's lips twisted into an uncomfortable smile. "Tommy picked up the cattle this morning. Jeff's helping him haul them up to stockyards in South St. Paul."

"What!" Teri howled. She rushed at Stitch, her hands like claws. Nedra grabbed her from behind, pinning her arms to her sides. "I'm going to kill you!" Teri shouted.

"Hold on, Teri," Nedra said.

"I want my cattle back," Teri wailed.

Stitch sneered. "Go to the store tomorrow and buy hamburger. That's where they'll be."

Teri surged against Nedra, but Nedra's hold remained fast. "Damn you! Damn you to hell!" she sobbed. Nedra eased her against the plank of the barnyard fence. "Lucky, Lucky," she wept, repeating the name of her pet cow over and over again.

Matt slinked to the back of the crowd, watching Eppy threaten Stitch with the shotgun. "Lord, why?" Matt muttered. He felt the Thompson farm slipping from his control. If Jeff did indeed sell the cattle, he'd have money to pay down the loan. Maybe somebody would help him pay it off totally.

Eppy jutted the shotgun toward Stitch. Her finger tightened on the trigger. "When is he coming back?"

"Shit, I don't know. I don't keep his schedule."

"I'm leaving this pile of donkey dung with you," Eppy said, lowering the weapon. "I've heard everything I need to hear."

"What are you going to do?" Nedra asked, keeping a hand on Teri, who was still weeping.

"Attend to family matters," Eppy said. She made for her car.

"Eppy," Nedra said, "you're going after Jeff, aren't you?"

"You bet."

"I want you to leave the shotgun behind," Nedra said firmly. She wrapped her hand around the barrel. It was clear that she out-muscled Eppy. "You can pick it up at my place later."

Eppy locked eyes with Nedra for a moment. "Just don't let that bastard get his hands on it," she said as she loosened her grip.

Nedra saw a mixture of disdain, amusement, and surprise swirling in Eppy's eyes as the weight of the weapon transferred into her hands. She didn't know what piece of emotion to fasten on to, or which to believe. But things had gone too far to care about Eppy Sinclair's opinion.

As soon as Eppy drove off, Helen moved beside Teri and slipped an arm around her. "Honey," she murmured, "oh, honey." After comforting her for several minutes, she turned to Stitch. "Why did you do such a thing? You know how much she loved raising cattle on her own little pasture. You ought to be ashamed."

"Hell, a man has a right to help out his nephew." He entwined his sausage-like fingers under his belt.

"You're an evil man," Teri muttered.

"You should look to yourself first," Matt Jensen broke in. Everything was gone now, all his dreams for a giant spread ruined because a boy had to go do things his way. He could have helped Jeff—helped them all—if only they hadn't wrecked the plan that he had worked out with the Lord through knee-numbing hours of prayer.

"You're going to pay for this, all of you!" Teri cried.

"Pay for it? Like you paid Ed?" Matt's mouth curled. "You put him in the ground."

"What are you talking about?" Nedra said.

"He's talking trash," Teri said, her crying bout suddenly over. "I didn't hurt Ed."

Matt glowered. "You didn't think I'd ever tell, did you?"

"Shut up!" Teri cried.

Matt dipped his head in her direction. "She killed her husband, that's what."

"Liar!" Teri screamed. "Liar!"

XXXI

EPPY IN HER GLORY—TERI SEEKS SALVATION—
EPPY'S SQUEEZE PLAY—TRAPPED

Eppy Sinclair swung her car up the long paved drive of Tommy Feldon's home. "Thank God," Eppy muttered, feeling that a lifetime had gone by. A six-wheel platform truck that held five Hereford cows was parked on the northside of a round-about. Eppy spotted the Thompson dog shut in the cab of the truck. Samson jerked his head around when he saw Eppy, and then went into a spasm of barking. "Well, old boy," Eppy said, peering up through the half-open driver's window, "I see you've been for a ride."

Recognizing Eppy, the dog sent his bark a pitch higher. He jumped around the seat and stuck his head through the opening.

"You've got a rotten master, you know," Eppy said. "If it wouldn't land me in jail, I'd rip his head off and give it to you to eat." Samson yipped even louder, his tail snapping around like a whip. "God," Eppy said, starting toward the house, "what I wouldn't give for a dog's ignorance."

She marched up the walk like she was taking possession of the estate. Tommy Feldon's house was a large, modern affair, fronted with white bricks and an entry way covered by an arch. She punched the door bell and then flung open the door when she heard a greeting and saw a form moving toward the door. "Jeff!" she yelled, stepping inside. She sank in the plush carpet. A ceiling fan churned the cool air. The house smelled of lavender.

Tommy Feldon gaped at Eppy Sinclair. Normally he had an easy, open demeanor of the successful farmer, one who had slid through the eighties unscathed, worked hard, and wintered in Arizona. He had on a work shirt and jeans, and he wore his graying hair slicked back. "Eppy," he said in a husky, commanding voice. Deep furrows appeared on his wide, tanned forehead.

"Jeff Thompson here?" Eppy said, craning her neck around the farmer. "Jeff! Get out here!"

"He's in back. We're having lunch on the deck."

"Get him."

Tommy called back for Jeff, then disappeared. A few moments later, Jeff emerged from the shadows, Tommy at his elbow.

"What are you doing here?" Jeff asked. He had a bruise that ran from his nose to his cheekbone.

"What happened to you?" Eppy asked.

Jeff shrugged. "Bumped myself."

"Tommy," Eppy said, "go back to your lunch. I'm taking the boy home."

"But he's staying a few days. Stitch said..."

"He's coming with me."

"Wait a minute," Jeff said. "I get some say in this. I'm staying."

"Are those the Thompson cattle in your truck?" Eppy asked Tommy.

"Sure," he said, his face blank. "We hauled them over here this morning. We're having a bite to eat before we load up my cattle and head up to the stockyards. What's the problem?"

"Just a little one," Eppy said. "Those cattle are not for sale."

Tommy turned to Jeff. "What's going on here? I thought you were selling them for your mother."

"I am."

"He's selling them for himself." Eppy let her black eyes burn into the boy. "You had no right."

"Listen," Tommy said, holding out his hands, "obviously there's been a mistake here. I though the boy was just delivering them. His mother called me two days ago. We worked out the arrangements. If there's a problem..."

"Looks like you've been duped by Stitch and the boy here."

Tommy's face reddened with anger. "I don't trade in stolen cattle. I'm taking those cows back right now!"

"Huh?" Jeff said, his face looking small under his bowl of blond hair. "You can't!"

"Hold on," Eppy said. "Keep them a while 'til I get things worked out." She pointed a thick finger at Jeff. "That's the one I want." She hesitated just a moment. "Oh, for Christsakes, I'm going soft. There's one more thing I'd better take back."

⌘

"Are you saying Teri murdered her husband?" Nedra said to Matt.

"That's exactly what I'm saying."

"Liar!" Teri screamed again.

"You killed Ed, and the Lord was a witness!" Matt glared at his neighbor.

Teri snatched the shotgun from Nedra's hands.

"Teri!" Nedra shouted as she grabbed for the weapon. She was too late.

Teri gripped the twelve-gauge and pointed it at Matt. "You think I killed one man. Well, watch me kill another!"

"No!" Nedra cried.

Teri two-stepped backward toward the barn. "Stay there!" She waved the weapon at Nedra, then back to Matt.

"Jesus!" Matt cried. "Put the gun down!"

Nedra moved forward. "Give me the shotgun, Teri."

Teri sawed the air with the weapon, her face swollen and red with anger. She pressed the trigger as Nedra reached for the barrel.

"Nedra!" Annie cried.

"Give it up," Nedra said firmly to Teri. "Now."

Teri yanked desperately at the frozen trigger. It didn't budge. She recoiled with disbelief.

"It's rusted solid," Helen explained quietly. "Now give the gun to Nedra."

"Tell everyone what you did!" Matt goaded. "Go on!"

With an angry cry, Teri flung the weapon at Matt. He ducked, and the shotgun crashed into the side of Stitch's utility truck, leaving a zig-zag gouge in the green paint.

"Hey!" Stitch cried. "You're gonna pay for that!"

"See," Matt said smugly. "She tried to kill me. Just like she killed Ed."

Behind the barn, the bull snorted and let loose a long, lonesome wail. Teri's head snapped around. "What's that?"

"That's the bull," Stitch said. "We didn't dare put him in the same trailer as the cows. I'm shipping him out separately."

"No!" Teri cried as she grasped at the gate handle into the barnyard pen.

"Go on!" Stitch cried. "You're just as stubborn and dangerous as that bull."

"Teri, come back!" Nedra shouted.

But Teri was around the side of the barn.

Nedra tore after her, knowing that a human in a bull pen could just as well be a paper doll. Teri would be no match for tonnage guided by cranky hormones.

⌘

Eppy gripped the steering wheel as tightly as a bully wielding a bludgeon. "You'd better give me an explanation, buddy," she said. "Right now, I'm about the closest thing you have to a friend except for that dog of yours, and in the brain department, he's about as worthless as your uncle Stitch."

Jeff looked out at the flat, wet fields rushing by.

"Why'd you and Stitch go in together on this?"

"I was desperate. Stitch said it'd be the only way to save the farm—the proceeds from the sale and then the money he'd loan me."

"He'd loan you money!"

"Sure. Twelve thousand."

Eppy hooted. "Stitch doesn't have twelve dollars. I should know. I've personally reviewed his finances at the bank."

"That can't be."

"The hell it can't," Eppy huffed. "By promising you what he can't deliver, he's made sure that you'll lose the farm. He's pulling the damn carpet out from under your gullible boots, and trashing your mother's sanity with it."

"I don't believe it."

"He helped you abort those cows, didn't he?"

"Not really." Jeff felt the fuzz on his upper lip. "I did the work. He just told me how to do things."

"You fool. You've given him more power over you. He can blackmail you from now 'til doomsday. He could threaten to tell the cops or your mom—I don't know which would be worse, and you'd be off that farm so fast you'd have third degree windburn."

Jeff blinked hard at Eppy, his mouth slack, his face splotchy.

"If you don't wind up in the slammer for cattle rustling, there's always the break-in at the vet office. That could get you a couple of years minimum."

Jeff worked his mouth around a bit and swallowed hard. "But he helped me plan it all. He showed me how to spring the lock and where to throw my stuff in case I ran into trouble—the flat roof of the Presbyterian church."

"That's just aiding. You did the doing. You're the one who'll go to jail."

"Like hell."

"Yep. That's just what you're facing, Jeff, my boy. Pure hell."

⌘

Teri Thompson stood in the middle of the bull's pen like a shabby matador sans swords. She was defenseless, but without fear. She approached the rust-colored hulk, which eyed her suspiciously.

"Come here, my baby," she cooed. "I need to touch you."

Loco's eyes rolled from side to side, the whites large and veined. The animal took one step back, assessing the situation. His chewing slowed, then stopped.

Nedra placed a foot on the wooden slat of the fence behind her. "Teri," she said softly, "back away. Now."

"Loco's the grandson of my first cow—Rusty." Teri stretched her arm, palm up, toward coarse, russet hide stretched over massive muscles. "Did you know that?

"No, I didn't."

"I bought him from the O'Malleys, right after Ed died. He was my first purchase." She waggled her fingers at the warm, mud-splattered creature. "Rusty was the comfort of my life. I don't know why people can't understand that."

"Maybe they just haven't appreciated the depth of your feeling."

"I never cared much for the bulls. But Loco here is all that I have left now." Teri was now inches from Loco, her hand almost touching the bull's broad shoulder.

"You have your children and everyone who loves you." Nedra observed the rolling eyes of the bull and wondered how much longer the animal would tolerate the commotion. "Now, back away from Loco."

"This is where I belong."

"No, you belong with us. Out here."

"I'm not coming out. Ever."

"Go ahead, stay in there, you pug-ugly bitch," Stitch jeered. "You murderer." The others gathered behind him.

"Shut up," Annie said to Stitch. "You're making things worse."

Stitch grinned. The bull's tail snapped sideways.

"I didn't kill Ed," Teri said. Her face was white and broken. "I...I...just didn't save him."

"What do you mean?" Nedra asked.

"I could have reached out when he fell in," she said, taking another step toward the bull. "But I didn't. I couldn't. All that corn pouring down, and there I was, my arms stuck to my side. I was so scared I couldn't move."

"Good thing you didn't try," Helen said, her voice low and smooth. "He was twice as big as you are. He would have pulled you right into the bin with him. You both would have been killed. Now come out of that pen, child."

"You're lying!" Matt cried. "The Lord knows it! I know it!"

Teri rested her hand on the bull's shoulder. The bull moved a rear leg forward. "I could have saved him, but I didn't. I'll have to live with that forever." Her voice flattened. "You know, I had wished him dead so many times, and then when it was happening, I let it. Maybe he deserved to die. He sold my Rusty, almost ruined the farm, and let our kids go in rags." She began to stroke the thick bovine hair. "I remember that corn shooting over him like water out of a fire hose, bouncing off his seed cap. He had this look of panic on his face. 'I can't move, Teri,' he said."

"You're lying," Matt repeated.

Teri showed a thin smile. "He never asked me to help him. I think maybe he knew he deserved to die. I just watched him disappear under all that corn, like a great yellow sea swallowing him up."

The bull pawed a groove into the soft mud of his pen. His ears were pinned back, and his head was low.

"For God's sake," Nedra said firmly, "get out of the pen."

"I let my children's father die," Teri continued. "When help came, we dug and dug and we couldn't find him. I think God buried him on purpose, so we wouldn't be able to revive him."

"That can't be," Matt said quietly, his voice drifting in the background.

"Yes, it can, Matt," Teri said.

"Nedra," Helen said quietly, "don't you have one of those tranquilizer guns?"

"This isn't *Wild Kingdom*," Nedra snapped.

"I'm telling the truth," Teri said. She stopped stroking the bull. "Why don't you, Matt?"

XXXII

A SQUIRMING BOY—A WESTERN TEASE—
SOME TRUTH—MORE TRUTH

As they neared the Thompson farm, Eppy said, "So, where'd you get the shiner?"

"Mrs. Osborne."

"Oh, Christ, not Lana."

"I promised her that I'd leave Carolyn alone. But she caught us together last night."

"What did she give you for your promise?"

"She was going to give me money. Five grand. Plus, she called Tommy Feldon, pretending to be Mom."

"Offering him the cattle?" Eppy said.

"Yeah. I was going to use the money to get ahead—get some decent herbicides and fertilizer. I could build a great windmill—Stitch said he'd help me—one that would generate enough electricity so we could sell some back to the utility." Jeff took off his cap and slapped it against a knee. "Stitch told me all about how I could do it. My mom can't run the place, but I sure could. All I needed was a chance."

The tires of the car hit the shoulder. Eppy steered vehicle back into the lane. "Listen. Your mother kept that farm going all these years. You don't have a thing to your name but that your mother didn't pay for it with money she couldn't afford to spend. You should be grateful, instead of blathering on about how she can't farm."

"I don't have anything to be grateful for. Her operation cost my dad his life."

"That's twisting things up, don't you think?"

"Think about it. The accident never would have happened if we didn't have the cattle." Jeff's voice took on a harsh edge. "We wouldn't have needed to store the feed corn in the bin."

"You're forgetting that Ed had already sold the cattle when the accident happened."

"Sure, but we had left over feed that we were going to store until corn prices went up. If we wouldn't have had the corn in the first place, Dad would never have fallen into the bin. He died because of mom's stupid cows and no matter what you say, you know it."

"That's it!" Eppy shouted. She swerved off the road and slammed on the brakes. She grabbed Jeff by his collar and yanked him close. "You listen to me, Jeff Thompson. You don't think your mother hasn't suffered every day of her life? She had a father that beat her and a husband that two-timed her all over town."

"You're lying." Jeff tried to wiggle from Eppy's grip, which only grew stronger.

"I saw it with my own eyes," Eppy hissed. "I caught your father prancing out of the Park View Motel in Mankato with his latest squeeze."

"That's bullshit."

"I told Ed to knock it off or else. All he could do was quiver and blurt out how sorry he was," Eppy said. "Yeah, he was sorry all right." She let go of Jeff. Her voice grew uncharacteristically soft. "I always felt kind of bad about that. Especially with your father dying not long after. I think I might have broken him. If you're going to blame anyone for that accident, blame me. Ed was probably so distracted by my threats—or heartbroken because I busted up his affair—that he got careless...maybe even lost the will to live."

"At least he loved something human. Not like Mom. She's always loved her damn cows more than anything. More than Dad. More than me. The wrong person died in the grain bin, if you ask me."

"Don't count on it," Eppy said.

"Who was it? Who'd you see Dad with?"

Eppy turned to the young man with a mixture of pity and wicked delight.

⌘

Loco kept his head low. His nostrils flared like great pink wings. His eyes looked ready to pop out of his massive skull; they were wild with animal blood lust. The huge bulk of his body hunched into itself. Nedra felt as if she were watching a giant spring, its coils pressed tighter and tighter. At any moment the trapped energy would explode.

"Hey!" Nedra swung herself over the top of the fence. "Hey!"

"My God, Nedra!" Annie cried, running up to the fence.

The bull jerked his head around from Teri. He fastened his eyes on Nedra and charged at her like a snorting torpedo.

Nedra feinted to her right. Loco's hoofs skidded in the mud. The bull followed her move. Nedra cut to the left toward Teri, who was standing motionless in the middle of the pen.

"Damn," Annie muttered, "I don't believe this." She found herself jumping into the pen. "Hey! Hey!" she cried. She waved her arms at Loco. With the animal momentarily distracted, Nedra grabbed Teri by the back of her jeans, yanked her to the fence, and hoisted her over like a sack of potatoes. Nedra heard Annie's shrill whistles and the beat of hooves bearing down on her. Nedra knew she didn't have time to send herself over the fence. She dove for the space under the bottom slat.

In a wild burst, Loco crashed through the wooden barrier. The stumbling bull scattered the group around Teri like a flock of startled ducks, then picked out a new target: Matt Jensen.

Annie scrambled through the broken fence to Nedra. "Are you all right?"

"Fine." Nedra grimaced as Annie helped her up. She gave her a reassuring squeeze. "Let's go!"

"Lord! Lord!" Matt yelled as he ran across the roundabout. His fancy Western shirt clung to his wet back. With arms pumping, he skidded to a stop at the side door of the machine shed. He opened the door, but couldn't close it in time. The bull wedged his way into the building.

Nedra and Annie, close in pursuit, heard cries and rampage from inside the shed. "Let's open the big door!" Nedra yelled. She motioned Annie back as she began to twist the handle on the large roll-up garage door.

"Stay to the side," Nedra said. Annie nodded and readied herself for whatever awaited them.

With a giant heave, Nedra rolled the door three-quarters of the way up. When she peered inside, she could hardly believe her eyes. Matt clung to the top of the John Deere tractor, with the bull below him, banging away.

"Get him away from me!" Matt screamed. His eyes were as big as eggs.

"Before we do that," a voice said, "I want you to tell me something." Teri walked to the middle of the yawning hole in the shed. "And I want the truth."

⌘

"I'll get you the best legal defense possible," Eppy said. "And I'll pay for it out of my pocket...if you finish answering my questions."

"I won't need a lawyer," Jeff said quietly. His face was streaked with tears.

"A lawyer is the least of what you'll need. Probably a phalanx of body guards to stop your mother from beating the crap out of you. Not that you don't deserve it. Now, answer my questions."

Jeff sniffed, then wiped his eyes. He felt absolutely broken open and drained. "I already told you, I used the drugs that I stole from the clinic on Mom's cows. What more do you want?"

"What about the last calf—the deformed one?"

"I tried giving that cow electric shocks early in its pregnancy. I wanted to try something different in case someone was getting suspicious. Stitch told me how to do. But I almost electrocuted myself trying to shock that damn Betsy."

"You had it all figured out." Eppy voice held no admiration, only a slight tremor at the cruel self-centeredness of someone related to her dear Helen. "I'm dropping you off at the police station. You'd better do all the cooperating you can before your Uncle Stitch has a chance to worm his way out of another crime. Maybe if you make a full confession, you won't wind up as meat yourself...in Stillwater Prison."

⌘

"You and Ed had something going. What was it?" Teri yelled at Matt.

"A business deal."

The bull glanced back at the group. Blood oozed from a gash above one eye.

"Come on, Teri," Nedra said, stepping toward the woman. "Let it go."

Teri paid no attention. "You tell me or so help me, we're leaving you right where you are." Loco butted the side of the tractor. The side molding clanged to the floor, escalating the bull's ire to a fit of frenzy. The group of onlookers hung back toward the edge of the building, terrified of the bull, but entranced by the spectacle.

"It's your own fault," Matt cried as the tractor quivered from another blow. "All you wanted was a little hobby farm for your little cattle operation. You didn't pay attention to your own husband. Of course he looked elsewhere."

"Another woman?"

"They were in my machine shed. It was the week before I moved to the farm. I dropped by to inspect the property. There they were, buck naked, sinning like the devil was right there goading them on."

"So," Nedra said, "you decided to blackmail them." The bull snorted and backed off a bit as he gathered himself for another strike. He shook his head, flinging drops of blood into long arcs.

"It wasn't blackmail. I wanted access to the stream running on the Thompson property, so I got Ed to sell me five acres that cut across to the water. His partner in sin thought she'd toss in ten thousand out of gratitude."

"Are you saying she volunteered to pay you?"

The bull banged the tractor again, but with less intensity.

"That's the way I see it," Matt said. "After all, I was willing to lend him twenty thousand short term to see his creditors through."

"Short term!" Helen cried. "You knew he could never muster up enough to pay you back in a hundred years."

"Ed told me he'd have half the money in cash within thirty days. The day I'm supposed to get it, Ed died."

Teri had what she needed to know. "That damn Ed. Here I thought he was just a fool who'd made a bad land deal. Turns out he was blackmailed."

Loco wheeled around, his energy lagging. His interest suddenly focused on something in the distance.

"I paid him for the land, right on top of the loan I gave him. It was a legit deal. I never got a dime, and til now I never pressed for it out of respect for your family. I am a Christian man, after all."

"And I'm Grace Kelly," Helen said dryly.

Teri followed the bull's gaze and saw Eppy's car rolling up the driveway. She was pulling a trailer.

Eppy scrambled out of the car and lowered the gate of the trailer. Loco let out a deep bellow, flicked his long tail, and trotted out of the shed. When Eppy spotted the bull heading in her direction, she dropped the lead line and let the animal back out on her own. It was Lucky.

"Where'd you get the trailer?" Helen called out.

"Borrowed it from Tommy Feldon," Eppy said, making her way to the group at the machine shed.

"What! That bastard!" Stitch ran for his truck.

In the machine shed, Matt jumped from the tractor, relief spreading across his face.

Lucky let out a deep *mooo!* as she plodded up toward the roundabout as Stitch's truck barrelled down the drive.

"I've got her back!" Teri cried. "I've got Lucky!"

"Now don't go getting goofy again about cows," Eppy scolded. "I want you to promise me that this will be your last cow. No more."

"That's a promise Teri can't keep," Nedra said with a smile. "Lucky is pregnant."

EPILOGUE

The following Saturday, the long rays of the early evening sun slanted across the pasture and wide lawn of the Sinclair farm. The rains had cleared and the rivers had begun to recede, sending their destruction toward the swelling Mississippi River and lower states. Nedra and Annie lounged in lawn chairs, their beer bottles resting close by. Helen and Eppy came out of the house and took nearby seats. Eppy cradled a lemonade and Amaretto.

"How's Lucky doing?" Helen asked.

"Fine," Nedra said. "All signs indicate a normal pregnancy."

"How did you ever know Lucky was pregnant in the first place?"

"I discovered it when I examined her the day Jeff tried to throw Annie and me off the farm. Given Jeff's reaction, I knew he was behind the cow problems.

The flame azaleas and big-leafed hydrangeas at the back of the Sinclair house tipped in the breezes, and the mock oranges in the nearby flowerbed filled the air with their fragrance. The sky was as clear as a blue sheet, and the sun fat in its descent.

"I have a question for you, Eppy," Nedra said. She caught Eppy's eyes. "What did you say to get Jeff to confess to his involvement with the break-in and aborting the cows?"

"I told him that his father wasn't perfect...that if anything, Ed was so rattled about my seeing him at the Park View Motel with Lana Osborne that he lost his senses at the corn bin. That cracked him. I squeezed him like toothpaste after that, and he spit everything out."

"Wait a minute!" Annie cried. "Lana Osborne!"

"That's right," Eppy said. "President of the School Board."

Annie let out a resounding laugh. "No wonder you won that battle over my contract."

"I told Lady Lana that if she didn't support you two young ladies," Eppy said, "I'd tell her husband about her affair as I was withdrawing my money from the bank. Naturally, the Board of Directors would want to know why one of their own was taking her business elsewhere. God, that threat works better than torture on money grubbers."

"You didn't!" Annie slapped the arm of her chair in disbelief and joy.

"I'm a heartless old bitch, my dear. Of course I did." She took a noisy, satisfied swig of her drink. "I just wish I could have had the satisfaction of snapping the handcuffs on Stitch myself."

"I'm sure that's a pleasure Joanne didn't want to share. She said that he could spend some time behind bars—felony theft for starters," Helen said. "He'll probably get off light, especially since they're going easy on Jeff."

"I know," Nedra said. "I didn't have the heart to press charges against him. Joanne said he gave a complete story at the station, one that verified our theories. He's a lost kid with a lost mother. I didn't want to add to their grief."

"I certainly hope he feels some remorse." Helen paused. "I'm glad that he's decided to stay on with Stitch's cousin. It's going to take a long time before he and Teri can mend things between them. I offered to put him through two years of college, and I think he's finally going to take me up on it."

"Matt was pretty clever, too," Annie said, "forcing Ed to sell him the patch of land, then loaning him money to get a credit hook into the farm."

"That loan business is a bag of hooo-eee," Eppy declared. "I'm sure Ed never saw a penny. It was pure blackmail with an installment loan as a cover. The principal was small enough not to raise the eyebrows of the bank lenders if it ever showed up on a balance sheet, but enough to let Matt get a claim on the land."

"Too bad Matt's getting away with his scheme," Nedra said.

"He won't" A self-satisfied smile stretched across Eppy's face. "Not totally."

"Now what did you do?" Helen asked.

"Being on the Board of Directors of the bank, I thought it only fair to have a little chat with Matt—unofficially, of course." Eppy grinned. "I pointed out to him that with the shenanigans he tried to pull, the bank would not look kindly on further borrowing. We stomped on his dream of owning all the land between here and Mankato."

"Eppy..." Helen started in.

Eppy held up her hand. "He can get funding elsewhere, but not from the bank in this town. At least officially. I suspect Lana's been paying him off for years."

"What about the ten grand?" Annie asked.

"Looks to me like it's found money. Lana can't claim it without admitting her affair with Ed, which she denies. With the sale of her herd—except for Lucky—plus the ten grand and a little gift from me, Teri can pay off that damn Matt." Eppy drained a quarter of her drink. "Now she only has to worry about me as a creditor. I made her sign Lucky and the calf-to-be as collateral for the loan. If she doesn't bring the farm around, they're joining the rest of the herd at the stockyards."

"Will that work?" Nedra sounded skeptical.

"I think reality is setting in. She's agreed to work with a farm management group out of Mankato, at my expense, mind you. They'll supervise her operation closely. She's promised to follow their recommendations even if it kills her. She's got three years to make it work or I'm pulling out. No exceptions."

"Teri can do it," Helen said. "Reverand Olson said he'd give her extra care too, and he'll help work out a reconciliation with Jeff when the time comes."

"How is Jessie handling all of this?" Annie asked.

"She's so mad at her brother," Eppy said, "she'll probably work twice as hard to show him up."

"I have one more question," Nedra said. "It's about your seeing Ed and Lana at the Park View Motel. How did that happen?"

"I own a majority share of the motel," Eppy said. "I had stopped by to see the manager—who is one of the minority stockholders—about his buying some of my shares. I don't think Ed knew that he was screwing his lady love on my property."

Nedra and Annie exchanged a surprised look, then burst into laughter.

"What do you think of life in a small town, now?" Nedra asked her lover.

"It's more interesting—and complicated—than I ever imagined. I *think* maybe I can get used to it," Annie said.

"You *think* you'll stay?"

"I'd better," Annie said, smiling sweetly. "Someone has to save you from rampaging bulls."

In the distance, a Palomino ambled toward the barn from the open pasture, setting off the other horses in the same direction. Sparrows dipped overhead and perched in a nearby apple tree. The shadows of the evening lengthened into twilight. After a long while, the women on the Sinclair farm stirred from their reveries and went into the house to crack open the battered cigar box filled with dominoes and the promise of good cheer.

Other Books from Madwoman Press

On the Road Again
The Further Adventures of Ramsey Sears
by Elizabeth Dean
Irreverent magazine columnist Ramsey Sears tours America, finding adventure and romance along the way. This is the critically acclaimed sequel to *As the Road Curves*.
$9.95 ISBN 0-9630822-0-5

That's Ms. Bulldyke to you, Charlie!
by Jane Caminos
Hilarious collection of single-panel cartoons that capture lesbian life from every vantage point—from dyke teenagers and lipstick lesbians to the highly-assimilated and the politically correct. This Lambda Book Award finalist is a must read.
"These funny cartoons depict moments in lesbian life with a fine edge." —Women Library Workers
$8.95 ISBN 0-9630822-1-3

Lesbians in the Military Speak Out
by Winni S. Webber
Women from every branch of the armed forces tell their stories about being women and lesbians in the military. Nominated for an American Library Association Gay and Lesbian Book Award.
"It documents voices previously silenced by legal and social censure . . . highly recommended reading amidst the confusing and often painful dialogue . . . concerning the role of gay and lesbian people in a democratic society." —*Minerva Quarterly Report*
$9.95 ISBN 0-9630822-3-X

Thin Fire
by Nanci Little
Elen McNally signs up for a three-year hitch in the Army, thinking it will get her a one-way ticket out of Aroostook County, Maine. A remarkable coming of age story. Nominated for an American Library Association Gay and Lesbian Book Award.
". . . compelling . . ." —*Lambda Book Report.*
$9.95 ISBN 0-9630822-4-8

Sinister Paradise
by Becky Bohan
A professor of classics on sabbatical in Greece finds a budding romance and her life endangered by an international arms-smuggling conspiracy. This fast-paced adventure is set amidst spectacular scenery in the Mediterranean. Bohan weaves a tight drama.
". . . a riveting tale of love and greed in a country of olives and deep blue water." —Minneapolis Star Tribune
$9.95 **ISBN 0-9630822-2-1**

Mrs. Porter's Letter
by Vicki P. McConnell
Nyla Wade, recently divorced and starting a new career as a reporter, discovers a packet of passionate love letters buried deep within the old desk she's just bought. Her journalist's curiosity piqued, she wonders if the writers, W. Stone and Mrs. Porter are still alive and embarks on a search to find out. First book in the Nyla Wade mystery series.
$9.95 **ISBN 0-9630822-6-4**

The Burnton Widows
by Vicki P. McConnell
Nyla Wade moves to Burnton, Oregon. In this misty, Northwest costal town, her unwanted probing of an old double-murder turns deadly, reopening old wounds and galvanizing local gay activists. Nyla's investigation puts her life in jeopardy just as she falls in love. Second book in the Nyla Wade mystery series.
$10.95 **ISBN 0-9630822-7-2**

Double Daughter
by Vicki P. McConnell
Nyla Wade goes home to Denver for a visit and finds clouds of menace hanging over the lives of friends, old and new. Although the threats appear to be the work of well organized anti-gay groups, Nyla suspects the source is closer to home. Soon, she's the next target! Third book in the series.
$9.95 **ISBN 0-9630822-5-6**

Fool Me Once
by Katherine E. Kreuter
Paige Taylor, mystery writer and private eye, is intelligent, urbane, and

can't resist a pun or the chance to travel. A routine dental appointment turns into a search for the dentist's wife who's disappeared along with a half-million dollars worth of Krugerrands. Someone is plotting the perfect murders, and as Paige gets closer to the truth her name is added to the list of targets.

$9.95 ISBN 0-9630822-8-0

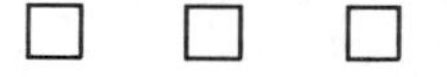